A Long
JOURNEY
Home

by Bill Muir

A Long Journey Home

Bill Muir

Methinx Publishing

MeThinx Publishing

methinx
Methinx Publishing
methinxentertainment.com

Printed in the United States of America
First paper edition by Methinx Publishing
ISBN: 978-1-7347696-1-6

Art & Design:
Contributing Editor: Kathryn Tedrick
Cover Art: Digital Coast Media, LLC

Chapter One

Daniel and Michael

In 1774, the city of Boston, Massachusetts, and its harbor was considered a powerhouse of shipbuilding, commerce, and the largest seaport in America. Although a God-fearing community, with numerous churches and religions, the city was a hard place, because it was open to the world and often drew riffraff to its shores.

Daniel Beaumont, a sixteen-year-old boy with deep blue eyes, and his friend Michael worked on the docks as longshoremen nearly every day. Their days consisted of loading and unloading the many ships that came and went throughout the year. It was hard, dangerous work, but the wages they earned helped support their families.

As they came to the end of their shift, the boys talked about what they would do after work.

"Are you going to do your magic tricks tonight?" Michael asked.

"Oh, yes," Daniel said with a smile. The wind blew through Daniel's dark, shoulder-length hair, but barely rustled his friend's short blond locks. "There's a new ship in port filled with sailors itching to spend their earnings in town," Daniel replied.

"Willing to make a wager on anything that might fatten their purses with more gold," Michael added with a grin.

The boys set their last crate of salted meat into the storeroom of one of the ships, and headed up to the deck, passing sailors and other longshoremen. At the gangway, men were crowded together, waiting for the bulwark to clear out so that they could depart. The workers talked among themselves, but one topic seemed to dominate their conversation.

"Stole it right off the ship in broad daylight," one sailor remarked to his mate.

"Don't that beat all?" Another replied. "The thieves must have nerves of stone to pull somethin' like that off."

Curious, Daniel turned to the men. "Did someone steal something from this ship?"

"Not this one," the first man answered. "They took it off the H.M.S. *Endeavor*. That British Frigate over there on the next dock."

Daniel and Michael exchanged looks of amazement.

"What would a British Frigate be carrying that would be worth stealing?" Michael asked.

"Don't rightly know," the second sailor said. "Whatever it was, it was packed in a fair-sized crate."

"That right," the first sailor said. "Four men carried it right past the dockworkers, sailors, and even the captain himself like it was nothing more than normal cargo being offloaded to a warehouse. It's rumored that the crate was full of stolen Spanish gold bound for King George's coffers."

The gangplank finally cleared, allowing the waiting men to depart the ship. Daniel and Michael continued talking about the fantastic heist as they left the dock and walked toward the small park, two blocks away from the harbor across the street from a general store. There, Daniel searched under the large walnut tree in the center of the park. He needed to replace one of his walnut shells that an irate sailor had smashed the night before. Searching the ground beneath a walnut tree, he found the one he wanted. The outer green husk had already split open, exposing the brown shell. Using his pocket knife, Daniel opened the shell and ate the ripe nut while cleaning the inside. As he put the two halves in his pocket, he heard a noise and looked up, spotting four men struggling to place a large crate on the back of a wagon.

Daniel placed a finger in front of his lips and grabbed Michael's arm, getting his friend's attention as he pointed out the scene taking place a hundred feet away. He then placed his lips next to Michael's ear and whispered, "That's the stolen crate from the ship. Let's follow them."

Michael shook his head *no* but reluctantly followed his adventurous friend. They kept their distance, tracking the men along the dirt road out of town until they reached a large farm. The boys slipped behind the broad trunk of an ancient oak tree. They watched as the four men removed the crate and awkwardly carried it toward a weathered red barn. While they worked, the men continuously looked around to see if anyone was watching. Their worried glances made Daniel shiver with excitement. Clearly, these men were up to no good.

"Look at that," Michael said, keeping his voice low. "I wonder what's inside that crate."

"Whatever it is, I think they stole it from the *Endeavor*," Daniel whispered to his friend.

Michael looked around the meadow, there was no one in sight. "They must be pirates," Daniel whispered, letting his vivid imagination run wild.

"What makes you think it was pirates?"

"Who else would be daring enough to steal something right out from under the noses of the British Navy?"

"Maybe it's just the man who owns the farm and a few of his friends transporting something he just bought," Michael offered.

"If that were the case, why are they sneaking around so much?"

"Maybe you're right," Michael admitted reluctantly.

"Of course, I am. Look, if it was legitimate, they wouldn't be acting so sneaky, would they?"

"Well, whatever it is, those men are big," Michael replied. "It wouldn't be a good idea to tangle with them."

As the idea of pirates fired up his imagination, Daniel's eyes lit with increased excitement. "I'll bet it's the King's stolen treasure."

"Treasure or not, it's trouble. We should leave."

As the boys watched, one man lost his grip, and a corner of the wooden crate hit the dirt with a thud. All four were sweating profusely.

"Sorry, boys, I lost my grip," a tall, lanky man apologized to his fellow accomplices.

"Just hurry and pick it back up before someone catches us," a dark bearded man snarled as he nervously looked around the meadow.

"He's afraid they'll get caught," Daniel whispered.

"I'm afraid *we'll* get caught," Michael said worriedly.

"They won't see us as long as we stay hidden behind this tree."

"As soon as they get inside the barn, we should leave."

"There must be a fortune inside that box."

Michael shivered. He liked to play it safe and was not very adventurous. However, Daniel was bold and never seemed to be afraid of anything.

"They must have heard about the treasure and followed the *Endeavor* into port," Daniel said. "I wonder where the rest of their crew is."

"I don't know, but if we're smart, we'll get out of here before we end up getting ourselves killed."

"Maybe their ship is still in the harbor."

"Are you crazy? You can't just sail a pirate ship into Boston Harbor. The authorities would be all over them."

Daniel looked annoyed. "It's not like they'd raise the skull and crossbones. They may be pirates, but they're not stupid. The safest place for a mouse to hide is in the ear of a cat."

"Why is that?"

"The cat would never think to look there."

"Wouldn't he feel it?"

"You're missing the point," Daniel said with a sigh.

"*We'd* be stupid to steal their treasure."

"Now, we're the mouse."

"As soon as they discovered it missing, they would tear the city apart looking for it."

"Nah, the redcoats would never let them do that. Once they leave, let's go down and get it," Daniel said, ignoring him.

"Haven't you heard a word I said?" Michael asked. "If this is treasure and if those are thieves, then we are talking about pirates here, *real pirates.* Besides, if four strong men are struggling with it, we wouldn't have a chance of hauling it back out."

"Not all at once," Daniel agreed. "We wouldn't necessarily have to steal it all, just enough to set up our families."

"And what would we say when our parents ask us where the money came from?"

"I'll think of something. Let's go."

"No way. It won't work," Michael insisted.

"Come on," Daniel said. "Where's your sense of adventure?"

"I've got plenty of adventure, except when it comes to pirates. I don't know about you, but I don't want to end up a slave on their ship or worse."

As the two friends quietly argued, the men opened the barn door and carried the heavy load inside. Several moments passed, and the boys remained where they were, waiting for the pirates to leave.

Ten long minutes later, the men came out of the barn. Two stood to watch while the other two men shut the doors and secured it with a heavy two-by-four, which they slid across the door's brackets. The three men grinned and slapped each other's backs, relieved that they had accomplished their task without anyone spotting them, or so they thought. They started to walk toward the farmhouse when one of the men stopped and looked directly at the tree the boys were hiding behind. After a moment, the man started to walk towards it. Michael panicked. He was about to take off running when Daniel grabbed his arm and shoved him against the tree trunk.

"Are you crazy?" Daniel whispered.

"Oh no, they're going to catch us spying on them." Michael squeezed his eyes shut as he and Daniel froze, not daring to move a muscle.

Placing his mouth next to his friend's ear, Daniel spoke softly. "Just follow me around the tree. If they see us, run for your life."

"Hold up," the man with the beard said, making both boys jump.

"What's wrong?" One of the men asked.

"I thought I heard someone talking."

"I don't hear anything," the tall, lanky man said. "You must have imagined it."

"No, I'm telling you…"

Just then, four women came over the crest of the hill and turn toward the town center. The men could now hear them clearly talking about what they planned on buying.

The men exchanged looks. Satisfied, one man walked into the back door of the farmhouse as the other three climbed on the wagon and left. As soon as they were out of sight, the boys sighed with relief.

Daniel tugged on Michael's sleeve. "Now."

"Now what?"

"Now we find the crate and see what's inside," Daniel said excitedly.

Chapter Two

The Crate

Checking to make sure the man was still inside the house, he dropped to the ground and crawled to the next tree. Fearfully, Michael followed right on Daniel's heels. Sitting up, Michael pressed his back against its trunk and panted with unsuppressed fear.

"They're going to come back and catch us. I just know it."

Daniel ignored him and crawled to the next tree.

"I don't know why I listen to you," Michael mumbled as he followed. "You're going to get us in big trouble."

"Or worse," Daniel said with a grin.

"Right like death," Michael groaned.

When they reached the last tree, they still had twenty-five feet of open ground between them and the barn door. Daniel got to his feet.

"Come on, duck, and run. When we reach the barn, grab the left end of the bar on the door, I'll take the right. We'll heave it out of the way and dart inside. I'll close the door."

"What if they come back? They'll know someone is inside as soon as they see the door is no longer barred," Michael fretted.

Daniel sighed. "Come on. Why would they come back?"

Michael gave in. "All right, but we had better hurry, just in case."

Daniel nodded, and the two boys crept to the door. The bar was more massive, and it took longer to remove it than they initially thought. When they dropped it to the ground, a cloud of dust rose into the air, making them cough and sneeze.

They checked once more to make sure no one saw them, just as the men had done earlier. The coast was clear. Daniel quickly opened the barn door, and the two boys slid inside, pulling the door closed behind them.

"What if they come back? We should leave not. We are only going to get caught," Michael fretted.

Daniel sighed. "Come on. Don't be a scaredy-cat. Why would they come back?"

"I thought I was the mouse?"

Daniel gave a deadpan stare to his best friend.

Michael gave in. "All right, but we had better hurry, just in case."

"You worry too much," Daniel whispered back.

"And my worrying has kept us out of a lot of trouble," Michael said.

Lost in his world, Daniel didn't hear a word.

"The pirates are gone. Let's just find the treasure, grab as much as we can, and leave. We can always run to the docks and tell the Brits we found their stolen cargo."

The barn contained several objects and paraphernalia: bales of hay from this year's crop, a heavy wooden work plow, farming implements. Two empty stalls for the workhorses when they weren't out in the pasture, and numerous crates of varying sizes. The boys started their search with the containers in the front of the barn, looking for one the same size as the object just brought in.

While they hunted, Daniel disturbed a nest of mice, sending the small rodents squeaking and scrambling throughout the barn. The boys exchanged nervous grins. They went back to work, but each crate they examined was wrong. It was either too big, too little, or the wrong shape. Their search seemed to take forever, and Michael grew increasingly anxious. Even Daniel felt himself grow twitchy. Both boys kept glancing at the door, hoping the pirates wouldn't return.

As they made their way through the middle of the barn, Michael found a crate that looked to be the right size and shape. "Daniel, come here. I think I found it."

His friend hurried over.

"I can almost feel that gold running through my fingers." Examining the crate, he realized they needed something to pry it open. "Look around for a crowbar."

"Where are we supposed to find one of those?"

"It's probably with the tools over there," Daniel replied, pointing to the wall.

The boys hurried over to the tools. In their haste, they knocked a couple of tools off the shelf, which hit the floor with a great clang. Startled, the boys dropped down and hid behind a bale of hay. Their hearts pounding, they waited for almost a minute before peeking around the bale to check the door.

"I hear footsteps," Michael whispered.

Daniel thought he did, too. His body tensed with waiting. They heard the sound of footsteps again. Someone was right outside the door.

"What are we going to do?" Michael whispered.

Daniel looked over at his friend and saw that his eyes were large and round with fear. "Look for something to fight with."

"Are you crazy? We can't fight them."

"It's that, or die." Shifting his position, Daniel started to lose his balance, and he reached back to catch himself. As he did, his hand came down upon something metallic. Snatching it up, he realized what it was. "I found it!"

"What?"

Daniel raised the crowbar and waved it at his friend.

"A lot of good that's gonna do us now."

Daniel frowned. Michael was right. If the pirates discovered them now, they would never be able to get their hands on the treasure. Hearing the footsteps getting closer, he tightened his grip on the crowbar. Then they watched in horror as someone opened the barn door and peeked inside. Both boys partially rose up into a crouch, ready for fight or flight. Still, to their amazement, the intruder closed the door, and his footsteps moved away, fading into the distance. Sighing with relief, they stood up.

"Whew! That was close," Michael said, wiping the sweat from his brow with his fingers.

"Come on. Let's have a look at that crate."

They hurried over to it. Then Daniel placed one end of the crowbar along the top edge of the lid and pried it partially open. Moving down the side, he tried again, opening the cover a bit more. The crate was now open enough that Daniel could see inside. He looked and sighed with disappointment.

"This isn't it. Keep searching."

Michael frowned. After their narrow escape, the only thing he wanted to do was get out of there. It wasn't going to happen. One look at his friend's face told him that

Daniel was more determined than ever to find the treasure. Sighing, he continued the search.

They moved to another section of the barn closer to the back, and a moment later, Daniel called his friend over.

"Here! This has to be it."

"I hope so," Michael said as he hurried over.

"No, this has to be it. There's a canvas sail thrown over it."

Daniel's excitement was catchy. Just then, an owl flew down from the rafters, scaring both boys. It snatched up one of the mice in mid-flight and flew back to its perch. Michael looked like he was about to collapse. "That owl scared me to death. I thought that man was coming back."

"Me, too," Daniel admitted. "Come on. Let's get this open."

"We should just leave. If those men find us, we're goners."

"No way, the treasure is under this sail. Just think, we'll be heroes, and our families will be set for life," Daniel said encouragingly.

"Not if those soldiers find out we stole their gold."

"We didn't steal it from them. The pirates did. We're just stealing from the pirates."

"If those men catch us, we'll be dead. But at least our families won't have to worry about us anymore."

"Come on. The sooner we get this open, the sooner we can get outta here."

Michael grabbed the sail and was about to pull it off, but Daniel's hand covered his, stopping him. His natural showmanship kicked in.

"This has to be done right."

"You want to do this right now? Let's just pull it off and get it over with."

Daniel shook his head; he wanted to make a production of it. Michael's hand dropped away as his friend searched for a corner of the sail. When he found it, he grinned and slowly started to pull, building the suspense as he did.

"Ladies and gentlemen, you are about to be amazed by the amazing treasure that lies beneath this magic cape."

Despite his fear of discovery, Michael found himself caught up in his friend's performance. *Let this be the stolen gold. It would really help our families. Let this adventure not be a waste.*

Drawing out the excitement for as long as possible, Daniel closed his eyes, crossed his fingers, and taking a deep bow, whipped the cover off.

The boys sagged with disappointment. There was no chest. No gold. Only a brand new, shiny, black wood-burning stove.

Suddenly, the barn door flew open, lighting up the interior. The man with the dark beard stood there, pointing a musket at them.

"I told you someone was in here," the tall, lanky man said, standing behind the bearded man.

"He has a gun!" The same words screamed out of both boy's mouths at the same time. They ran to the back of the barn, desperately looking for another way out.

Chapter Three

Showmanship

"What are you doing here?" One of the men demanded. "Are you stealing my wife's new stove?"

The reason the men had seemed so furtive wasn't that they were pirates. They were keeping an eye open for the farmer's wife. It was a gift for her, and they did not want her to see it and spoil the surprise.

In their haste, the boys ended up in a corner along the back of the barn.

Trapped!

Frantic, Michael looked around. He was about to turn away when he spotted a thin sliver of light leaking out between two bales of hay.

"Help me out," he whispered, pointing to the light. Daniel grinned, and together, they rolled the bale away from the wall, revealing a hole just large enough for them to crawl out. Michael dropped down on all fours and scrambled through, followed by Daniel.

When he realized what was happening, the farmer and his companion ran out the barn door and watched as the boys scampered up the hill. "I better not see you around here again. My wife has waited a lifetime for this stove. In fact, if anything comes up missing, she will be the one to hurt you. That's a promise!"

The boys ran all the way to a cliff that overlooked the Boston Harbor. Their sides ached from their run, they dropped to a sitting position on the ground to catch their breath. As their breathing slowed, they listened to the seagulls call out to each other.

The familiar smell of salt, brine, and fish reached their nostrils as they watched a large ship as it entered the harbor only to see it slow to a stop next to the wooden dock. Two other ships had already dropped anchor and were in various states of loading and unloading as longshoremen scurried about like a busy colony of ants.

One merchant ship stood taller than the rest. She was a galleon, a towering, sluggish, behemoth used for transporting cargo. Even though she was slow, the ship wasn't an easy target because she carried heavy cannons, making a direct assault difficult. She had three masts. The forward masts had square-rigged lateen sails on the mizzenmast and a small square sail on her high rising bowsprit.

"Someday, I will own a ship like that," Daniel said, his voice dreamy. "And when I do, I will enter this harbor on a morning, just like this."

"Yeah, right, and someday I'll be the King of England," Michael replied.

Standing up and throwing his arms wide as he bowed reverently, Daniel responded, "Your majesty, I am at your service."

Michael clicked his heels and tapped Daniel on the shoulder as he proclaimed, "Commander, your loyalty is deeply appreciated and sail the world in the name of your king."

As the *Majesty* sailed past them, Daniel watched in awe.

"She's as tall as this cliff," he said. "I feel like I could lean forward and touch the top of her. Look at that masthead. Whoever carved her must have been a master woodworker."

Michael continued to study the ship, and she entered the harbor.

"The colors they painted on her are very nice. She looks like a siren, calling the men to sea. Probably why she's called the *Majesty*. You know, my father's ship wasn't nearly as large. Isn't she beautiful?"

Unfortunately, his friend had absolutely no interest in ships other than to load and unload them. Micheal's attention wandered.

"I'll tell you who's beautiful, Alice Franklin. I think she loves me."

"You know, she's 48 feet tall," Daniel said.

"She's not an inch over five feet," Michael replied.

The boys looked at each other, realizing they were talking about two very different things.

"I think I love her," Michael said.

"I can see why. She is the biggest ship that sailed the Atlantic Ocean."

Michael reached out and spun his friend around.

"Don't talk about my future wife that way!"

Both boys laughed and headed to the busy port.

As Daniel and Michael walked along the wooden dock, a crate broke free of its rope bindings and crashed to the ground five feet in front of them.

Both boys jump back.

A grimy dockhand pushed Daniel aside.

"Dangerous place, boys. I would suggest you run back to your mother's side. It's a lot safer there."

Insulted and not wanting to leave, Daniel looked him in the eye and said, "It's okay. We're longshoremen, but we're finished for today."

"Then I suggest you git yerself off the docks. Yer in the way."

"Come on," Daniel told Michael. "Let's go empty of few pockets with the best show in Boston."

"I said get out of here," the dockhand snarled. "Before I put ye back to work."

When the boys took off, they could hear him laughing in the background.

Across the cobblestone street from the docks, happy sailors, returning from the sea with money to spend, filled the crowded taverns and shops. As usual, the streets were crowded with pedestrians, shopping, working, or just going about the usual routine of their day.

Down the alley behind the Dancing Bear Tavern, Daniel entertained the crowd with his much-practiced magic tricks. In front of him, a muscular, ugly sailor, who stood over six feet tall, laid his money on the table and leaned menacingly over it. He studied the three walnut shells lined up on a small empty crate. Daniel slid the walnut shells across the top of the box in a fast tempo. A showman at heart, he looked up at the crowd as his movements came to a stop, indicating to them that it was time to guess.

"Under which shell is the pea, my friend."

"The left one," the crowd said.

"No, the right one," someone else shouted.

"It's the one in the middle," a couple men declared.

The ugly sailor looked confused. Perspiration ran down his face from his temples. He glanced at his money, gave the kid a cursory look, and studied the walnut shells.

Daniel decided to goad him a little. "Do you want to bet or give someone else who's smarter, a chance to win some easy money?"

The sailor's hand rubbed his five-day-old beard. His eyes focused on the shells, trying to see through them. It was useless.

"I tell you what," Daniel said. "No bet. Go ahead and guess this time."

"Okay," the sailor replied. "No bet."

The sailor pointed to the middle shell, and Daniel picked it up, revealing the pea.

"Too bad, you should have bet," the boy said. "Listen, if you want to raise the ante, you can."

Feeling confident, the sailor reached into his dirty pants pocket and pulled out some more coins and slapped them down on the table.

Standing behind Daniel, Micheal leaned forward and whispered, "You don't have enough money to cover that bet."

Daniel looked nervous, but it was nothing more than part of the show he was putting on for the crowd. Daniel weaved the walnut shells around each other. He would stop, and just when the group started shouting their guesses, he would continue changing the walnuts position on the table. Standing behind him and next to Michael was another sailor. This one had a better view of where the walnut with the pea was.

"Okay, which one is covering the pea?" Daniel asked.

"The left one, no, the right," the excited crowd shouted.

The ugly sailor looked confidently at his friend. They had agreed to use hand signals that would indicate which walnut to choose. The cheat held up his index finger, and the ugly sailor smiled with glee. The money was his. Daniel was going to lose.

"The left one."

"This one?" Daniel asked.

"Yes, now let's see it, and give me my winnings," the sailor demanded, growing impatient as he grinned to the crowd.

Daniel lifted the walnut, but there was no pea underneath. The sailor and his co-conspirator exchanged shocked looks.

Daniel playing to the amazed crowd smiled, and decided to give the man another chance. "Okay, I'll let you choose another."

The ugly sailor squinted at Daniel, then the two remaining walnuts.

He then reached deep into his pocket for his remaining wages and placed it on the table.

"It's the right one." the sailor declared, again turning to the crowd with a confident smile. His friend standing behind Daniel nodded his approval of his choice.

"Are you sure?" said Daniel.

The sailor laughed as he shoved the boy's hand away and reached for the money. Daniel lifted the shell on the right, but there was no pea underneath it. Daniel then revealed the pea under the middle shell. The sailor's hand slammed down on the table, sending everything into the air, including the money.

"You cheated me!"

The crowd scrambled on the ground, scooping up the coins as quickly as possible. Daniel ducked down, grabbed what he could, and ran out of the alley, into the grasp of another large, scruffy-looking man.

Chapter Four

George Beaumont

The crowd on the busy street paid no attention to the town drunk, and the boy in his arms. Daniel looked up into the man's face and realized it was his uncle.

"Where might you be going at this time of day?" asked George Beaumont.

"Uncle George! I was just going to the store to buy food for dinner," Daniel nervously replied.

"First, you'll buy me a drink with that money in your hand, or I'll tell your mother about your extra activities," George threatened.

Daniel had no choice. If his mother found out that he made extra money by doing his sleight of hand tricks, she would be distraught. She didn't like the idea that he had to work at the docks, but it was honest work as opposed to his magic.

George laid a hand on his nephew's upper back and steered him toward the front of The Dancing Bear, a white three-story wooden structure that was a favorite of the sailors. A large sign showed a black bear drinking a pint of ale while doing a jig. Colors and objects, like black bears, red lions, an eagle, and even likenesses of famous men, made the taverns easily recognizable, as many people could not read. The second and third floors had rooms rented out by the day or by the week. Aside from being a bar and hotel, the tavern served as a living room for many of the neighbors. Most houses were small and crowded with children, with very little heat to keep them warm.

Although it did a brisk business, often taking most or all of the sailor's hard-earned wages, the tavern looked worn and well used. A long wooden bar, scarred from fights as well as general use, was the centerpiece of the room. Wooden trestle tables with benches filled most of the space. When the pub was crowded, which it usually was, there was barely enough room for the barmaids to get through.

Sailors lead a hard life, and most drank too much, which often led to bar fights. The damage was often extensive. Although the combatants usually paid for the mess, the owner couldn't see the point of buying anything expensive. Chances were the new stuff would soon be broken anyway. George and his nephew entered the tavern and headed for the empty table in the center of the room. A barmaid came over to take their order, but as soon as she saw who it was, she placed one hand on her hip and shook her finger at George.

"Good afternoon, Mary."

"Don't you good afternoon me, George Beaumont. I told you about yesterday. No money, no drinks."

"Ah now, Mary, don't be that way. I'm good for it."

"Like I haven't heard that line before."

George winked at her. "Besides, my talented nephew is picking up the tab."

Mary gave Daniel the fisheye, her disbelief evident on her face. Daniel remained silent until his uncle smacked him on the back of the head.

"Go ahead, boy, show her the money."

Reluctantly, Daniel pulled some of the coins out of his pocket. He didn't want to display it all. Otherwise, his uncle would spend everything on drinks, and there would be nothing left to purchase food. His earnings as a longshoreman were not enough to get them through a month, especially with his uncle mooching off them both regularly.

"Are you willing to use it for his drinks?" Mary asked.

Daniel hesitated, but when his uncle fixed him with a threatening look, he replied, "Yes, ma'am."

An hour later, two empty mugs sat on top of the table. A third, half-filled mug was in George's hand. Daniel studied his uncle's face. He knew the man was tipsy.

"I'm not going to have any money left to buy food if you keep drinking," Daniel whispered. He was careful to keep his words respectful. His uncle had a quick temper. When he was drunk, he could get as mean as a treacherous storm at sea.

For the moment, the alcohol made George kind, even interested in Daniel. "What do you want more than anything else, son?" George asked, slurring his words.

Daniel looked out the tavern's window at the *Majesty* sitting next to the dock. He longed to sail away with her and live a life of adventure and danger, just like his father had before he ran out on his mother and him. Sadness welled up inside, and the thought that taunted him, whenever he and his mother had a problem with George was, *You should have been the one to run away, not my father.*

When he spoke, he wanted to tell it like it is, but he forced himself to swallow those bitter words. Saying instead, "I'm not your son."

"Excuse me, nephew."

Swallowing his anger, Daniel's voice filled with wonder, and he daydreamed. "I would love to set sail on the *Majesty* or at least see what she looks like on the inside. I've seen plenty of ships, but the *Majesty* is different. I've heard that the captain's quarters are fit for a nobleman, and I'll bet the rest of her is just as grand." Daniel fixed his eyes on his uncle.

"Father took me aboard his ship once, but I was too little to remember much of what he showed me. And from that day on, I knew I wanted to captain a mighty vessel someday."

Before George could respond, two men rudely interrupted their conversation as they crowded around the table, towering over Daniel and his uncle.

"You're behind on your gambling debts, George," the first man said.

"I know, I know," George slurred as he looked up. "I promise. You'll get your money tomorrow."

"You get paid to drink?" the man asked. "Seems to me if a man can't pay his gambling debts, he shouldn't have money to drink either."

"How much does he owe you? Daniel asked.

George contributed very little to the household. His money went for drinking and gambling, along with a portion of Daniel's hard-earned wages.

"Twenty-two dollars," the man replied.

Daniel was amazed. "It would take a sailor half a year to earn that much!"

"It's that, or if he doesn't pay it now, his life is forfeit."

"I told you, tomorrow," George said. "I'm good for it."

One of the men grabbed Beaumont from behind and placed him in a chokehold with his arm. Using his other hand, he grabbed George's right hand and slammed it down on the wooden table, pinning it flat. It was time to demonstrate how serious they were.

"Sorry, that's the wrong answer," the man said.

The other man pulled a knife and slammed it into the tabletop between two of George's fingers. Alarmed, Daniel jumped to his feet.

His uncle gasped for breath. "Tomorrow."

"There are no more tomorrows for you," came the response.

Short on breath, George gasped for anything to delay his punishment.

"If the kid shows you a trick you can't figure out, will you wait until tomorrow?" he choked.

The two men exchanged glances. What did they have to lose? They figured he didn't have the money on him, so they nodded.

"If the boy can do that, we will give you another twenty-four hours." One of the men said.

Daniel quickly pulled out a deck of cards and two handkerchiefs. Looking at one of the men, he said, "I want you to tie one over my uncle's mouth and the other over his eyes."

Puzzled, one man did so and stepped back after making sure George couldn't see anything or put anything in his mouth.

"That's an improvement," yelled someone from across the bar.

Daniel spread the cards out in a fan shape, using both hands. The faces of the cards were visible only to the two men.

"Pick any card."

The man who had done most of the talking picked the six of hearts. He showed it to his partner and the people who had gathered around the table. Daniel collapsed the cards into a deck and reached into his pocket for a small piece of charcoal. "I want you to write your name on the face of the card with this."

While one man marked the card, Daniel turned to the other man. "Pick a number between one and fifteen."

"Fourteen."

Daniel then took the card back from the man and placed it in the deck. By now, most of the patrons in the bar had gathered around to watch.

"That card is the only one like it in the deck. I am now going to hand the deck to my uncle, who will cut them so that the card ends up in the fourteenth spot."

George cut the cards three times. Then standing up, he made a show of counting off thirteen cards out loud, flipping them onto the table. He and his nephew had done this trick before, and they were always ready for a performance, should the occasion arise. He then turned up the fourteenth card. It was the queen of diamonds.

"That's not it!" The first man shouted as everyone groaned in disappointment. "Sorry, George, but you knew the consequences."

One of the men reached for the knife, still buried in the table. The crowd grew silent.

Chapter Five

Cards and Bacon

The patrons in the tavern held their breath and studied Daniel. They saw no nervousness in him even though the trick hadn't worked.

"Wait!" Daniel shouted, holding up his hand. "The trick isn't over." Taking the remaining deck from his uncle, he laid it on the table.

"As you know, I had you tie handkerchiefs over my uncle's eyes and mouth before I started the trick. Now here comes the interesting part."

George reached up and pulled off the handkerchief covering his mouth. Then opening his mouth and stuck out his tongue, revealing a folded up card inside, which Daniel took.

"And this, my friend, is the card you chose," he said, opening up the card to reveal the signed six of hearts.

The crowd went wild and started clapping. Neither man could figure out how Daniel and his uncle had accomplished the trick.

"I don't know how you did that, but you have saved your uncle's life for another day," the first man said. "George, you have until noon tomorrow. Twenty-two dollars, all of it." The man pulled the knife from the table and wiped it on George's sleeve. The man left the table, and when he reached the door, he looked back and mouthed the words ' twenty-two dollars'.

Daniel's uncle sighed and rubbed his neck and said. "Go on. Get out of here, and tell none of this to your mother," he said embarrassed.

As his nephew rose to leave, George grabbed his arm. "Thanks, kid. I owe you one."

Daniel hurried out of the tavern and down the street. He stopped in front of the large window of the butcher shop. Daniel studied the prices of meat, chickens, slabs of beef, and pork, hanging on display, most of which he could not afford. Reaching into his pocket, he counted the money and frowned. He had hoped to buy a few extra things they needed for their pantry, but there just wasn't enough. The store owner, a pleasant-looking fellow with a ready smile, stood in the doorway, watching him.

"What will it be today, Daniel?"

"My mother sure would love to fry up some of that bacon for dinner," Daniel replied.

"Come on in, and I'll get you some."

Daniel headed for the door, but before he could step inside, the ugly sailor from the alley grabbed him from behind and jerked him to a halt.

"You stole that money from me, you little thief," the angry man growled.

Reaching down, he grabbed the young man and pushed him against the wall. The sailor held him in place with his right arm against his chest.

"Turn your pockets inside out," growled the sailor.

As the few remaining coins fell to the wooden sidewalk, the sailor scooped them up with his left hand and stuffed them in his pocket.

"This ain't all of it. Give me the rest."

"I don't have it. My uncle used it for drinking money."

"You'd better not be lying to me, boy."

"I'm not. I swear."

The sailor shoved him to the ground and walked down the street. Inside the store, the butcher saw the whole thing through the window and felt sorry for Daniel. It was a shame the young man's father had run out on his family. Moreover, this puzzled him. Captain Beaumont had always been so responsible. Had he not disappeared, Daniel would not have had to deal with such unscrupulous men.

Daniel looked up at the butcher and sighing, he sauntered down the street. Before he got too far, the butcher came out and ran after him. When he caught up, he handed the boy a hunk of bacon wrapped in brown paper.

"I know you're good for the money," the store owner said.

"Thanks, Mr. Anderson," Daniel replied gratefully and headed for home.

Chapter Six

Mother and Son

Later that evening, bacon snapped and crackled as it fried in a pan on the wood stove in the kitchen. Temperance Beaumont, Daniel's attractive but tired-looking mother, mixed the dough for biscuits. The table where she worked had one chair for the man of the house and benches along the sides for everyone else. Standing next to her, Daniel used a knife to peel potatoes. The two talked and laughed together. He loved the smell of freshly baked bread and couldn't wait for the delicious smell to fill the house.

Because they were poor, their home was small, with only two bedrooms. Two beds and a wardrobe for Daniel and George took up most of the space in one bedroom. Temperance slept in the other bedroom. Aside from the stove, table, and a small pantry, two upholstered chairs sat in front of the fireplace with a small table between, holding little more than a candelabra with three candles.

"You should have seen the look on the audience's faces when I lifted the shell," Daniel said.

"You're going to get hurt doing tricks like that, especially if a sailor thinks you tricked him," his mother warned.

"That will never happen, mother. You worry too much."

As Temperance deftly formed another biscuit, she sighed and smiled.

"This is when I miss your father the most," she said in French, "Preparing dinner and waiting for him to come through that door."

"I miss him too," replied Daniel. "Mom, you never told me why he ran off and left us."

"He didn't."

Daniel gave her a quizzical look.

"I don't care what your uncle or anyone else said. I don't believe it. He wouldn't do that to us."

"Then what happened to him?"

"I don't know. Daniel, but I know that he would never abandon us. You are so much like your father, especially your love of the sea."

Daniel kept peeling the potatoes, his mind turning back to the *Majesty*.

Temperance switched to English. "You must be very careful while working around ships. It's a dangerous world."

"Don't worry, mother," Daniel reassured her.

"I couldn't bear to lose you too," she said from a place deep in her heart.

Daniel reached out and hugged her as he said, "You worry too much."

"That's what mothers do. Now set the table for two. I doubt your Uncle will be joining us.

Though the dinner was meager, the two sat at the table for over an hour talking, Temperance shared with Daniel his father's sea adventures as a captain. Daniel hung on to every story even though he had heard them before. He loved every minute of it.

Until Uncle George slammed open the front door, stepped inside, and fell flat on his face, drunk. Rising to his feet took forever, but he finally managed to stand up, weaving in place. "The kid saved my life today."

Temperance gazed at her son with a puzzled expression on her face. Before he could say a word, George continued.

"That trick was amazing. I never get tired of seeing it. Show her, Daniel, the trick you did in the tavern that saved my life. See if she can figure it out."

Before Daniel could say a word, George collapsed onto one of the chairs and immediately fell asleep. Loud snores filled the room.

"I don't want you anywhere near that tavern. Do you hear me?"

Daniel nodded.

* * *

The next day after work, the ugly sailor from the day before stood outside the tavern, talking and laughing with a couple friends. When he spotted Daniel heading for the alley that led to the back of the building, he and his friends quickly surrounded him.

"Hey, it's that cheat," the sailor said. "Planning on cheating another sailor out of his hard-earned wages?"

"Just leave me alone," Daniel replied nervously.

"Yeah," a skinny red-haired man said, giving Daniel a shove. "Why don't you show us some more of your magic tricks? Come on, pull a coin out of my ear," he snickered.

The other men laughed.

"Oh, wait!" the skinny man said. "You can't. You're not a magician. You just like to cheat people, don't you?"

His words caused the other two to grumble in agreement.

"Why don't we break his arm," one man suggested. "He only needs one arm for the shell game."

"You're right," a third man agreed. "Maybe we should break both his arms so that he can't cheat anyone else."

"Look," Daniel said, "I didn't cheat you. It was sleight of hand. You guessed wrong.

"Yeah? So how about we try it again, but this time I win," the ugly sailor said.

"I'm broke," he protested. "You took everything I had."

"Ain't that too bad," the skinny man said. "We want to play anyhow."

"Ahhh, forget it," the ugly sailor said. "We're not interested. Are we mates?"

"Nah," they all replied in unison.

"Say, who taught you to do tricks, anyway?" The third man asked.

"Must have been his old man," the ugly sailor sneered. He had done some checking on Daniel the night before and learned the story about Captain Beaumont's disappearance.

"Leave my father out of this," Daniel snarled.

"Why? You gonna fight me? You think you're man enough?"

The men snickered.

"What happened to him, anyway?" The skinny man asked.

"He was a great captain, not scum like you…" Daniel's words trailed off. He would never admit to these bullies that his father had walked out of his life.

"Oh yeah? Who you calling scum?" The skinny man asked.

The ugly sailor's expression grew nasty. "Probably ran off, couldn't stand the thought of having someone like you for a son."

Daniel's face turned red with anger, and he balled his fists. It was apparent the man knew all about the disappearance of Captain Beaumont.

"He couldn't have been much of a captain if he had to run away," the ugly sailor added, looking around at the other men. "Must have been a coward!"

Daniel flew into a rage and attacked, punching the man in the face. The others circled around the two and egged them on as the punches flew. Daniel took a hard jab to the stomach that doubled him over. He retaliated by kicking his opponent in the shin. As they fought, a crowd began to form, most of them cheering for Daniel.

Locked together, the two rolled across the sidewalk until a ship's captain, Captain Herring, heard the commotion. He pushed through the crowd and broke up the fight.

"Stop this fighting, or I'll have the two of you thrown in the brig," he said, pulling them apart.

Captain Herring shoved him into the arms of the sailor's friend. "You! Get him out of here, and don't let me see you hanging around here again, or I'll just have to have a talk with your captain. Twenty lashes ought to cool you off."

The ugly sailor righted himself and jerked away from the skinny man who had a hold of him. He turned to Daniel. "Stay away from me. Or next time, there won't be anyone around to save you."

As the men walked away, grumbling, the captain turned his attention to Daniel. "Haven't I seen you working on the docks?"

"Yes, sir."

"What the devil are you doing picking a fight with a bunch like that? They're nothing but trouble. You could end up with a knife in your gullet."

"He called my father a coward," Daniel retorted. His left eye was closed and turning black and blue.

Who is your father?"

"Captain Henri Beaumont."

Captain Herring was surprised. "I know, Henri. He's a good friend and an excellent captain."

Daniel shook his head. "He's been gone for a long time."

The captain softened his voice. "I've known your father for many years. We grew up together. Trust me. He would never desert you and your mother. There has to be a logical explanation for his disappearance."

* * *

The next afternoon, the tavern was full and noisy. A man sharply dressed in an officer's uniform walked up to a crowded table of dockhands.

"Captain Nathaniel Stewart is offering to advance any man six months' salary, if he is willing to sign on today with the *Majesty*," the first mate said.

Two men immediately stood and took him up on his offer, but most of them ignored him. He was about to leave when George, who sat alone at a nearby table, called him over. "How much would that amount to?"

"Twenty-four dollars," the first mate replied.

George stood. Here was the answer to his woes. "I'll take that salary and that job."

The man smiled and handed George a slip of paper. "Hand this to the sailor at the bottom of the gangplank we sail at dusk."

Behind the tavern, Daniel performed another of his card tricks, attracting a more massive crowd than the day before. Suddenly, a hand grabbed his arm and pulled him out of the alley.

"I owe you for yesterday," George said, plastering a false smile on his face. "How would you like to see the inside of the *Majesty*."

"You're kidding, right?" Daniel asked, yet hope sprang up inside him. It was a dream come true.

"Come on." George urged his nephew.

"Let me grab my tricks," Daniel said as he raced back to the table, apologized to the crowd, scooped up everything, and shoved it in his pocket.

His uncle escorted him to the *Majesty*. When they reached the bottom of the plank, he showed the paper to the man standing guard, who nodded. Daniel figured the article had merely been a note granting them permission to tour the ship. As they walked up the plank, he became very excited.

"Hurry up," George urged him. "The ship is leaving today, and I have to get you on before they pull up the gangplank."

After stepping onto the deck, George led him everywhere. Daniel studied everything he saw. They passed the galley, examined the canons, walked past the captain's large stateroom, and then entered the crew's sleeping quarters.

"Thanks so much, Uncle George…"

As he turned for one last look, his uncle clubbed him on the back of the head, knocking him unconscious.

Chapter Seven

All Alone

On the floor in the belly of the grand ship laid Daniel unconscious. His body was motionless under the swaying hammocks like a discarded towel.

"Get up!" A sailor named Hawkins shouted as he threw water on Daniel, who was face down on the floor.

The shock of the cold water brought the young man to his feet. As he looked around the large dark room, he saw hammocks hanging from the rafters, and felt the deck rock beneath him. There was one hammock for every two seamen. The rest slept in bunk beds piled two and three high. The movement of the ship often dismantled the cots, dumping the men on top of each other. Each sailor had one blanket.

For a moment, Daniel stood dumbfounded. Where was he? Why had his uncle knocked him unconscious? He didn't know the answers, but as the realization of where he was hit him, he panicked. "I have to get off!"

Hawkins laughed. "You'll be home in a couple years."

"No, you don't understand," Daniel said.

"We're miles from shore," the sailor replied. "I'm afraid you're stuck here until the return trip."

"No listen, I have to get back home."

"No, *you* listen, if you don't die at sea from the storms, or if pirates attack, you'll be back in two years."

"There's been a mistake. I'm not supposed to be here. I have to get back home," Daniel pleaded. "My mother needs me. She won't be able to survive if I'm not there to support her financially."

Hawkins laughed again and handed him a mop. "You have cleaning to do."

By now, his panic was nearly out of control. Daniel dropped the mop and darted past the sailor in an attempt to escape. Hawkins simply reached out and wrapped his muscular arms around the young man, stopping him.

"Just where do you think you're going? Ain't no way off this ship, unless you can swim a few leagues without drowning. While you were here taking a nap, we left port several hours ago." He picked up the mop and roughly shoved it into Daniel's hands. "Listen up, kid. Your uncle sold you to the *Majesty* for six months of wages. During that time, you belong to him. So you'd better get busy and earn your keep, or it'll be the whip or the plank for you."

He grabbed Daniel by the arm, marched him out of the crew's quarters in the bow, and down a long corridor to a room, where they kept the animals that supplied the ship with meat, milk, and eggs.

"Agg, it stinks in here," Daniel complained. He scrunched his nose.

"Just wait until we've been out to sea for three months. This is nothing," Hawkins laughed. "Smell or not, get to work and clean up this mess."

Daniel looked around the large room. Stalls held cows and bulls. A penned area contained dozens of pigs, and there were numerous rows of nests stacked two shelves high for the chickens. It would take more than a broom to clean this mess up.

"Once you muck out this room, feed the animals."

40

Daniel got to work. His mind was racing. *What can I do? How can I get home?*

How do I get off this ship?

Chapter Eight

Cabin Boy

It was a dirty job that took two hours to complete. While he cleaned, Daniel looked for a way to get to the top deck of the ship. However, there was no exit other than the doorway the sailor leaned against, blocking it.

The longer Daniel cleaned, the more seasick he felt. "I need some fresh air. I'm going to be sick."

"Just throw up in the bucket. You'll get your sea legs in a few days."

The rocking motion of the boat made him sicker until Daniel grabbed the bucket and threw up. There wasn't much in his stomach since he hadn't eaten since breakfast.

Hawkins felt no sympathy for the young man. "Now, get back to work."

"What am I supposed to do with this?" Daniel asked, indicating the bucket and the filth he had cleaned up.

"Toss it through the porthole. We can't have you hauling it through the ship and spilling it."

Daniel frowned. Once more, a possible escape route was blocked. He poked his head out the porthole and stared across the horizon until Hawkins pulled him back into the room.

"Next time I catch you doing anything other than your job, it will be the whipping boy."

* * *

On deck, the helmsmen gently guided the round, wooden wheel in front of him. Captain Nathaniel Stewart stood behind him, along with the first mate.

"Speed?" Captain Stewart asked.

The first mate ordered a sailor at the front of the ship to drop a log attached to a rope. Another man turned a sand dial. When the wood reached the stern of the vessel, another sailor called its position.

The first mate, Peter Hodge, made his calculations and turned to the captain. "Four knots, sir."

Captain Stewart, speaking in French, ordered more sails. "Plus, voiles."

"More sails!" The first mate shouted.

Sailors climbed the masts and untied the massive sails wrapped around horizontal poles. As they opened up in full splendor, the sails billowed, capturing even more wind.

The Captain smiled. "That's better."

* * *

When Daniel finished his job, Hawkins took him to a warm, dry room near the galley where the provisions were stored and showed him which barrels held feed. Besides the grain and food used for the animals, the storeroom contained tightly sealed barrels of water, hardtack, salted meat, and pickled vegetables, as well as coffee, sugar, ale, and rum. He would later learn that the cook added rum, and lemon juice to the water to diminish its foulness. However, there was never enough to last an entire voyage.

"Just be careful and don't spill any of it," Hawkins warned. "If the rats get into the food, we'll starve."

"Rats!" Daniel knew that rats were a problem at sea. He had seen them while loading and unloading many ships. For some reason, he'd had a romantic idea that there wouldn't be any on a ship as grand as the *Majesty*. It was a foolish notion.

"Where there's food, there are rats."

When Daniel finished feeding the animals, the sailor took him next to the mess. He stood in line and eventually received a plate of food. Looking around for an empty place on one of the benches, he finally found an open space at a table with several muscular sailors. Looking down at the slop on his plate, he made a face. It didn't smell that great either. Although the meals served at the beginning of a voyage were usually better, made with fresh goods like meat, vegetables, butter, and soft bread. However, if the cook wasn't any good at his job, it didn't make a whole lot of difference.

One of the sailors sitting across from him noticed Daniel's expression. "Let me give you a piece of advice. The meanest man on the ship is the cook. Don't do anything to make him mad. If you do, he'll make your life on this voyage more miserable."

His warning came too late. The cook, whose nickname was Grubb, also saw Daniel's expression. He marched over to their table, grabbed him by the scruff of the neck, and jerked the young man off the bench.

"You don't want to eat my food? Make room for someone who does."

When Daniel stood up, his stomach growled.

The sound brought a grin to Grubb's face. "We'll see how you feel after you've gone hungry for a while. Now get over there and start scrubbing the dirty pots and dishes."

Daniel went to the galley and found an enormous mound of plates, cups, forks, spoons, pots, and pans. More would come later, as the crew of seventy-five finished eating. A large tub of saltwater stacked with additional tableware waited. Washing the dishes in freshwater would be a waste of that precious commodity. As he dug into the monumental task, Daniel muttered to himself. "Is there no end to the work on this ship?"

Once his task was finished, and everything secured in its place so that the rocking of the boat would not break anything, Hawkins put him to work mopping.

Daniel walked through a jungle of clothing, hung up to dry. Grabbing a mop, he swabbed the floor, working his way through the corridors on that level. As he scrubbed, the ship shifted as it altered course, and the door to Captain Stewart's stateroom swung open. A servant was inside, but for some reason, he gave Daniel a dirty look before closing the door. Time passed, and he grew bored with the sweeping. To entertain himself, he began daydreaming. In his mind, he imagined what it would have been like to watch his father studying charts. To have seen his father commanding his vessel through storm-ravaged waters, or playing his violin. Daniel missed him so much. Life at home had deteriorated rapidly. Without his father's income, he and his mother were barely scraping by. Things worsened when Uncle George had moved in with them. If it hadn't been for Daniel's mother, life would have become unbearable.

* * *

Nighttime finally descended, and the ship quieted down as tired sailors headed for the crew quarters to snatch a few hours of sleep. When Hawkins finally sent him to bed, all of the hammocks were full. Daniel sighed and searched for an empty space on the floor to bed down. He was so tired, and his muscles ached, which surprised him. He was

45

used to hard work as a longshoreman. What he didn't realize was that his turbulent emotions wore him down as much as the physical work.

As he looked around, a man in a nearby hammock yarned, stood up, and stretched. He was a veteran sailor who had sailed the seas for the past twenty years. Feeling sorry for the young man, he touched Daniel's shoulder. "Never sailed before?"

Daniel shook his head. "No, sir, my uncle shanghaied me. He sold me into servitude and took the six months' wages that should've been mine, or at least, gone to my mother."

"Rough, that happens a lot, even to grown men. Especially when a man has a debt, he can't pay. Yer, not the first person to find himself at sea without knowing how he got there. They'll work you to the bone."

"You got that right."

The inner ship was dark, and the hull of the vessel moaned as it pushed its way through the ocean waves.

Daniel looked at the sailor and wondered how long he had sailed. His body seemed to be thirty years older than he thought the man to be. Life was hard on the men who labored on the high seas.

The sailor looked at Daniel, "Call me, Mitch. They say these boats are sailing jails for people like us. Hard work, tight quarters, bad food, and for some, the only good prospect is death."

"I have to get off this ship."

"Yea, we've all uttered those words. I have to go above deck and take my turn at the watch. Why don't you take my hammock? When the seas get rough, the hammocks sway. At any rate, we only sleep four hours at a time. Mark my words, in a couple weeks, you'll get used to the way things are done aboard ship. It won't make the work any easier, but it will help once you accept your fate."

Daniel nodded and fought back the tears. He was grateful that he hadn't cried, he didn't want Mitch to think he was weak. Daniel climbed into the hammock. It was the first soft thing he had experienced since he arrived on the ship. An hour later, he was still awake, gently swinging in his hammock. He was so tired and distraught that he allowed the tears to run freely now that no one could see him. He thought about how he had lost his world and everything precious to him. Closing his eyes, he pictured his mother sitting with him around the table, laughing. He wondered if he would ever see her again. That thought served to stiffen his determination. *One way or another, I will find a way back home.*

The stench of dozens of unwashed bodies in the cramped sleeping quarters was overwhelming. The men fell into their beds fully clothed after putting in a hard day's work, they smelled of stale pungent sweat. Burying his nose into his arm, he covered his ears, trying to stifle the loud snores that echoed around the room. Hammocks hung only inches apart, and the cots ran end to end with little room between them.

The hammock next to him contained a fat sailor snoring so loudly that Daniel knew he would never get to sleep. Still, he was bone tired. He tried to sleep for nearly an hour but finally gave up. Slipping from his hammock, he tiptoed around the sleeping sailors, heading for the door. He was almost there when a man entered the room.

Daniel ducked down. He watched the sailor make his way across the room and slip into the hammock, he'd just vacated. He was about to stand when the man next to him turned over in his sleep and threw an arm around him. Daniel held his breath and froze.

When the man's snores deepened, he gently removed the sailor's arm and laid it on the

cot. Slipping from the room, he went above to the deck to escape the ship.

Chapter Nine

The Brig

Except for an occasional lantern, the upper deck was dark and quiet. Although deep in his mind, he knew it was impossible, Daniel looked for a way to escape. There was none. He walked to the railing on the lee side of the ship. Under the full moon, the water danced alongside the boat, and Daniel felt the grand mystery of sailing fill his soul. *This is why men go to sea.* He smiled for the first time since waking up to this nightmare.

The only way off this boat is to jump overboard. In his desperation, he forgot about not knowing which direction to go and didn't stop to think that he might never make it. He swung one leg over the railing.

Before he brought up the other leg, Mitch walked out of the shadows. "You'll drown before you reach the shore. We're too far out. Go back to bed. Your nightmare will be over in a couple of years."

Daniel's face fell. He brought his leg back down and stood at the railing, studying the stars. Looking up, he spotted the dinghy. Daniel was used to heavy labor, but the small boat needed careful maneuvering, which was usually a two-man job. He tried, anyway. Struggling to lower the boat, he guided it over the rail toward the water. However, the vessel got away from him and slammed into the deck instead.

Hawkins, who was on post, ran over and grabbed him by the arm. "You shouldn't have done that, boy."

He marched Daniel below deck and threw him in the brig.

As soon as the man slammed and locked the gate, Daniel jumped to his feet. He quickly wrapped his hands around the bars and shook the door.

"Let me out of here! I have to go home."

"Quiet down," Hawkins shouted. "If you wake up the sleeping men, they'll skin you alive and feed you to the sharks."

Daniel's frustration overwhelmed him. He wanted out, had to get out. He shook the bars one last time and sighed. The door wouldn't budge. He stood there, wondering what to do next when the hair on the back of his neck stood up. He wasn't alone.

Turning, he put his back against the bars and stared into the dark recesses of the cell, trying to see by the dim light of a lantern hanging too far away to be of much use. As he strained to see, he could just make out a dark figure squatting on the floor in the corner. The next roll of the ship made the lantern sway, briefly casting more light into the cell.

What he saw made his blood run cold. It was the man's face; his long stringy hair framed his head in wild abandon. His maniacal expression sent chills up and down Daniel's spine. The man's eyes had a cunning look. Then he gave Daniel a wide, gap-toothed grin and began to cackle, making him want to crawl through the bars and escape, but he couldn't.

He was trapped.

"What are you in for?" Asked a cultured voice with a British accent.

Daniel spun around, thinking someone outside the cell had spoken.

"I asked you a question, boy."

Daniel turned back around in confusion. The voice did not match the man's appearance.

"Trying to escape the ship in a dinghy."

"That's bad," the man replied. "You'll walk the plank for that."

Fear filled the boy's eyes. "No. Really?"

"No," his cellmate chuckled, "But the whippin' will hurt."

"That's not good."

"My name's Richard. What's yours?"

"Daniel." The young man sighed and plopped down on a bench against the wall. He looked at the man. "What are you in for?"

"Stealing from another sailor."

"That's not good either," Daniel said. "Why did you steal anyway?"

"I was trying to steal the keys off of a lieutenant. He thought I was going for his wallet. That's how I ended up here."

Daniel gave him an exasperated look. "But why? I thought this was a merchant ship, not a pirate ship."

"I am not a pirate," Richard replied. "I was trying to solve a mystery."

The man's words pricked Daniel's curiosity. "What is it?"

"Don't know, that's why I called it a mystery."

Daniel figured the old man was crazy and lost interest in his fabricated story.

"I need to get back home."

"Soon enough, my young friend soon enough. In the meantime, you should try to make this trip easier, not harder."

51

Bored, Daniel pulled a deck of cards out of his pocket and started practicing a card trick.

"You any good at that?"

Daniel nodded.

"Why don't you show me?"

He shuffled the cards, spread them out, and had the man pick one. After returning the card to the deck, Daniel slowly fanned them open. There was only one card whose face was not showing. When Daniel turned it over, it was the man's card.

"Very good."

The man smiled, tapping the card deck. "This is how you can make the trip easier."

A surge of hope filled Daniel's mind. "How?"

"Tell me the trick, and I'll tell you to have to make your trip easier."

Daniel smiled, "I can't give away a magician's secret."

"Then, I can't tell you how to ease the journey."

"Ok, but don't tell anyone."

"I promise."

"When you were looking at your card, I flipped over the cards and hid that from you by leaving one card back to cover them. When you slid your card in, it was upside in the deck. Then I turn the cards over when I put them behind my back. When I pulled them back out, your card was easy to spot."

"Very nice."

"Now, you tell me the way to make this trip bearable."

"Entertain the men. Life at sea is boring. Keep them happy, and they will look after you for making their lives easier. This will make them your friends."

"Do you really think it will work?" Daniel asked.

"Trust me. First chance you get, do tricks at the tables in the mess hall. Entertain the men, and they will take care of you."

Daniel nodded and thought about the man in the cell. While the man looked crazy, the conversation indicated quite the opposite.

"Are you really crazy?"

"No. It just stops me from getting beaten the way you will be tomorrow."

Richard's last words made Daniel's guts twist.

"Listen, kid, don't worry about that now. It'll be nasty, but you'll get through it," Richard said.

"Tell me more about this mystery of yours," Daniel said. "At least it'll take my mind off everything else."

Chapter Ten

Legends and Tricks

Richard sat up on his bench and rested his back against the wooden wall. By the expression on his face, it was apparent he was delighted to talk to someone about this so-called mystery.

"This ship is not just going to some port to deliver goods."

This statement piqued Daniel's curiosity. "It's not? Where's it going then?"

"Ever hear of The Golden Chest?"

Daniel shook his head and leaned toward the man.

Richard smiled. He knew he had Daniel's interest now. "It's said to be filled with a fortune of gold and jewels."

Daniel sat up straight. "Where did it come from?"

"It belonged to a famous pirate. Ever hear of Black Bart?"

"Who hasn't? He was one of the most successful pirates in the world! It is rumored that he plundered 400 ships before he died in a battle against Captain Challoner Ogle, who was sent by the British government to find and capture him."

"That's true. The Brits also captured the vessels from his fleet, which contained an enormous amount of gold," Richard said. "They certainly fattened the King's coffers. Nevertheless, the good Captain Ogle didn't find all the treasure. Before Bart's men were tried and executed, some of the guards overheard them talking about a massive chest and the vast fortune it held. The pirates were tortured for its whereabouts, but no one talked.

They took the knowledge of its location to the grave. People have been hunting for The Golden Chest ever since."

"Didn't that happen back in 1722?" Daniel asked.

"Yes."

"If no one has found it in all these years, why is this ship looking for it now?"

"Rumor is that new information has surfaced along with a treasure map Captain Stewart suspects will lead us to the gold," Richard said. "That is part of the reason that the first mate was looking for recruits in Boston, last chance for any labor."

"This is a pretty large crew," Daniel said thoughtfully. "How much would each of us receive?"

"No one knows for certain, but from what the pirates said in their cells before their death, it would be more than enough to give every man onboard a lifetime of wages. We could all spend our time relaxing on the beaches and away from this wooden casket they call a ship."

Daniel's mind churned with ideas about what he would do if he could get his hands on that much gold and jewels. He and his mother would never be poor again. It might even be enough to buy a ship.

***

The next morning Daniel awoke to the sound of approaching footsteps. He scooted back on the bench until he reached the far corner. Shrouded in the darkness of the brig, he foolishly hoped the man wouldn't see him. It didn't help. Hawkins approached the cell and unlocked it with a skeleton key. Raising the lantern he held, Daniel saw that there was a whip attached to his belt.

"Let's go, boy."

"Are you going to whip me?"

"Nah, worse, you're going to work for the cook."

Daniel didn't know if this was a reprieve or not. "I've heard bad things about him."

"Whatever you heard, it ain't true," the sailor laughed. "It's worse. He's drunk and lazy. Now move it. You'll be doing all the work, so I hope you can cook."

Hawkins entered the cell, grabbed Daniel's arm, and dragged him through the corridors to the mess. When they arrived, they found the mean cook's head lying in a dish of food on one of the tables. They stopped next to him.

"Here's your help," Hawkins told Grubb.

The cook looked up. Seeing Daniel, he said, "You're kidding, right?" The cook lowered his head and fell back to sleep. When he awoke, he saw Daniel sitting alone across from him at the table.

"Get to work!"

"What am I supposed to do?"

"Everything, but start with cleaning the pots and then fix breakfast."

Daniel went to the galley. Although he had cleaned up the dirty dishes and pots from last night's meal, he discovered still more dirty pots crammed in the storeroom. Grubb hadn't touched them since the previous voyage. Getting them clean would take a lot of hard work. Daniel sighed and got busy scrubbing.

While he worked, he thought about his mother and the dishes they used to do together. He had never liked doing dishes, but he treasured the time spent with her, talking and laughing about old times. They even discussed what they would do if his father ever came home. If only things hadn't gotten so bad after his father's disappeared.

He put the first dirty pan into the cold dishwater. His mother's pots never got this dirty. The job seemed to take forever, and when he was finally finished, he went to the storage room to see what he could make for breakfast.

Remembering the chickens he saw yesterday, he thought about making eggs. When he entered the storeroom, however, he discovered a twelve-year-old boy milking the cows. Walking over to the chicken pen, he opened it and reached for the first nest. Before he could take a single egg, the boy stopped him.

"I'll get the eggs as soon as I finish milking the cows."

"I thought maybe the crew would have them for breakfast," Daniel told him.

"Can't, you need them to make bread."

"Make bread? I can't make bread."

"You'd better learn fast. The loaves they brought on board will be gone by the end of the day. Grubb started his drunk early. It's doubtful he'll be up to making any. If there's no bread for the Captain's table in the morning, there'll be hell to pay."

"I don't suppose you know the recipe, do you?"

"Actually, I do. I've helped make bread in the past. Once I'm finished here, and the men have eaten breakfast, I'll show you how."

"Thanks, uh, what's your name? I'm Daniel."

"Samuel. Is this your first voyage?"

"Yes."

"Give it some time. You'll soon learn everything you need to know."

Returning to the galley, Daniel made coffee and then started two huge pots of oatmeal. When breakfast was ready, two men helped carry the kettles into the mess, placing them on the serving table, next to the coffee, fresh milk, and sugar. The crew filed in.

Having served the men, the boys ate. Afterward, Samuel left to continue his duties, but Daniel decided it was time to see if Richard was right. He pulled out a deck of cards and shuffled them. This caught the attention of a few sailors in the room.

"Hey, what can you do with them cards?" One sailor shouted, gaining the attention of the others.

Daniel grinned. "Watch closely." He shuffled the cards a bit more then proceeded to spread them out on the table. Looking at the man across from him, he said, "pick a card."

The sailor grinned. He was pleased that he would be the one to participate in this particular trick. His hand wavered over the cards, finally stopping midway and choosing one.

"Now show it to everyone else but not to me," Daniel said.

The sailor got to his feet and did just that. It was the ace of spades.

Daniel picked up the remaining cards and shuffled them once more. He stopped shuffling and held the deck in his left hand. "Whenever you're ready, tell me to stop and place the card back in the deck."

Grabbing all but a few cards, he began dropping stacks of six to ten from his right hand to his left. He was about a third of the way through the deck when the sailor told him to stop. Daniel held out his left hand with the pile of cards he'd accumulated, and the sailor placed the ace of spades on top. Then adding the remaining cards to the deck, the young man shuffled them a few times more.

"Now, I will say the word 'shazam,' and the deck will reveal your card."

Daniel spread the cards out on the table the same way he had at the beginning of the trick. With his fingers, he spread some of them out a little more until he came to a card with a blue back.

"What have we here?" He said as he picked up the blue card. "What was the card you picked?" Before the man could answer, Daniel, turned over the blue card, revealing the ace of spades. "Was this it?"

The crowd burst out with exclamations of surprise and glee. When the trick began, there was no blue-backed card in the deck. The men clapped and cheered.

"If you like, I'll show it to you again in slow motion."

"Yes!" Everyone shouted as they crowded around for a better look.

"Let's put the blue card here," Daniel said, placing it on the table. He then shuffled the cards and spread them out as he had the first time. The blue card was face down above the line of red ones. "Who wants to pick this time?"

Naturally, everyone did. The room grew loud with "me's" and "I do's." Finally, Daniel picked a man who had worked his way over from the other side of the room.

"How about you? Pick any card you want."

The man chose a card. It was the three of hearts. He grinned and showed it around, making sure Daniel could not see what it was.

Daniel repeated the trick as he had done before. Then, saying the magic word, he spread the deck out beneath the blue card that was still face down on the table. There was no blue card in the deck this time. Passing his hand over the cards, he spread out a bit more, but none of the cards appeared to be any different from the others.

"Hmm, I don't see any cards revealing themselves."

The men groaned.

"Why didn't the trick work the second time around?" The man who chose the card asked.

"Well, we still have this blue card." Picking up the blue card, he looked at it before revealing it to his audience. "Was your card the three of hearts?"

The room exploded with sound. If they were amazed the first time he performed the trick, they were totally astounded the second time. That blue card had lain there, untouched, in front of everyone, during the entire second trick. The sailors tried to figure out how he had done it. Although some of them came up with a few ideas, they were utterly baffled over how he had accomplished the trick the second time. Daniel's illusions were winning them over.

The loud banging of a wooden spoon against a pot caught everyone's attention. "Okay, everyone out!" The cook shouted. "Show boy needs to wash the dishes."

The men groaned and complained as they filed out. The closest sailors patted Daniel on the back. They were happy and hoped he would continue to entertain them throughout the long voyage.

"Will you show us another trick at lunch?" Mitch asked.

"Sure thing," Daniel replied.

His response brought cheers and good wishes. Life on board a ship was monotonous and boring. Daniel's entertainment brought a bit of laughter and happiness to the sailors they usually wouldn't have.

After cleaning up the dishes, Samuel returned long enough to show Daniel how to make bread. He caught on right away. After all, he had watched his mother do it so many times that he quickly mimicked her. It was another of his many talents. He used to make her laugh whenever he lowered his voice and pretended to be his Uncle George or one of the townspeople. As he mixed up batch after batch and set them on the tables to rise, he realized that he needed to learn the characteristics of some of the men on board, especially the officers. Mimicking them was a sure-fire way to get a laugh or two.

Once the loaves were finished, he started peeling potatoes. At that point, the cook woke up. Even though the kitchen looked better than it ever had, Grubb gave it a critical eye, and when he spotted a cricket hopping across the floor, he screamed at Daniel.

"Look at that! You didn't clean upright!"

As soon as Daniel finished with the potatoes, Grubb made him hunt down the cricket. When he caught it, the cook grabbed it and tossed it into the ocean through the porthole. "It's fish bait now."

The rest of the day passed with Daniel helping the cook make lunch and the evening meal. In between, he performed more card tricks for the eager sailors. The pile of dirty dishes and pots seemed endless. When he finished the last of them, he swept and cleaned both the galley and the mess. For the first time that day, the cook had a smile of anticipation on his face. He sent Daniel to bed and headed off to pass the night away, drinking and singing with the men who were off duty. He did this every night, which was why he couldn't get any work done during the day.

In the crew quarters, Daniel grabbed one of the few remaining hammocks. No one protested. He had entertained the sailors so thoroughly that no one would deny him a hammock. Still, he was unable to doze off. Sleeping sailors were too close and their snoring too loud. Although he smiled when he entertained the men, it did nothing to relieve the loneliness and emptiness he felt. He missed his mother, his friends, and his old life. More than ever, he was still very much alone, but at least now, he had a reason to remain onboard – The quest for the Golden Chest.

Chapter Eleven

A Mother's Worry

In the Port of Boston, Temperance Beaumont walked the docks, asking if anyone had seen her son. She had a sketch of Daniel from a couple years ago. He hadn't changed much in the past two years, so it was a good likeness.

"Have you seen my son? I have a picture of him."

"Sorry, ma'am," one of the sea captains replied. "Does he like the sea?"

"Yes, his father was a captain of a ship, but he went missing a long time ago." She couldn't bring herself to say the words that he had abandoned them. "It's been hard on Daniel without his father."

"Chances are, he's joined a crew to search for his father," the captain said.

She had heard those words so many times she wanted to scream. Instead, she said, "You don't understand. Daniel's a good boy. He would never leave without telling me first."

"I'm sorry, ma'am. I haven't seen him." The captain walked away.

She sighed heavily. Daniel had been gone for nearly a week. Since then, she'd spent each day asking everyone she passed the same question. First, she had spoken with the town's people. No one had seen him, not his friends, or anyone else in town. After that, she had taken to the docks. The longshoremen he had worked with had no idea what had happened to Daniel either. With each passing day, her despair grew. Had he really sailed away on one of the ships? Had something terrible happened to him?

George swore he didn't know. He, in fact, made it worse. He'd decided not to tell her that he knew Daniel was aboard the *Majesty*. Naturally, he wouldn't confess his part in it, nor how he had tricked his nephew just so that he could pay off his gambling debts. Since he didn't know if the boy would make it back home alive, he lied. "For all we know, he could be lying at the bottom of the bay."

His words broke her heart, but she refused to believe him. Temperance told herself that her son was not dead. Late that afternoon, she sat drinking tea with a friend.

"How can you be so sure he is still alive?" The friend asked.

"I know he is. If he wasn't, I would feel it here." She tapped her chest. Her words faded to a whisper. "I would know."

Chapter Twelve

Life at Sea

Daniel settled into his new work routine, which meant doing everything the cook was paid to do. He tried his best to appease the meanest cook in naval history; at least, that's how he saw him. One night, he made a delicious stew that the men loved.

"It's the best meal we've ever eaten on board a ship," they all told him.

Their praise angered the cook and made him jealous. He made his helper's life even harder. The following day after lunch, Daniel cleaned up the kitchen and then headed to the supply room to plan the evening meal. As he determined what he would need, Grubb staggered into the room, drunk as usual. In his jealousy, he'd decided to show the young man up. It was an impossible task.

"Get out of here. I'm fixing dinner."

"Let me help. That's what I'm supposed to do."

"What do you think you're doing?" Grubb snarled.

"I'm trying to help you," Daniel replied.

"Why?"

"You seem to need a friend."

"I have plenty of friends."

Grubb pulled a flask out of his pocket and gulped a healthy swallow. He staggered, but before he tripped over one of the barrels, Daniel grabbed his arm and held him steady. An idea struck the young man, and he wondered if there was a reason why the cook drank so much.

"What happened?"

"Whadda you mean?" Grubb's words were slurred.

"Something happened that causes you to drink so much. Did you lose someone you loved?"

Daniel didn't know what made him ask, and he figured the cook wouldn't answer the question. He was in for a surprise.

Grubb's expression turned melancholy. "I wasn't always this way. I had an attractive, even-tempered wife and a handsome young son."

"Did something happen to them?" Daniel asked.

"My wife wanted to move to the Virginia Colony. She had something wrong with her, and the harsh winters in Boston were making it worse. She would become sick, usually for the entire winter. Some of the women took turns caring for her and our five-year-old son. Don't get me wrong, she was grateful, but it made her feel helpless. I was afraid of losing her to the illness. So I sold everything we owned and bought passage for the three of us on a ship heading south. We were only a couple days out of port when a bad storm blew up." Grubb sniffled and wiped the moisture from his eyes with a dirty sleeve.

"It was a bad one. I lost them both. When we reached land, I joined the first ship I could find, hoping another storm would come along and take me, too. It hasn't happened yet."

"I'm sorry. That's terrible."

Daniel's words cut through the melancholy, and Grubb realized he'd allowed himself to become vulnerable in the young man's eyes.

"Stop lollygagging around! Go clean the animal pens."

Daniel headed for the door, but before he could walk through it, Grubb grabbed his arm.

"You tell anyone what I told you, and I'll throw you off the ship. Don't want anybody's pity. I couldn't take it."

Daniel nodded and left.

As the days passed, turning into weeks, and then months, Daniel continued to make friends with the crew. Entertaining them at mealtimes became part of his routine. Although the cook still mistreated him, no one else did. Their store of fresh food had run out long ago. With no more citrus onboard, their source of vitamin C was gone. Some of the men battled scurvy, leaving them with muscle weakness, tiredness, muscle and joint aches, a rash on the legs, and bleeding gums. As the ship headed further south and they arrived in a warmer climate, malaria and yellow fever would also become a problem.

Then Grubb started showing some of the signs of illness. Tired and always drunk, the cook soon allowed Daniel to take over the meals again. Working only increased his aches and pains. It was enough to dampen his jealousy, but not for long.

After another bout of stormy weather that lasted for two days, the sea was still rough. The men had to settle for salted meat and hard biscuits, as it was too dangerous to use the stove or light a fire. No one was happy with the meals, but they knew that once the weather cleared, the food would get better.

With not as much to do in the kitchen, Daniel decided to clean the storeroom. As he worked, he spotted a rat. He had to do what he could to prevent rodents from eating everything. If that happened, the crew would starve until they reached the next port.

Snatching up a medium-sized empty container, he cautiously herded the rat to a corner of the room where he trapped it in the box. He couldn't just throw it out the porthole. It would swim to the ship and climb up the side. He carried it to the upper deck and headed for a side railing.

Daniel stopped and listened to the sound of the gentle waves slapping against the side of the boat. Coupled with a gentle sea breeze, they made a soothing sound that usually helped put him to sleep in his bunk or hammock. As he listened, he carefully watched the water's surface for the denizens of the ocean. The lookout had spotted them a couple days ago.

Sharks.

Then he saw one, swimming alongside the ship.

"Waiting for someone to fall overboard?" He called out to the shark. "How about a little snack?"

Opening the container, he heaved the rat over the rail and into the water, directly into the path of the killer fish. The rat squealed as it hit the surface. It wasn't frightened for long. The shark sped toward it, its mighty jaws fully open, exposing five rows of razor-sharp teeth. Within seconds, it swallowed the rat in one gulp.

"If that weren't a rat," Samuel said. "I'd feel right sorry for it."

"It's them or us," Daniel said.

He wasn't as unfeeling as his words portrayed. However, he knew that rats would not only eat their food supply, but they also carried rabies and other diseases. Enlisting the help of some of the crew, they kept a man on guard day and night. Whenever a crewman spotted a rat, a well-thrown knife took care of the problem.

When Daniel finished cleaning the storeroom, he checked on the animals. With the waves finally calm, he would be able to cook a decent meal for the crew. Grubb, however, had other ideas. His jealousy, that the crew liked Daniel's cooking better than his, made him decide to fix a hot lunch and coffee. Still drunk, Grubb leaned over the boiling water. As he did, the cloth in his hand came too close to the flames and caught fire.

He threw the cloth away before it could burn his hand, but it landed in an empty but greasy pot. The fire greedily consumed the grease, making the flames rise higher and threaten to go entirely out of control. Had Grubb been sober, he would never have done what he did next. He picked up a kettle of coffee and threw it at the flames. The water did not put it out. Instead, the fire spread, catching the wall between the galley and the storeroom on fire.

Grubb's alarm grew, and fear seemed to close his throat so that he couldn't speak aloud. *Oh no! What am I going to do? If I call for help, the Captain will find out. I'll be punished, maybe even keelhauled. If I don't call for help, the entire ship may go up in flames. Then we'll all be dead.*

Everything he tried only made things worse. A moment later, Daniel entered the mess. When he saw the fire and the direction it was taking, he dropped the basket of eggs he carried on a nearby table and ran back to the storeroom. He had to smother the fire before it destroyed their food stores. Thinking fast, he broke into the salt barrel and scooped up a bucketful. Returning to the galley, he tossed the precious stuff onto the flames until they went out. The salt would run out sooner, but at least he'd minimized the damage.

Daniel returned the bucket to the storeroom and returned to the galley, finding a sobered up cook. Fear had done the job.

"I'll get one of the carpenters to fix this up before Captain Stewart finds out," Daniel said. "He won't tell anyone if I promise to show him how to do one of my tricks, which I will."

Grubb looked at him in surprise. "You would do that for me, even after the way I treat you?"

"Sure, why not. We're in this together."

Grubb was so pleased and surprised that from that day forward, he never said another mean word to Daniel, although he was still nasty to the other sailors.

"I'm indebted to you, young sir. I don't know why you're doing this, but I owe you. If the officers ever discovered what happened, I would receive a whipping at the very least. What do you want in return?"

"I want to find that treasure."

"Sorry, I don't have any insight into that. That is the Captain and the officer's job to figure out that goose chase. Something else?"

"I'd like to be able to go up on deck and looked around. At night, I could look at the stars, and who knows what I might see during the day."

"I have a job that will allow you to do just that," Grubb said.

That day was his first good day since waking up onboard the *Majesty*.

* * *

From that day forward, things changed. Daniel studied the stars at night and the sea during the day. As they continued into warmer waters, he became fascinated with the

70

way seagulls would follow the ship. Occasionally, he would throw them a few pieces of hard biscuit infested with weevils. He enjoyed watching the graceful white birds dive for it, squawking for more. The day the dolphins showed up was a special one. Daniel remembered his father's stories about them. He was thrilled to see firsthand the things the dolphins were capable of doing.

One day, a sailor named Charlie, who wasn't an excellent swimmer, fell overboard.

"Man overboard!" Samuel shouted.

Several crewmen grabbed a rope and hurried to the place where the man had fallen into the sea. It took precious time to rig a harness and lower a man over the side. Charlie might have drowned, but the dolphins came to the rescue. They kept him afloat until the man in the harness could reach him and wrap his arms around him. As the men on the deck pulled them up, the dolphins gave off joyous cries. Some jumped high into the air, while others seemed to walk backward across the surface of the ocean on their tail fins.

It had been forty-two days since the ship left the Port of Boston. With his newfound freedom, Daniel fell in love with sailing all over again. He was happiest with a gentle sea breeze to cool him off as he listened to the men singing in the background. *I want to become a Captain, and finding that treasure will help make that happen.* With those thoughts, came a new determination. He would find it return home and buy a ship, and see that his mother wanted for nothing. After that, he would go back to the sea.

* * *

One day, Daniel ran into his former cellmate.

"Hey, Daniel, I see things are looking up for ya."

"That they are, Richard. I see they let you out of the brig."

Richard winked, "Off for good behavior."

"Well, all's well and ends well," Daniel smiled disarmingly and began to walk back to the galley.

Richard took his arm and led him over to a rail. No one else was nearby. "Say, have you found out anything more about what I was telling ya?"

Daniel nodded his head. Now that he had the freedom to walk the ship, he decided this would be an excellent opportunity to check into it further.

Richard looked around again, a sign of his own paranoia. "Check the room that has the guard posted."

"Think the map is there?" Daniel questioned.

"Why else would there be a guard?" Dawson smiled.

Daniel nodded again and headed back to the galley.

This extra help might give me the edge I need to learn about the treasure of Black Bart. The Golden Chest may soon be mine!

That night after the evening meal, Daniel entertained the men as usual. It was standing room only. They loved watching him perform, cheering and screaming as they tried to guess how he'd completed the trick. This was entertainment like they had never seen. It kept their spirits high throughout the day, even between performances. They loved trying to figure out how Daniel had done it, and they looked forward to seeing the next one. Each day when Grubb entered the mess to tell everyone to leave so that Daniel could cleanup, the men always groaned. Yet they returned to their duties with smiles and lively discussion.

Chapter Thirteen

Sharks in the Water

Now that Daniel had the freedom of the ship, life was more comfortable. He still had a lot of work to do, but no one gave him a hard time. His growing friendship with Grubb made the monotonous routine of shipboard life easier to bear.

One day after cleaning up the dirty luncheon dishes, Daniel decided to begin the hunt for evidence of the treasure that he and his former cellmate had discussed. Entering a part of the ship that was off-limits, he snuck down the corridors, carefully peeking behind every closed door. Daniel was about to open the next one when he heard someone coming. As the approaching footsteps grew louder, he dropped to the floor, slid around the corner, and hid, pressing his body as flat and close to the wall as possible.

A wave of fear passed over him. If the sailor caught him, he might lose his newfound freedom. He had no plausible explanation for being in this part of the ship. He was so tense that when the sailor started to whistle, he jerked in surprise, and his left hand slid away from the wall. Just then, the sailor rounded the corner and stepped on his fingers. Daniel wanted to scream, but he gritted his teeth and remained silent, hoping the man would not look down to see what he had stepped on. He didn't. Daniel waited until he could no longer hear the man's footsteps. Then rose to his feet, shook his throbbing hand, and continued to explore.

Opening the next portal, he peered inside. He saw no expensive tooled leather box and no treasure. Continuing on, he checked behind the next door. Nothing. He was about to turn the corner when he spotted a man guarding the door of the next room. He grew excited as the thought, *This has to be the one.* Now, he had to think of a way to make the guard leave his post. Thankfully, he did not have to wait too long. The guard moved away from the door in the direction of the head. Daniel waited until he was out of sight and sound, then he snuck into the quarters.

He searched the area until he came upon a small chest of drawers. Finding the drawers locked, he pulled out the picklock and got to work. In no time at all, he had the drawers open. Among the papers inside, he found the box he'd been looking for. He had to pick another lock to see what was inside. When he opened the lid, he found a map. It was old and faded, but it was a map. *Well, now I have proof of Rochard's claim. Though I better return to the kitchen before I am missed too much.* He was about to leave when he heard footsteps approached the door. He quickly hid behind some stacked crates. No sooner had he dropped to a crouch, when two men walked through the door. They walked to the center of the room, straight toward Daniel, who tried to make himself even smaller.

"Why haven't you sent the message?" One of the men quietly asked the other when they came to a stop.

"We're not close enough yet," the other replied. "As soon as we are, I'll release the carrier pigeon."

"How do we know it'll reach him?"

"Pidge is an old hand at it. Rest assured, if our friend's ship is anywhere close, this bird will find it," the second man assured him.

Hearing these words, Daniel realized they had a couple spies on board. *I have to find out who they are and warn the Captain.* Trying not to make a sound, he peeked around one of the crates for a look. The men's backs were to him so he couldn't see their

75

faces, but he did notice one man's shoes. Usually, sailors went barefoot or wore black leather shoes with a brass buckle and leather soles. This man wore boots, which was something sailors never wore on the deck of a ship.

When the men finally left, Daniel waited until he could no longer hear their footsteps. Obviously, the current guard was one of the conspirators. He suspected that the men were spies for the British and that the "him" they spoke about was a British officer. Nevertheless, he had no way of being sure. Knowing the guard would soon return, Daniel tried to sneak out. However, as soon as he approached the door, he heard the guard talking to a crew member.

He had returned to his post, and Daniel was trapped inside.

Looking around frantically, Daniel spotted a porthole and rushed over to it. Opening the hatch, he stuck his head out and spotted a four by four, extended rail. Hope punched through the panic. Taking a moment to take a deep breath and calm down, he deliberately slowed his breathing until he felt better. The way was dangerous, but he had no choice. Climbing through the porthole, he grabbed the rail and pulled the hatch closed. As he slid along the rail, he looked down at the crashing waves, soaking him to the skin. If he lost his grip, he would fall into the ocean, and if not rescued, either he would drown, or the sharks would get him. Daniel swallowed hard. *Don't think of that. Just hang on and climb up to the deck.*

Moving hand over hand, he made his way to the next window. If the cabin beyond was empty, he could probably reenter the ship that way. The next porthole, however, led into the Captain's quarters. Although his back was turned, he looked up from the chart he was studying and turned toward the window. Daniel jerked back, hoping the Captain hadn't spotted him. As he did, his hand slipped, and he dropped closer to the choppy water. He swung back and forth unsteadily as he tried to reach up and grab the rail.

His hands grew slick with sweat and saltwater, and his right hand lost its grip. As he slipped closer to the surface, a shark spotted his movement and swam toward him. Its body moved through the water like a bullet through the air. Nothing could stop it. Nothing could keep it from making a meal of Daniel's legs. When it was close enough, the shark propelled its body upward, and its jaws opened wide.

Time seemed to stand still. The sound caught young Daniel's attention. He dropped his head to see what had caused it and found himself staring into the terrifying jaws of a man-eater. All color left his complexion as he frantically pulled up his legs, but he was too close to the surface. If he couldn't pull his body higher, he was a goner. To make things worse, the shark's actions attracted the attention of others. Two more sharks sped toward him like a couple torpedoes. Daniel opened his mouth to scream, but a wave of saltwater crashed into the side of the ship, smothering any sound he might have made. Before the first shark could clamp its jaws around Daniel's legs, the other two jumped into the air, slamming into its side, and knocking it back into the ocean. Its powerful jaws slammed shut, clamping on nothing more than air and water.

Fear gave Daniel added strength. He made his body swing harder, grabbing for the rail each time his hand got close. It took two more tries before he finally caught the rail and pulled himself up and onto the deck. Fighting to regain control of his breathing, he looked over the side at the sharks below. What he saw filled him with awe.

The other two sharks weren't sharks at all. They were dolphins, and they had saved his life. They continued to attack the shark until battered and bleeding, it swam away to escape them. The trail of blood it left attracted other sharks, and a feeding frenzy began. The sight was terrible to behold. It wasn't long before his attacker was no more. Daniel then looked for the dolphins, worried for their safety. They were fine. Swimming alongside the ship, they jumped and called out to him. He waved, wishing he had some fish for them. When they joined the rest of their pod, Daniel sighed with relief until a hand reached out and grabbed him.

"Taking a swim?" Mitch said with a smile.

Daniel wiped his nose with the back of his wrist, "small accident, took a bit of a tumble. Still don't have my sea legs."

Mitch continued to smile as he spoke, "be careful, I won't always be here to save you."

With that, Daniel raced back to the kitchen.

***

When he entered the galley, the cook approached.

"I really appreciate the great meals you're making for the men," Grubb told him. "After supper, why don't you take off the rest of the evening? I'll do the dishes."

Surprised, Daniel smiled. "Thank you, Grubb. I think I'll watch the sunset afterward."

After entertaining the men after the evening meal, Daniel thanked everyone for their enthusiasm and went up on deck. While he watched the sunset, some of the men on duty approached, wanting him to perform another trick. The young man pulled out his deck of cards and began another trick. Their eyes watching his hands as he shuffled the cards, no one noticed the Captain had joined them, until the last moment. The men froze, fearing punishment, but the Captain smiled.

"Go on," he said. "I want to see it, too."

As Daniel continued the trick, the first mate walked up to the Captain.

"Someone has been in the room," Peter Hodge said in a quiet voice.

With a look of concern on his face, the Captain left before the trick was completed. Daniel watched them leave, worried they might figure out that he was the intruder. He wanted to tell someone about the spies on board, but not knowing who the culprits were, he decided to wait. Daniel would look for the man wearing boots. Once he discovered who the man was, he would go to the Captain. If he raised any suspicions, one or both of the spies might escape in one of the dinghies before he discovered who they were.

He quickly finished the trick, and the men returned to their duties.

"Hey, Daniel," Charlie called out to him. "I think I figured out how you performed that trick last night. When Willie replaced the card, you pushed it off-center so that it didn't align with the rest of the cards. Right?"

Daniel grinned. "Nope, that's not what I did. Sorry."

Standing alone at the railing, he looked up at the stars and wondered if his mother was looking at the same stars.

She was.

Chapter Fourteen

All Ashore Who's Going Ashore

Far away from the *Majesty* and off the coast of North Carolina, the *Swift Bounty*, a privately owned sloop, carried its owner and his family, along with a small amount of precious cargo south. They lived in Roanoke, and they were sailing to Fort Caroline, a colony that would eventually become part of the state of Florida.

The *Bounty* was fast and could sail in only eight feet. Its owner, Captain Samson Flint, had chosen this ship because of its speed. He hoped it would give him a better chance of escape, should pirates ever attack.

His hope was in vain.

The captain's family consisted of his wife Margaret and their sixteen-year-old daughter Rebecca. Their life was one of privilege. Besides the sloop, the family-owned a massive mansion in Virginia with plenty of servants to care for it. Both sides of the family were wealthy. Unlike Daniel, Rebecca had servants to grant her every whim, who, like her parents, spoiled her. Whatever she wanted, her father made sure she received it. Her mother supplied her with the most exquisite gowns money could buy.

Rebecca, however, was a bit of a tomboy. She loved sneaking around the ship in sailors' clothing, which she had secretly purchased before they set sail. The outfit consisted of a navy blue doublet and off-white breeches, a navy blue cotton waistcoat and drawers, a white linen shirt, and a black pair of men's sailing shoes in the smallest size she could find. To complete the look, she piled her long golden tresses atop her head and secured it with pins under a knit cap.

Late one evening, when the sky and water were black as pitch, pirates pulled alongside the ship in several dingies. They tossed ropes with grappling hooks over the side that caught on the railings. Then like an invading army of ants, the pirates swarmed over the sides of the ship and snuck aboard.

The pirates silently took out one of the men on watch, knocking him out before he could make a sound. The others crept closer to the remaining sailors on deck, including the captain. They waited while two pirates hurried to Captain Flint's cabin and softly opened the door. Inside, Margaret's back was to them. She did not see the invaders until a calloused hand clamped over her mouth. They dragged the struggling protesting woman to the deck. They marched her over to her husband, placing a single-shot flintlock pistol to her head.

"Toss yer weapons to the deck and put up yer hands," the Pirate Captain shouted. "Or yer woman will be the next casualty."

Under other circumstances, Captain Flint would order his crew to fight, but when he turned around and saw his wife, he knew he had no choice.

"Do as he says," he ordered his crew.

Once the men complied, the pirates searched the ship for anything of value. Aside from some jewelry belonging to Margaret, and the money they carried for their trip, the pirate's haul was disappointing.

When everyone was on deck, Samson and Margaret frantically examined the crew's faces, searching for their daughter. When they didn't see her, hope blossomed. Maybe she had managed to hide somewhere, and the pirates hadn't found her.

"Listen up, as of now you are under the power of meself, Captain Jacques Dupree," the Pirate Captain shouted as he approached Samson. "This is a fine ship yer got here, Cap'n. And since you've little else worth taking, I'm thinking it will make a good addition to me fleet."

Samson wanted to spit back a nasty remark, but he realized that the lives of his family and crew hung on the precipice. Acting foolishly could get them all killed.

"I'll give you fine gentlemen," Captain Jacques Dupree said with a wicked grin, "A choice. Either you join me crew, or I set you afloat in yer lifeboats."

At first, no one said a word. None of the men wanted to become a pirate, but none of them wanted to die either. That still could happen as a pirate, but joining the crew would give them a chance to jump ship and possibly escape with their lives, once they reached port.

"If I may say something," Samson said to Jacques Dupree.

"I guess I can allow that," the pirate laughed.

Samson looked at each of his men. "Living like a pirate won't be easy. Your lives will constantly be in danger. Not only because of the escapades, you will take part in, but also, if captured, the authorities will hang you. Still, we're so far out to sea that your chances will be better with them than in a lifeboat. I suggest you take the captain's offer."

"Does that include this one?" A pirate asked as he dragged what appeared to be a young man up from below deck. "Found this one hidden in one of the storage rooms."

Once Margaret and her husband got a good look at the 'young man' Samson's face went deadpan. His wife had to bite her lip to keep from crying out. It was their daughter, dressed in her sailor outfit. Both Captain Flint and his wife knew that if the pirates discovered she was female, her fate would be worse than death.

"This one is almost too purty to be working on a ship. What did you use him for, Cap'n?" Dupree asked with a sneer.

Samson thought fast, but his wife replied before he could open his mouth.

"He's our cabin boy," she replied.

"Maybe I should make him *my* cabin boy," the Pirate Captain said with a laugh. His men chortled.

"The one I have now is getting a bit long in the tooth."

This brought more laughter and snide remarks.

"You're nothing next to Captain Flint and his wife," Rebecca sneered. She had lowered the pitch of her voice, and the combination of fear and anger roughened it for her.

Her words brought her a sharp slap across the face. Some of Samson's men grabbed their captain by the arms to hold him back. No one treated his daughter that way. One sailor's calm whisper brought him to his senses.

"If you go to her aid, they'll wonder why the 'lad' means so much to you."

Captain Flint relaxed and nodded his thanks. Still, it was a struggle to keep the anger inside. He believed his wife, and he would not live much longer. If possible, he had to save his daughter's life.

"When we get back to the ship, put his crew in the brig for a while," the Pirate Captain said. "That should soften them up."

During the capture of the *Swift Bounty*, the pirate ship *Leviathan* had drawn up alongside her. More pirates came aboard and began escorting members of the captured crew to their ship. Others took their places and manned the boat, preparing it for its new owners.

"What about my wife and me?" Captain Flint asked.

Captain Dupree seemed to think it over, but it was just for show. "Well now, I suppose being a captain in all, ye could run a ship with a pirate crew. Course I doubt I could ever trust you."

Samson remained quiet. He knew the pirate would never allow him to live.

"Being a fair-minded man," Dupree said, grinning at his men, "I'll give ye a choice. You and your wife can take a dinghy and be set afloat. Course, you'll probably both die before anyone rescues you, or I can shoot ya both now and put you out of your misery."

Samson quickly sent his daughter a warning look. He hoped she remembered what he'd taught her about situations like this. "If it's all the same to you, we'll take the dinghy."

Rebecca did remember, but her mind screamed in protest. She wanted to open her mouth and beg the Pirate Captain to let her go with them. Sneaking a glance at her mother, she saw Margaret's eyes pleading with her to remain quiet. Grief encircled her heart. She didn't care if she died, as long as she was with her parents, but the pirates would never allow that to happen. She straightened up and put on a brave face. If this would be the last time her parents saw her, she wanted them to believe she was courageous and had a fighting chance to somehow escape her plight and live.

* * *

While Daniel fixed breakfast, he overheard two men talking. The ship would be arriving into port within two days to restock and resupply. When he completed his morning duties, he left the galley in search of Richard. He finally found him topside, scrubbing the deck.

"Can you talk?" Daniel asked.

"As long as I keep swabbing the deck, no one will care."

"Once we reach port, I'm going to sneak off the ship," Daniel said.

Richard shook his head. "If they catch you, you'll get forty lashings for sure."

"I have to get a message to my mother."

"Good luck to you. I hope for your sake, you don't get caught."

Daniel walked the deck, planning his escape and returned to the ship. He considered asking the Captain for a brief shore leave. However, considering the way he arrived on board as a member of the crew, he figured his chances of receiving permission were nil. He thought about how worried his mother must be. His thoughts formed his resolve. Somehow, he had to leave the ship long enough to get a message to her. Paying little attention to where he was going, he left the upper deck and walked the corridors below. As he passed Captain Stewart's quarters, he overheard him speaking to the first mate.

"Once we arrive in port, I have something special I want you to do," the captain said.

"What's that?" Peter asked as he walked over and closed the cabin door.

85

Daniel wanted to stay and listen through the door, but he couldn't risk being caught snooping. He had already pushed his luck by searching for the map the other day. He headed for the galley, still thinking about a solution to his problem. He continued to ponder as he prepared lunch. Once he had served the men, he grabbed his lunch and scanned the room for Richard, finally spotting him at a table in the corner. He sat alone.

Daniel hurried over and sat across from his former cellmate. "What's the procedure once we get into port?"

"Still looking to jump ship?" Richard kept his voice pitched low to prevent anyone from overhearing them.

Daniel nodded.

"Once we arrive, if the water is deep enough, the boat is docked. If it isn't, the Captain will anchor it offshore. The crew will use dinghies to transport the cargo back and forth."

"Do you know if the water there is deep enough for docking?" Daniel asked.

It was clear by Richard's expression that he was thinking hard. "Yes, I believe it is. Good thing, too, it would be hard for you to sneak onto a boat to get to shore. Once the Majesty reaches the dock, a guard ties it to the dock and then stands at the end of the gangplank. There will be a guard on duty the entire time we're in port."

"So, how am I supposed to get past the guard?"

"Well, there are a couple things you can do," Richard said as he scratched the three-day stubble on his chin. "If I wanted to sneak ashore, I might hide in the supplies. Once the crates leave the ship, the dockworkers take the cargo to the merchant's warehouse. You can wait there until the coast is clear and then do what you had to do."

"That seems like a pretty good plan," Daniel said.

"There's just one flaw. Once you're inside the warehouse, the foreman usually opens a few crates to inspect the contents. If he happens to pick the one you're inside, you'll be discovered and hauled back to the ship."

"That's a chance I can't take. Any other ideas?"

"You could try leaving from either the aft or the bow side of the ship. You'll need a sturdy rope unless you're up for a swim, but I wouldn't recommend it. Chances are someone would hear the splash when you hit the water."

"Leaving from the front or back of the ship, as opposed to the port side, makes sense."

"If you make it to the dock without being seen, you can mingle with the people there and head into town," Richard said. "The only other way I can think of is to have someone distract the guard at the end of the gangplank so you can sneak past."

"The only way that would work is if I could carry some of the cargo off with me. The dockworkers wouldn't know who I am, but one of the crew could still spot me. I think your second idea is the best."

"No matter which way you choose, it will be dangerous and nearly impossible. No one would see you if you went out hidden in a box of cargo, but there's still a chance of discovery once you reach the warehouse."

"Anyway, I could talk the dockworkers into just letting me go about my business?" Daniel asked.

"It's highly doubtful. I know. I tried it once."

"What happened?"

"I picked the wrong box. When the foreman discovered me, he had a couple burly men drag me back the onboard ship, straight to our captain. Hence, the forty lashes I mentioned earlier. The pain will eventually go away, but the scars are with you for life."

"Well, I still have time to consider which way to try. If I opted for the distraction, could you supply it for me?"

Richard looked downcast. "You know I would if I could, but if you were caught, I would be punished, too. And frankly, I don't need any more scars on my back."

Daniel was disappointed, but at the same time, he understood. "Then I won't try that way. If I get caught, I don't want anyone else to be punished for my crime."

* * *

For the next two days, Daniel weighed the pros and cons of all of his plans. On the evening before they reached port, he dreamed he had stowed away inside one of the cargo bins. Then the dream became a nightmare. The warehouse foreman caught and dragged him before Captain Stewart. He awoke to the sound of his own screams as the first mate delivered his punishment. He woke up in a cold sweat, panting.

As soon as the ship docked, Daniel made his decision. He had initially planned to take the chance of discovery at the warehouse, but his dream shook him so severely that he changed his mind. The day seemed to drag on forever. Whenever possible, he'd casually stroll past the port and aft sections to determine his escape route.

When the sun finally set, he made his way to the rear of the boat. Somewhat hidden from view, he watched as the men worked by the light of torches and lanterns. Gathering his courage, he was about to slip over the side when the first mate, Peter, who had just returned from his particular assignment, saw him.

"You'd better go below. With so many men carting cargo back and forth, you might get hurt. Even with the lanterns, it's difficult to see, especially when you're struggling with heavy cargo."

Daniel deflated like a balloon. He had to obey the first mate, but this would make it more challenging to return to the deck unnoticed. He started walking toward the opening that led to the deck below, thinking that as soon as the first mate looked elsewhere, he would change course and head for the front of the ship. He never got the chance. The first mate walked with him until Daniel went below.

The corridors proved to be as dangerous as the deck above him. Daniel tried to squeeze past the dockworkers, but he kept getting in the way, making some of the men angry. The only thing to do was to go with the flow, and before he knew it, he was inside the cargo hold. He wondered if fate was telling him to climb into one of the boxes, after all. He looked for something to hide in. It had to be something already empty. If he displaced the contents to climb inside one of the containers, it would be a dead giveaway.

Daniel finally spotted what he was looking for. He knew it was empty because the lid was slightly askew. Typically, the tops of the containers holding cargo were firmly in place, to not lose the precious cargo. He was about to climb inside the box when one of his crewmates, Mitch, shoved it aside. Looking up, he spotted the young man.

"You'd better find somewhere better than this," Mitch warned him. He had a sneaking suspicion of what Daniel had in mind. "I'll turn my back as you get out."

Daniel jumped out of the way and hurried back into the corridor. He would have to return to his original plan. But, for now, he needed to get out of the way. When he finally reached a clear passageway, Grubb found him.

"You need to start fixing dinner."

Trying not to look disappointed, Daniel headed for the galley to prepare the evening meal.

"Now that we're in port, we'll be taking on fresh supplies." Grubb rubbed his hands together enthusiastically. "That means fresh meat and vegetables and some good eating until we run dry again."

"That's great. The men will enjoy it."

"I think most of the new supplies are already on board," Grubb said. "Why don't you make that stew everyone loves so much?"

"Good idea."

Daniel forced himself to appear happy. He retrieved the items he needed from the storeroom. Returning to the galley, he began chopping up vegetables, but his mind was firmly on his escape plan. After dinner, he entertained the man as usual, and then returned to the galley to clean up. By the time he was finished, no one else was around.

Daniel looked out the porthole and made a decision. Going up on deck was still too dangerous. The quickest way for him to leave the ship would be through the porthole in the galley. Retrieving a rope from the storeroom, he fastened it to one of the heavy iron stoves and slipped through the porthole. The smell of saltwater and fish-filled his nostrils as the waves gently rolled against the side of the ship. He did not slide down immediately but walked along a small wooden ridge to check his options. He was too high up to jump down to the dock.

Returning to the rope, he slid down it until he was a foot or two above the dock. Then bracing his feet against the side of the ship, he pushed off, and when he was over the dock, he released the rope. When his feet hit the wooden pier, it made so much noise that he looked around to see if anyone noticed. No one had. The sounds from loading and unloading the ship covered him. Daniel mingled with the workers and started walking away from the ship.

Above him on the deck, Mitch looked down and yelled, "Too late. The Captain is coming back."

Daniel hesitated for a moment. He was off the ship. Surely, he could slip by without Captain Stewart noticing him. Deciding it was worth a try, he took another step.

"I wouldn't. It's too late. The Captain will see you, and even though he likes you, he'll still order forty lashes. He can't play favorites. It'll upset the crew. You'll have to wait for the next port."

Although he wanted to deny it, Daniel knew that Mitch was right.

"I'll distract the guards so that you can sneak back on board."

True to his word, the crewmen descended the gangplank and engaged the guard in conversation. His speech animated, he pointed toward something, making the guard turn away to see it. Daniel waited until he saw some men returning from the warehouse. He slipped in behind them and made it back on board without incident. A few moments later, Mitch joined him.

"Look, I get it. You don't want to be here, and under the circumstances, I understand why. If you jump ship now, you'll have to find a way to get back to Boston. The trip could be dangerous, thanks to the war." He grinned. "Besides, we can't lose a great cook like you."

"I just wanted to get a message to my mother so she wouldn't worry."

"Sorry, we'll be staying a couple extra days at our next port. Maybe the Captain will let you send one to her from there."

Crestfallen, Daniel, remained on deck. It took another hour before the old cargo was finally off the ship, and the new supplies and cargo onboard. Although less crowded, the deck was filled with men preparing the vessel to leave port.

"Cast off," Captain Stewart told Peter Hodge.

"Cast off!" The first mate shouted to the crew.

Finding a secluded spot, Daniel watched as the ship left the harbor. He felt helpless with a mixture of anger and sorrow. Jumping ship was hard enough, but he had made the crew so happy with his cooking and entertainment that leaving unnoticed was next to impossible. He realized that the only reason the crewmen did not turn him in was that he would be unable to perform his cooking and entertainment duties until he recovered from the lashing.

Daniel sat down on the deck and buried his face in his hands. He was determined to try again when they arrived at the next port, hoping that Captain Stewart would allow him to get a message home to his mother.

* * *

Back in Boston, his mother shivered as an odd feeling overwhelmed her. Somehow, she knew that something had upset her son. It had been so long since he disappeared. Earlier that evening, she'd discovered the reason behind his disappearance. George had returned home, drunk as usual. She had helped him to his bed. Temperance was about to go outside to commune with the stars when she heard him mumble something that froze her in her tracks.

"Sorry. I had to…had to sell your services to the Captain, Daniel. Those men would have killed… killed me. I…had to pay off my debt. You'll…you'll be back in two years. I promise I'll…make it up to you."

Righteous anger flooded Temperance's emotions. She was so angry, she stomped back to the bed and shook George. "How could you?" She yelled when he finally opened his bleary eyes. "How could you force my son into servitude onboard a ship? The waters are too dangerous. What would happen if pirates captured him? What happens if the British attack the ship? If he lives through the attack, they will imprison him for treason. They might even hang him." Her voice had risen to a shriek. "How *could* you?"

George didn't answer. He passed out without a word.

Chapter Fifteen

The Captain's Quarters

The next evening, Daniel was about to set out the food for the evening meal when the cook approached him.

"The man who serves the Captain's table is sick. You'll need to do it tonight."

Daniel's stomach filled with butterflies. He felt like he was about to serve a king, and when he realized that he didn't know the proper way to handle a formal meal, he grew queasy.

"What am I supposed to do?"

As usual, Grubb was already well into his drink. He tried to show him but did a terrible job. Every time he told Daniel how to do something, he changed his mind and taught him another way, leaving the young man thoroughly confused.

"Okay, let's try this," the cook said. "Here are the plates and utensils you'll need."

"Why are there three plates? Is one for the soup bowl?"

"The small one is for bread. Then the medium one goes on top of the large one." Grubb paused. "No, wait. Maybe the medium one is for the bread, and the smaller goes on top of the big one."

Changing it around, he and Daniel stared at the setting. It didn't look right.

"It looked better the other way," Daniel suggested.

The cook changed it back. "Uh, okay, let's move on to the napkin."

"They use napkins?"

"Captain Stewart is a gentry. He wants his meals properly served." He picked up one of the cloth napkins. "Now, there's a certain way this has to be done." He tried to fold the napkin properly, but his addled brain couldn't remember how. Frustrated, he folded it into quarters and laid it down on the right side of the plate. "Now the silverware goes like this. The fork is on the right side and the knife and spoon on the left. No, that's not right. Maybe the knife and fork go on the right and the spoon on the left."

He changed it around, but even Daniel realized that the setting still wasn't right.

"Anyway, the food has to be served in the proper order." He paused yet again. "I just...I don't remember how."

By now, Daniel was in a total panic. He ran out of the room and headed for the crew's quarters. Searching the bunks and hammocks, he finally found the Captain's steward, Tom Jenkins. Waking him up, he said, "You have to tell me how to serve the Captain's table. Grubb is too drunk and doesn't remember how."

"I'm sick. Go away." He groaned.

"Please, Tom, I don't want to mess it up," Daniel begged.

Tom shook his head no. "If I show you, you might replace me. Serving the Captain is the cushiest job on board, so I'm not telling you *anything*." He rolled over, furthering the point that he was not about to help the young man in any way.

Daniel ran back to the mess, where he found Grubb still trying to figure it out. "Okay, I think this is the way it's done."

Daniel studied the setting as the cook explained the proper order to serve the food.

Grubb looked up. "You got it?"

Daniel nodded. He stacked the dishes, utensils, and napkins he needed on a tray. He was about to take them to the Captain's quarters when the cook stopped him.

"Wait. You can't go dressed like that."

"What am I supposed to wear? These are the only clothes I have," Daniel said.

"Not true. I picked up some stuff for you while we were in port." The cook took the young man to the supply room and handed him a package wrapped in brown paper with a string tied around it. "I meant to give this to you earlier, but I forgot."

More like you were passed out drunk. Daniel took the package. He had a puzzled expression on his face.

"Go ahead. Open it up."

Daniel did so. Inside the paper, he found two sets of sailor's clothing.

"The top one is for everyday use. The bottom is for more formal occasions, like when you have to serve the Captain."

"I don't get paid until I've been aboard for six months. I'm sorry. I can't pay you back until later."

"Did I *ask* for money?"

"No," Daniel replied hesitantly.

"This is a gift."

Daniel was about to protest, but the cook held up his hand.

"Why would you do this for me?" Daniel asked.

"It's my way of saying thanks for saving my bacon. I'd have received a whipping, maybe even keelhauled, if you hadn't covered up the fire in the galley. Now put on that outfit and go serve the Captain and his officers."

Daniel quickly changed. Then, gathering the tray with the dishes, he took it up to the Captain's quarters. When he arrived, he knocked. The first mate opened the door. Daniel entered the room, realizing that it was nothing like the rest of the ship. His earlier glimpses through the porthole and open doorway hadn't allowed him to really see the interior. The room was clean, orderly, and fit for a king. Grubb's words came back to him. *Captain Stewart is a gentry.* Apparently, he hadn't been kidding.

Unlike the rest of the ship, the room had two large windows. Looking through them, he saw the most beautiful view he'd ever seen: a cloudless blue sky and clear seawater. Once more, he made up his mind that someday he would become the captain of his own ship.

The first mate cleared his throat, bringing Daniel back to the present. He moved to a round mahogany table and began to set out the dishes. Naturally, he got it wrong because the cook still hadn't gotten it right. One of the officers smiled at Daniel and corrected the place settings.

"First time serving a captain?" The man asked.

"Yes," Daniel replied as he studied the setup.

"Better get the food before the Captain arrives," Peter said.

"So, you're taking Tom's place while he's sick?" Another officer asked.

"Yes, sir."

He left for the galley and returned with the food. A moment later, the Captain sat down. Daniel served him. Like the place settings, he got it wrong, but Captain Stewart smiled and showed him the proper order.

Picking up a ladle and a tureen of soup, the young man filled their bowls. As he finished filling the last dish, Daniel accidentally spilled some on one of the officers.

He shrank back. "I'm sorry, sir," Daniel said, horrified.

The man smiled. "Don't worry. It's not the first time someone spilled something on me."

The officers liked the young man and were patient with him. As the meal progressed, Daniel stood to the side and listened. The Captain related a tale about a sister ship that had been boarded by pirates.

Daniel thoroughly enjoyed the conversation. After serving the main course, he returned to the galley for dessert.

"How's it going?" Grubb asked.

"Pretty good, the officers have been nice and showed me the proper way to serve them."

"That's good. I knew you'd do okay."

Loading the plates with dessert on to his tray, he hurried back to the Captain's quarters. All the officers wanted some. Daniel served them. As they tasted it, smiles lit their faces.

"Who made this?" The Captain asked.

"I did," Daniel replied. "It's something my mother loved to make."

"This was excellent," Captain Stewart said.

The men applauded him.

"Say," Peter said. "I've seen you perform magic for the men down in the mess. How about showing us one of your tricks?"

"I'd love to," Daniel replied.

He pulled out his deck of cards and showed them the first one he had revealed the crew. Captain Stewart and his officers were impressed. Before this, they had been speaking in English.

This time, the Captain spoke in French. "The lad's pretty good."

"Thank you, sir," Daniel replied in French.

The Captain looked at him in surprise, returning to his English dialect, "You speak French?"

"My father was French and a captain on a merchant ship similar to yours."

"Really? What is your father's name?"

"Henri Beaumont."

"Henri Beaumont? I knew your father. He was a gentleman and an excellent Captain. His death was tragic," the Captain said.

A confused look crossed Daniel's face. "Dead? I'm sorry, sir, but my father ran out on us."

It was the Captain's turn to be puzzled. "Who told you that?"

"My Uncle George, he is my father's brother."

"Believe me when I tell you. Your father died in a tragic accident."

Daniel was shocked into silence. When he was finally able to speak, he asked, "How?"

"It was your uncle's fault. Whatever happened to George anyway?" The Captain asked.

"He's a drunk. He told my mom and me that my father abandoned us."

"George is a dirty scoundrel. Your father wouldn't have done that. He was a good man and loved you both very much. Before I became a captain, I was his first mate. He had a painting of you and your mother hanging on the wall behind his desk."

Daniel didn't know what to think. Why did his uncle lie? A dark voice in his head echoed words he didn't want to believe. *The accident was George's fault!*

The other officers left, leaving Captain Stewart and Daniel alone. They talked about Henri Beaumont for the next hour.

"I knew your mother, too. She was the most beautiful woman in the colonies. I have to tell you, Daniel. I had my heart set on her, but your father was much better looking. I didn't stand a chance."

Daniel grinned. "My parents really love…I mean, they loved each other. My mother still does. For some reason, she never believed that my father had deserted us.

"All this time, we believe that he left us for the sea. It made me feel unimportant, which really hurt because I admired him more than anyone. The bullies at school teased me a lot, too. It made me feel unworthy and ashamed. Growing up with my alcoholic uncle, I had to learn how to protect my mother and myself from his frequent outbursts of anger."

"That's unfortunate."

"What happened that day?"

"George was in the crow's nest. Your uncle had a hangover from the night before. We had just sold our cargo and made a big profit. The crew celebrated the night before. Like everyone else, George had a little too much rum."

Captain Nathaniel Stewart took the last sip of his after-dinner drink, a glass of scotch. "I was on deck talking to your father. We stood a couple of feet from the area beneath the crow's nest. Suddenly, we heard George cry out. He was climbing down and lost his grip. He fell, kicking and screaming. Captain Beaumont shoved me out of the way, saving my life. Before he could get to safety, however, your uncle landed on top of him. The fall banged up George a bit. I rolled him off your father and discovered that Henri was badly injured."

"What happened next?" Daniel asked.

"Some of the men helped me carry him to his quarters. The surgeon examined him and discovered that George had accidentally kicked him in the head just before he landed. Doc told me that Captain Beaumont had a severe brain injury. He died two days later. That was when George started drinking all the time. He couldn't face what he had done to his brother and your family." Captain Stewart paused a moment before asking, in hopes of changing to a more positive subject, "Do you like to sail?"

"Very much," Daniel replied. "Even though we believed that my father had deserted us, I have always loved to watch the ships come into port. I've dreamed of becoming a captain for as long as I can remember."

"Did your father ever teach you anything about running a ship?"

"No, I was too young."

"Why don't you meet me on deck tomorrow? I'd be willing to show you a thing or two. I feel I owe it to your father."

* * *

Daniel stood behind the tiller, a wooden wheel, dressed in the outfit he had worn since his arrival onboard the ship. He had thought about wearing the new outfit that Grubb had given him, but he didn't want to get it dirty.

When Captain Stewart approached, he looked at Daniel and frowned. "I will not have one of my men dressed this way," he told the first mate. "Peter, take him down and give him a change of clothes."

When they were out of the Captain's hearing, Daniel told Peter about the clothes the cook had given him. The first mate examined them and nodded his approval.

"Save the one you wear to serve the Captain's table. Wear the other."

When young Daniel returned to the deck, he looked handsome and well dressed.

For the next few hours, Captain Stewart taught him how to steer, read the wind, and batten down the hatches. He also showed the young man how to read a sextant. It was one of the best days of Daniel's life. He couldn't stop smiling, especially when he realized that he loved the wind in his face and the smell of saltwater, just like his father.

When he returned to the galley to start the evening meal, he found Grubb yelling at Tom.

"Captain's orders! He wants Daniel to replace you, which means you'll be working somewhere *else* from now on."

"We'll see about that," Tom said. Angered beyond reason, he stormed out of the galley. Seeing Daniel, he stopped for a moment. "I told you this would happen."

"I didn't know. Captain Stewart didn't tell me. I didn't try to take your job."

"Yeah, right. You just made him feel sorry for you because of your old man," Tom shouted. "Mark my words. You'll regret this."

Tom went up on deck to stew. He stood by the railing on the port side, his mind an angry whirl of emotions. Hawkins found him there later.

"I heard you lost your cushy job. What happened?"

"Magic boy stole it. While I was sick, he took my place. I knew this was gonna happen. That's why I wouldn't tell him the proper way to do my job."

"Apparently, that didn't make any difference," Hawkins said.

"He whined to the Captain about his old man, making the officers feel sorry for him. It's not right. Just because he lost his old man and can do a couple of card tricks, doesn't mean he should be allowed to take over my job."

"I know what you mean," Hawkins agreed. "I had him doing the dirtiest jobs, just like a newbie should. I don't know how he did it, but cook and everyone else took a liking to him. They've spoiled him."

"He has to pay," Tom grumbled.

"So, what are we going to do about it?"

"I don't know yet, but I'm going to figure out a way to ruin his life."

"Count me in," Hawkins said. "It's past time we put that boy in his place."

Daniel was in trouble. He just didn't know it yet.

Chapter Sixteen

Captain Stewart and Daniel Beaumont

The days flew past, and Daniel found himself frequently sitting at the Captain's table, talking with Captain Stewart. As their relationship grew, the young man felt more like the man's son than a crewman. One night after the evening meal, the officers left, leaving them to speak in private.

"You have at least one spy, maybe two, onboard the *Majesty*," Daniel said.

His words startled Captain Stewart. "I can't say that I'm surprised by the war going on, but what makes you say that."

Although they were now good friends, Daniel did not intend to admit that he was in the secret room when he made this discovery. "I was gathering eggs and overheard them talking in the corridor."

"What did they say?"

"One man asked the other one why the message hadn't been sent yet."

"Did they mention what the message was or who was supposed to receive it?" Captain Stewart asked.

"No, but they were going to use a carrier pigeon. One man said they weren't close enough yet. The other worried about the bird finding some other captain at sea, but the first man reassured him that as long as the boat was in range, the pigeon would find his target."

"Did you get a look at their faces?"

"No, it was too dark. I did, however, notice one man's footwear," Daniel said.

"Their footwear?"

"One man wore shoes like everyone else on board. The other had on boots. I would've told you sooner, but I didn't know if you would believe me. I decided to look for the man with the boots. Then I would come and tell you."

"Then, you found him?"

"Not yet."

"What did the men sound like?"

"Excuse me?" The question puzzled Daniel.

"How did they speak? Did they sound like the rest of the men, or do they speak in a more refined voice?"

"One man sounded like the rest of the crew. The other, the man with the boots, I think, talked more like you."

"Refined?"

"Yes. He definitely sounded like an educated man. Do you think he's a spy for the British?"

"That's a possibility. Although, I don't know what he expected to learn on my ship." He spoke the last three words slowly, as though something had just occurred to him. He thought back to the day when one of his crewmen told him that someone had gotten inside the room where the Black Bart's treasure map was located. The intruder hadn't taken the map, but that didn't mean the spy hadn't seen them. "Whoever he is, I don't want you repeating this to anybody, especially my officers. Until we discover his and the other man's identity, we must be cautious."

* * *

Down in the mess, Tom and Hawkins were the only ones left. The galley was clean, and Grubb had gone on deck for an evening of cards and rum. Tom stood up and checked to make sure no one was out in the corridor. Returning to his table, he sat next to Hawkins.

"Any ideas yet?" Hawkins asked.

"Not yet, but I'll think of something."

* * *

Daniel's lessons on how to be a captain and run a ship continued. The more he learned, the more he felt that he was on the road to making his dreams come true. Every afternoon, Captain Stewart worked with him. Teaching him how to read maps, defeat pirates, and all the other things he needed to learn.

"Have you been practicing with the sextant?"

"Every chance I get," Daniel replied.

"Good, let's go up on deck. You can show me what you've learned. Why don't you talk me through the process while you do it," Captain Stewart said when they reached the bow.

"First, I need to focus the telescope on the horizon. I can choose the sun, the moon, a planet, or a star. Next, I have to measure the angle of the horizon with the arc by looking through the telescope and aligning the horizon I see with the one reflected in one of the two mirrors. After that, I have to lock the arm with the clamp and record the degree measurement on the arc."

"Fantastic, Daniel. What's next?"

"I need to read the micrometer measurement, which measures fractions of a degree. Then I must add the measurement to the degree measurement on the arc and record the instrument error. It should be zero, but will normally have some measurable error. To account for this error, I have to subtract this error from any sightings I take."

"*Excellent*, now what?"

"I need to sight the celestial object again and move the sextant's arm, with the second mirror, until the object just touches the horizon. The celestial object is superimposed on the horizon. Then I have to measure the angle of the sextant like before and record the measurement along with the exact time I took it."

He showed the results to the captain, who then checked them for himself.

"You're still a little off." Seeing the sad expression on Daniel's face, he added, "Don't be discouraged. It takes a lot of practice before you get it right, but don't worry, you're getting close."

* * *

In the crew sleeping quarters, Hawkins and Tom laid in hammocks strung next to each other. They had taken the far corner of the room, keeping away from the other sleeping crewmen. It was mid-afternoon, so the room wasn't full. They had just awoken from their four-hour sleep and were talking about ways to get even with Daniel.

"We could throw him overboard," Tom said.

"I thought you wanted him to suffer. Drowning is too easy," Hawkins replied. "How about poisoning him?"

Tom thought some more and smiled. "I've got a better idea. Daniel ruined my life, and now I'm going to ruin his. And I know just how to do it. We'll make him look like a thief."

"That'll certainly get him into trouble with the Captain," Hawkins said.

"It will make the crew turn on him, too."

They continued to make plans for young Daniel.

* * *

His sextant lessons over, Daniel listened while Captain Stewart continued to talk about ways to outrun a pirate ship, should they attack.

"It is necessary to know these skills," Captain Stewart spoke to Daniel. "Though even more necessary to be able to think on one's feet. You can never really predict pirates."

"However, it stands to reason to know the fundamentals, right?" Daniel asked.

Captain Stewart smiled, "Absolutely."

"Captain," Daniel asked. "Can you clarify something for me?"

Nathaniel Stewart replied, "Depending on what it is, Daniel."

Daniel took a deep breath before he spoke. "Since we are on the topic of pirates. Should they attack us, I need to know. Is there really a treasure map aboard the *Majesty*? I have heard rumors from some of the crew. I wanted to verify those rumors with you if that is okay?"

The young man could not read the Captain's poker face as he tactfully answered his question. "There is, and when the time is right, I'll show it to you."

* * *

In the Captain's quarters, Tom snuck inside and looked around, trying to decide what to steal. At first, he thought he should take some money, but he rejected it. Tom saw a few personal items but decided they weren't important enough. Then his gaze fell upon the gift that Mrs. Stewart had given her husband before he left on this journey. Tom smiled. *Yes, this is the perfect thing. It will make him very angry.*

Stuffing the gift into a small sack he carried, he opened the door and checked the corridor. It was empty. Then hiding the bag in his shirt, he left the Captain's quarters and went in search of a place to hide what he stole.

* * *

That evening, Daniel gathered up everything for the officers' meal. Taking it to Captain Stewart's quarters, he correctly laid out the dishes and waited. The officers sat around the table and talked until the Captain entered the room and sat down. The meal began. Everyone was in good spirits until halfway through the main course, when Nathaniel realized that something was missing.

"Did you put my wife's gift somewhere else?"

Daniel's brow wrinkled, and he looked at the place where it was usually stored. "No, sir, I haven't touched it."

"Have the rest of you seen it lately?"

"It was there this morning," Peter replied.

Captain Stewart stood up so hard he knocked his chair over. "Call the crew to the deck."

"What about the ones who are sleeping?" The first mate asked.

"All of them. I don't care what they're doing. We've got a thief on board, and I'm going to find him."

Daniel prayed that Richard hadn't done it as he and the other officers hurried from the room. By the time the Captain joined them, the first mate had everyone lined up on deck.

"We have a thief in our midst," the Captain barked. He found Richard and gave him an accusing look.

"Not me, Captain," Richard said.

"Someone stole the gift my wife gave me just before we set off on this voyage. I will give you until noon tomorrow to return it. If it's still missing, I will punish everyone until the thief admits who he is."

The crew exchanged glances. They wondered who would do such a thing. If no one stepped forward, they would have to find out who the culprit was before noon.

"Rest assured. The thief will be caught and punished." Giving everyone a final angry look, Captain Stewart left the deck and returned to his quarters.

That night, the crew conducted a massive search. As they did, they wondered who would be so stupid as to steal something from the Captain. There was no music or singing that night. There was a thief among them, and if they didn't find him soon, they would all pay for his misdeeds.

At noon the next day, the men lined up on deck. All but two were utterly baffled.

"Well? Which one of you did it?" Captain Stewart asked.

Tom stepped forward. "I know who did it. I saw him hiding it."

"Who?" The Captain asked.

"Daniel."

There was an audible gasp of surprise, and everyone turned to look at Daniel.

"You're a liar," Daniel said hotly.

Captain Stewart didn't believe it, yet he felt disappointment rise in his throat. "Show me where it is."

Tom led Daniel, the first mate, and the Captain to the crew's quarters. Moving to the opposite side of the room where he and Hawkins had slept, he stopped by one of the cots in the corner.

"He put it under there. I saw him."

"No, I didn't," Daniel insisted.

"Yes, you did." Tom snapped back.

The Captain jerked the bunk bed away from the wall and looked down. His wife's gift was there.

Daniel continued to deny having anything to do with it. "Why would I do that, especially after you've been so good to me?"

"Why, indeed?" Although he didn't want to, Captain Stewart started to believe Tom's accusation.

"You must believe me, sir," Tom said. "I'm a witness. I saw him stuff it under that bunk."

"Put him in a cell," the Captain said to the first mate.

Although Daniel continued to deny his guilt, Captain Stewart walked out. He stopped as he reached the doorway. "I trusted you, Daniel. Looks like you're more like your uncle than your father."

Daniel hung his head.

* * *

Daniel was alone in his cell until Richard came to talk with him. "I know you're innocent."

"Who could have framed me? Who have I hurt so badly that they would want to do this to me?" Daniel asked him.

Richard thought about it a moment, then the answer came to him. "*Tom*, your accuser. Ever since you took his job, he's been whining and complaining to everyone about you."

"You're right, but how can I prove it?" Daniel asked.

They thought about it until Richard got an idea.

"I think I know a way," Richard said.

* * *

Later that night, Tom and Richard entered the sleeping quarters at the same time.

"Nice move, making Daniel look guilty," Richard said. "I was getting sick and tired of Captain Stewart fawning over him."

"I didn't do anything but tell the truth. He's guilty."

"Aw, come on, Tom, you can tell me. I know you set him up. Frankly, I don't blame you a bit."

"I didn't," Tom insisted.

"Hey, you're smart, and you loved your job."

Richard continued to stroke Tom's ego, but it didn't look like the former steward was going to admit his guilt. Nevertheless, Daniel's former cellmate wasn't ready to give

112

up yet. He continued to act as though he thought that Daniel got what was coming to him. Finally, Tom gave in.

"Okay, I admit it. I set the boy up. He stole my job and deserves to be punished."

At that moment, Captain Stewart and the first mate walked out of the shadows.

"Get him out of here," the Captain ordered.

In his cell, Daniel jumped to his feet when he heard Tom protesting as the first mate opened the door.

"Come on out, Daniel. You're innocent. This here is the culprit."

Daniel had to hide his smile. As soon as he cleared the door, the first mate shoved Tom inside, slammed the door, and locked it. As Daniel walked away, Captain Stewart joined him.

"I'm sorry I didn't believe you. I have no excuse."

"I'm just glad you found out who did it. You really have known me that long to know if I would do something like that or not."

"Nevertheless, I should have believed you. When Richard came to me to set up the trap, I realized that what he told me was more like something Tom would do than you. I had no right to say you were like your uncle."

Daniel nodded, and they shook hands.

Chapter Seventeen

Finding the Spy

Now that he'd told the Captain, Daniel decided to work harder at finding the spy. During meals, he studied each of the men at the tables. Captain Stewart felt that since the spy wore boots. It must be one of his officers, but he wasn't sure. They all seemed dedicated to him, following orders and making sure the voyage went smoothly. Then he had an idea. What if the spy was one of the sailors pretending to be a lesser educated man? Could such a person hide his aristocracy? Why not? It was far easier for a rich man to pretend he was miserable than a commoner trying to pretend he belonged to the upper class. He simply wouldn't have the education or the money to pull it off.

The next time he was alone with the captain, Daniel said, "Whoever he is, he has gone back to wearing sailor shoes instead of the boots. Why did he wear boots that day? Had he just come aboard?"

Captain Stewart pondered the question. "I suppose it's possible. Nevertheless, it would be difficult. What day did this happen?"

Daniel thought back. Then his eyes lit up. "Remember that day, *The Merchant Queen* pulled up alongside us?"

"The captain and four of the *Queen*'s officers came aboard to discuss the sighting of a British warship. We sailed together for the better part of the day. I was in conversation with their captain and didn't pay any attention when her officers returned to their ship."

"That had to be when he came on board," Daniel said excitedly. "Would you recognize his face if you saw it?"

"I think so. Still, he might be hiding. I'll make some discreet inquiries. Somebody had to be watching when the *Queen*'s officers returned to their ship."

* * *

Like Captain Stewart, Daniel was familiar with most of the men on board. He was confident he would recognize someone new. Each time he moved among the crew, he looked for someone different. When that didn't bring any results, he decided to continue looking for the spy among the *Majesty*'s crew.

Daniel suspected almost everyone. The first man he checked out was the cook. Grubb was always drunk, or was he? Could he be pretending? Was the story about losing his family just a tale? That evening, as he prepared the meal, Daniel started a conversation.

"How old was your little boy when he died?"

Grubb gave him a puzzled look. "He was six."

"Did he die before your wife?"

"No, it was a good thing, too. His loss would have driven my wife to her grave that much sooner."

Daniel wracked his brain for an idea that would trip up the cook. "It must've happened a long time ago."

Grubb stopped slicing a loaf of bread. He peered at Daniel suspiciously. "What's with all the questions about my family?"

115

"Just curious," Daniel said. "I thought that maybe if you talked about it, it would help."

"Well, you're wrong. I don't like to talk about it, and I would appreciate it if you would just mind your own business."

"Sorry."

Daniel was dissatisfied when he headed for the Captain's quarters. He hadn't come up with good enough questions. Since Grubb did not want to talk about it, he couldn't bring it up again. That night when he lay in his hammock, he thought about whom he would question next.

* * *

Daniel kept at it until he questioned every man in the crew. He also spent time looking for the boots, checking parts of the ship that had little activity. Whenever he lay down to catch four hours of sleep, he thought about everything he had learned, especially the clues revealed when he'd overheard the spies talking. He concentrated on the sound of the men's voices, but the encounter had been so brief, he couldn't be sure. He continued looking for the boots. That search also proved futile.

Daniel cleaned up the dishes and started to head back to the galley. He still didn't know the identity of either spy or what they planned to do. Nevertheless, he was confident of one thing. Whatever they were planning, it had to do with their unusual cargo.

* * *

One morning after breakfast, he found his former cellmate taking a break on the deck. The area around the railing where he stood was otherwise unoccupied. Daniel decided to brainstorm with Richard.

"How's the search going?" Richard asked.

"Not good. The Captain and I have a couple suspects, but no way to prove their guilt or innocence one way or the other."

"I know you've been checking the ship for a stow-a-way, did you happen to stumble upon information about the treasure yet?"

Daniel turned his head and pretended to watch the dolphins following the ship. He hadn't told Richard about finding the map. Not knowing who the spies onboard might be, he couldn't reveal that secret to anyone.

"No," he lied. "Why do you ask?"

"Just wondering."

For some reason, a chill ran up Daniel's spine. Was *Richard* the traitor? His former cellmate had questioned him repeatedly about the treasure. Was it because he really didn't know, or did he want to find out if Daniel could confirm his suspicions? If Richard was a spy, telling him might put the young man in danger. He decided to play it cool.

"What could a spy do on a large ship?" Daniel said in hopes of baiting Richard.

"Well, I suppose there are several things he could try. He could stir up trouble and cause a mutiny. He might even throw the cargo overboard."

"I could see the mutiny," Daniel said. "Do you think the crew would side with the British, given a chance?"

"Anything's possible. Folks are conflicted. They don't know whether to side with the colonial army or remain loyal to the crown."

"I just don't see what throwing the cargo overboard would do, unless it's something important to the patriots' cause. Do you know if we took on weapons at the last port?"

Richard shrugged. "Haven't a clue."

"Do you think they would try to sink the ship?"

"Nah, a ship like this would be a valuable commodity to the enemy. They could use it to transport men and supplies, or they could refit it as a warship. Sinking it would be a waste."

They grew silent as they watched the dolphins. Suddenly, something white fluttered past them and headed out to sea.

"The pigeon," Daniel explained. "They just released the pigeon! I've got to warn the Captain."

Richard studied the bird until they lost sight of it. "I don't think it was a pigeon. It looked more like a dove. Cap'n must have released it to see how close to the water we are."

"Are you sure?" Daniel asked.

"Would I tell you that if I weren't?"

Daniel wondered. If he were a spy, he certainly wouldn't admit that he'd seen the pigeon. To be on the safe side, he would ask Captain Stewart.

* * *

That night at dinner, Daniel studied the men around the table. After serving the first course, he decided to ask a few questions.

"Why would someone release a dove clear out here?"

"We wouldn't this far out to sea," Captain Stewart replied. "We only release a dove when we went to check how close we are to land."

As the captain responded, Peter, the first mate, gave Daniel a puzzled look. Then he realized that the young man must know there was a spy on board.

"Are you sure it was a dove that you saw?" The Captain asked.

"It might have been a pigeon," one of the officers suggested.

"I don't think so," Peter said. "We're too far out. Pidge would never make it to land."

"Pidge?" Captain Stewart asked.

The first mate laughed and thought of something to cover the slip of his tongue. "That's what I call them all, Pidge. We'd have no reason to keep a pigeon onboard."

Daniel turned his back to get control of his excitement. He'd discovered one of the spies! He distinctly remembered one man telling the other that Pidge was an old hand at delivering messages from one ship to another. Once the meal was finished, Daniel couldn't wait to be alone with the captain. The other officers left, except for Peter, who remained behind. Daniel wondered if he should tell the Captain and confront the first mate now.

He decided to take the dirty dishes back to the galley, hoping that by the time he got back, the first mate would be gone. When he returned, however, the Captain had left his cabin on an errand, and Daniel found himself alone with the traitor.

"Captain got called on deck. It seems they're having a bit of trouble up there."

Daniel turned to run out the door, but before he could get away, Peter clapped a hand over his mouth and dragged him into the corridor, where his men were waiting. With the Captain busy with what was happening on deck, he was unaware of what was happening below. The first mate's men, one of which Daniel identified as Charlie, took Daniel into the bowels of the ship. Daniel struggled and tried to call for help, but the corridors were suspiciously empty. It was though someone had cleared them out ahead of time.

Halfway there, Richard, who had just come out of the room where they kept the animals, overheard the commotion and changed directions to find out what was going on. As soon as he saw the men holding Daniel prisoner, he knew his friend was in trouble.

"What's going on here? Why are you treating Daniel like a criminal?" He asked the man who seemed to be in charge of the group, he went by Thompson.

"Nothing. Just keep to yourself. The first mate just wants to talk with magic boy."

"Then where is he?" Richard asked.

"He had to help Captain Stewart with a problem topside, but he'll be here in a minute. Just run along. Things are fine here."

Knowing he couldn't fight them all on his own, Richard pretended indifference and left to find help.

"Get back to your posts," Thompson said. "Two of us can handle this one until Peter arrives." As the others moved away, Daniel stomped down hard on the foot of the man holding him. His captor cried out and immediately released him, grabbing his foot and hopping to keep his weight off it.

Daniel slipped past the other sailor, who raised the alarm, bringing the others back at a run. Weaving in and out of the cargo, the young man used the commotion to cover the sound of his flight. He headed for one side of the room and worked his way up until he reached the front corner. There he hid behind a stack of barrels.

"Spread out," Thompson yelled. "Someone block that door. He's in here somewhere. If he gets out, he will head straight for the Captain."

The room grew quiet except for the sound of footsteps made by the men searching for Daniel. The young man was glad for the silence. Listening hard, trying to pinpoint where they were, he slowed his breathing, believing it would give him away. The fear he'd felt when trapped in the barn was nothing compared to this. This time, he knew the danger was real. These men weren't hiding a surprise gift for someone's wife, and there was no hole in the wall to escape through, and no one to help him. Still uncertain if Richard was the other spy or not, he had no idea if anyone would be coming to his rescue or not.

Panic nearly made him run from his hiding place for the door. Reason told him it was a foolish move. Instead, he carefully checked the area around him. Seeing it was clear, he tiptoed from his hiding place to another pile of crates and ducked behind them. Sweat ran down his face in streaks.

"Come on out, Daniel," Charlie taunted. "We ain't gonna hurt you. The first mate just wants to have a little talk with you."

The other men laughed.

"You'll be given a choice, and if you make the right one, you have nothing to fear," Charlie continued.

Daniel didn't believe a word. If they caught him, he thought they would murder him. Checking once more, he slipped from behind his present location and scooted to the next. There he leaned against the wall and once more slowed his breathing. As each move brought him closer to the door, his excitement grew, overshadowing some of the fear. He dared to hope that he would make it. Checking the area around him, he spotted one of the men thirty feet away. Daniel ducked back and waited. Seconds later, he looked again. Seeing no one, he headed for the next hiding place, but this time, someone spotted him, and a shout went up.

"There he is, heading for the door!"

Daniel ran as fast as he could, but it was no use. The men closed in. The one at the door was waiting with open arms and a sneer on his face. There was little hope of escape. The traitors moved in rapidly and surrounded him.

"I think our friend here needs a little convincing," Thompson said. "What do you say? Should we soften them up with a little beating?"

The men agreed. As they started to close in, Richard returned with several men in tow, including Mitch and Samuel, and a massive brawl broke out. One man grabbed Daniel from behind and pinned his arms, while another raised his fist to punch him. The young man kicked out and nearly lost his balance when the man holding his arms, suddenly released him. He turned to find Richard grinning at him.

"Go on. Head up to the deck and warn the Captain."

Daniel nodded and ran into the hallway while Richard fought with the other man. When he reached the deck, he spotted Stewart and ran to him.

"Captain Stewart, I know who the spy is. It's…"

The Captain turned around to hear what Daniel was saying, when someone in the ship yelled, "Pirates!"

Looking up in alarm, Nathaniel ran for the helm. Daniel followed.

"I have to tell you," Daniel insisted.

Grabbing the wheel, Captain Stewart looked down at him. "I'm sorry. We have bigger problems now. We'll talk about it later."

"But, it's your first mate!"

The Captain turned to Peter, who was reaching for his sword. "Arrest him," he shouted to the other officers.

The officers surrounded the spy, and a sword fight ensued. Even though he was outnumbered, the first officer was quite a swordsman. It took nearly ten minutes to disarm and subdue him.

"Thanks, Daniel," the Captain said. Turning to his men and shouted orders for battle.

The ship's bell rang loudly, bringing every available man scurrying to his post. The pirates were about to attack.

Chapter Eighteen

Pirates!

Captain Stewart turned to his first mate. "Are you one of them?"

"One of who?" Peter sneered.

"The pirates! Or are you a spy working for the British?"

The first mate remained silent. Disgusted, Captain Stewart ripped the man's shirt off him, and there on his arm was a pirate tattoo. A skeleton holding a glass with a devil next to him, also holding a drink.

"So, it's greed that drives you, not patriotism or loyalty to the crown. You're under arrest." Turning to one of his officers, he said, "Throw him in the brig."

The Captain now turned his attention to the problem at hand. "Listen up," he shouted. "We're going to try and outrun them. Unfurl the sails and man the oars!"

The men quickly followed orders. Capture by a pirate ship appealed to no one. They would either end up dead or be conscripted into the pirate crew. Neither choice was alluring. The *Majesty* was a fast ship, and for a while, it pulled ahead, leaving the one flying the Jolly Roger in its wake.

"Keep going, lads, it's working!" One of the officers shouted.

The Captain nodded, but he held back his enthusiasm for the moment. They weren't out of danger yet. Still, things were looking better. They had a chance of escaping their fate.

"Daniel, I have to let you in on a little secret."

"Another one?"

"This ship will easily defeat one pirate ship." Captain Stewart smiled

"Any more secrets?"

"I think that's all of them."

Then, the sailor in the crow's nest shouted, "Land Ho!"

"Where?" Captain Stewart asked.

"To the port side."

Captain Stewart raised his spyglass and spotted the land. He shouted course corrections to the men. Now was not the time to be land-bound. He was about to lower his telescope when he spotted something that made his blood run cold. Around an approaching point of land that jutted out like a giant finger, a second ship, sporting the skull and crossbones, came into view, heading straight for them.

"Man, the cannons!" Captain Stewart shouted. His orders echoed around the ship as his officers repeated the command. "We have a second enemy ship to the port side!"

Daniel grabbed a sword and remained near the Captain. As a young boy, he and his friend, Michael, had participated in numerous mock sword fights with wooden blades, but he had never used wielded a real weapon. He knew he would never win a sword fight against a seasoned pirate, but he had to do what he could to protect his captain.

Boom!

"*Now* we have a problem, Daniel. I didn't count on two pirate ships," Captain Stewart said.

A sudden blast from the cannons of the approaching pirate ship shook the deck so hard that Daniel had difficulty staying on his feet. The returning fire from the *Majesty* had him slapping his hands over his ears. The sound of cannon fire, along with the shouts of defiance coming from the men, was deafening.

Then the first pirate ship added their cannon fire to the chaos as it pulled closer to the merchant ship. Cannonballs blasted holes into the side of the boat. Two hit the mainmast, which came crashing down to the deck. Men screamed and shouted even louder as they scrambled to keep their badly damaged vessel afloat. The dead lay still and silent. Another blast shattered the rudder. Sailors left the oars, grabbed swords, pistols, and anything they could get their hands on to use for a weapon, and ran the sides of the ship. With no one manning the oars, and the sails shredded and useless, the mighty vessel slowed to a halt.

The two enemy ships veered around the *Majesty*, surrounding her on both sides. Throwing grappling hooks tied to the end of thick ropes, the pirates pulled the three ships together. When the vessels were about three feet apart, the pirates jumped onboard the galleon and attacked. The *Majesty*'s crew fought valiantly. Sailors and pirates alike fought and died, but the merchant ship's sailors were outnumbered two to one. It was a losing battle.

"Get below," Captain Stewart shouted to Daniel.

"I want to help," the young man argued.

Captain Nathaniel Stewart ran his sword through a pirate and briefly turned to his young steward. "You're no swordsman. Up here, they'll kill you. Down below, you stand a chance. Go to the galley and stay with the cook. You're young enough that the pirates will probably make you join their crew."

"I don't want to join their crew," Daniel protested.

"I know, son, but doing so will give you a chance to escape later when you're on land."

Daniel opened his mouth to protest again, but Nathaniel stopped him. "You're mother has already lost her husband. She doesn't need to lose her only son as well. Now, do as I say! You have to stay alive so that you can tell her that your father didn't abandon you!"

Hearing those words, Daniel gave in. More than ever, he had to get a message to his mother. Then he remembered the treasure! He had to get the Captain's map before the pirates did. He grabbed Stewart's arm. "Sir, the map."

"The map?" Then the Captain's expression cleared. He reached into his pocket and produced a key. "It's in my chest."

"Aye, sir."

"One more thing," Stewart said. "It's lost to the rest of us, but promise me you'll find a way to go after it. I'll rest better in the afterlife if I know you got it before the pirates. You and your mother deserve the treasure more than us anyway."

Daniel squared his shoulders and gave the Captain an earnest look. "I'll do my best, sir."

"That's all I can ask." He smiled fondly at Daniel for what neither of them hoped would be the last time.

Slipping through the pairs of battling men wasn't easy. Daniel ducked flying blades, shoved a pirate aside, and even ran his sword through the leg of another, allowing an overwhelmed crewman to finish him off. As soon as he was below deck, he ran for the Captain's quarters and slipped inside. *He must have moved the map to this location to keep it safe*, Daniel thought. His hands shook as he slid the key into the lock and opened the chest. The map was on the bottom. Daniel carefully folded the paper and stuck it under his shirt and inside the waistband of his trousers.

He was about to leave until he saw one of Captain Stewart's coats hanging over a chair, he pulled it on. It was a bit loose in the shoulders but otherwise, fit him pretty well. The coat's bulk would further hide the map's presence. Daniel also grabbed an oilskin, used to keep papers safe and dry. He couldn't take any chances.

After checking to see if the corridor was empty, he headed for the mess but lost his sword before arriving there, where he found several inches of seawater covering the floor. A cannonball had blasted an enormous hole in the galley. He found the cook in the entrance, bleeding badly from his injuries.

Daniel ran over to him, lifted Grubb's head out of the water, and held him in his arms. The cook moaned and opened his eyes. When he saw it was Daniel, he began to weep.

"I'm sorry for being so mean to ya."

"It's okay," Daniel replied. "You weren't always mean to me."

"I don't want to die. I'm afraid."

"You'll be okay. I'll get help," Daniel said, but looking at the man's wounds, he knew that Grubb's time had run out.

"No!" Grubb grabbed his arm. "Don't leave me. It's too late. I'm a goner."

"Okay. I'll stay."

Grubb choked up blood and shuddered. "I was only mean because it was my way of protecting you. You're a good man, Daniel."

It was the first time someone had called Daniel a man. In the 1700s, life was hard and often too short. At sixteen, he was old enough to do a man's job, and in a couple years, he could marry and have a family of his own, if he wanted to. Thinking about the past several weeks, Daniel felt sorry for Grubb. The cook's life had not been an easy one.

Chaos reigned above and below as the pirates infiltrated the hold of the ship. When they saw him, the pirates ignored him. Seeing his youth, they didn't feel he would be any threat. Daniel remained with Grubb until the cook coughed again. Then pinning the young man with an expression that begged forgiveness, he died. Daniel closed Grubb's eyes and gently laid his body down. With a look of determination, he headed back on deck.

Unarmed, he ran through the smoke and fighting men to one of the busted railings and pulling free a wooden belaying pin. Maybe he couldn't compete with a sword, but this would do just nicely. Working his way toward Captain Stewart, he used the pin to knock out a couple pirates. He continued to do this whenever possible until strong fingers wrapped around his wrist and squeezed, forcing him to drop his club.

"Ow!"

Daniel looked up into the meanest face he had ever seen. It was the pirate captain.

"That'll be enough of that," the Pirate Captain growled. Lifting his head, he shouted. "Surrender, and I'll let the last of ye live!"

Captain Stewart looked around. Not many of his men were still on their feet. Many were dead, others wounded, and on the verge of death. "Do as he says. Put down your weapons and surrender," he ordered his crew.

It was all over. The pirates had won.

Chapter Nineteen

Captain Jacques Dupree

Shoving Daniel aside, the Pirate Captain walked over to Captain Stewart. "Me name's Captain Jacques Dupree, the scourge of the high seas, and yer about to hear me terms for surrender."

With everyone's attention focused on Captain Dupree, Daniel snuck down below, hoping to find more fighters. He couldn't remember seeing Richard above, and he hoped he would find him below. He found him in the cargo hold, face down in two feet of water. Hoping to find him still alive, he waded toward his former cellmate and turned him over. Unseeing, blank eyes stared up at him. Richard was dead.

In the darkness, a sailor, who had been hiding from the pirates, said, "He was pumping out the water. While he worked, he told me about what a great person you are. Then a cannonball burst through the side and killed him."

Daniel bowed his head, and a single tear streaked down his cheek. He was in too much shock, his mind too numb to do more as he left the cargo hold and headed back to the deck. Daniel stayed in the doorway, hoping to keep out of sight. However, he was not happy with what he saw: Captain Dupree with his sword tip held to Captain Stewart's throat.

"Yer men are loyal to ye. If I allow ye to remain, there'll be nothing but trouble. I think I'll send ye out to sea."

A small dingy was lowered, and Captain Stewart was marched at sword point to the rail.

"Off with ye now," Captain Dupree said with a laugh.

The pirate guarding Captain Stewart and shoved him overboard. As he swam to the dinghy and climbed inside, the pirates roared with laughter. The *Majesty*'s crew wanted to lash out at them, but overwhelmed and unarmed, they were helpless. Daniel looked around and saw the bodies of his crewmen. He did not recognize Samuel and Mitch among them. I hope they at least went down fighting, Daniel thought. Though neither of them struck him as deserters or cowards.

"Alright, mateys," Captain Dupree said when the laughter quieted down. "Search the ship, bring any other prisoners up here!"

Several pirates went down to find any missing persons, each going as a pair to prevent being overtaken by the enemy. Dupree's men were strong, but they had a bit more brains than the average sailor. It took them no time to find Daniel and three other members of the *Majesty*. The next order was to keep the prisoners in small groups with several guards to each. Further limiting any hope for a mutiny.

"Peter's dead, Cap'n," one of his lieutenants Enos reported. "Someone got to 'im before we could."

"Such a shame," Dupree said sarcastically.

Captain Dupree and a few of his men headed for the galley. They would take any foodstuffs worth salvaging. Although a cannonball had devastated much of the galley, a single pot of chicken stew remained undamaged on one of the cookstoves. Grabbing a wooden spoon, he leaned over the pot, sniffed, and scooped up some.

A pleased smile crossed his face. "Bring one of our captured crewmen here," he ordered the other pirate.

The pirate returned shortly with one of the *Majesty's* crew, it was Tom

"Who's the cook on this ship?"

"Grubb, but he's dead," Tom replied.

Captain Dupree growled and placed his hand on his sword. It looked like he would run the poor man through.

"But it's okay," Tom stammered. "Daniel's been doing most of the cooking. He's a young man we took aboard in Boston."

Captain Dupree turned to his man. "Find him and bring him here."

"Why?" Tom asked.

"I want him," Dupree said with a snarl.

"What for?"

"That be none of yer business. If you know where he is…"

"I can point him out to you," Tom said.

Up on deck, Tom pointed Daniel out of one of the other groups and watched as the pirate grabbed him by the arm and pulled him across the deck.

"Captain Dupree won't treat you like Stewart did," Tom sneered. "Now, maybe you'll get your comeuppance."

Before they could go below, Captain Dupree appeared on deck, and the pirate took the young man over to him.

"This the one?" the captain asked.

"Aye, sir."

"Ah, the one so handy with a belaying pin. I hear you're the one who does the cooking. Is that true?"

Daniel replied in French, hoping to delay the inevitable.

Captain Dupree wasn't stupid. He figured this was a ploy, and he decided to outsmart the young man. "I could use someone who understands both French and English."

Daniel played dumb and shook his head.

With a calculating look, the captain grabbed one of the *Majesty*'s crewmen and placed his sword to the man's throat. Speaking perfect French, Dupree ordered, "speak English, or he dies."

"Okay, I'll talk! Yes, I do the cooking."

"That's more like it." Turning to one of the pirates, Captain Dupree said, "Tie him to the mast." He then looked at the rest of his crew and shouted, "Aye lads! Search the ship, bring back anything of value," he turned to the captured crew, consisting of about twenty men in total. "I'm sure you boys will oblige?" He then threw back his head and laughed a hearty and dark sailor laugh.

Daniel watched helplessly as the pirates put the captured crew to work, hauling anything of value up to the deck for inspection. Captain Dupree sat on a barrel and watched as his first mate related their new treasure to him. Dupree told him what to keep and what to throw overboard.

After the plunder had been sorted, everything was loaded onto the two pirate ships.

Tom spoke up, "What about us?" He was in the last group still on the *Majesty*. Most of the other men who were captured were still onboard the *Swift Bounty* while they did their unloading.

Captain Dupree smiled, revealing a gold tooth, "I may be a pirate, but I keeps me word. I won't kill ye, but you'll have to wait until we have loaded everything up."

"What about the boy?" The pirate who had been guarding Daniel asked.

The pirate captain donned a more somber look, "take him to the *Leviathan* but don't hurt him. He speaks French and is a fine cook. Throw him in a cell for now."

The pirate guard cut Daniel free from the mast as another tied the young man's hands behind his back. He was then roughly escorted to another dinghy that was lowered the moment Daniel stepped a foot in.

"Everything's loaded, Cap'n," the pirate first mate, Abner declared.

Captain Dupree smiled and ordered his men to round up the survivors of the *Majesty* and load them up as well.

"You said you wouldn't kill us!" Tom screamed as he wrestled against his captors.

"Aye," the captain said, "Never said I wouldn't shanghai ya! Consider yourselves new slaves of the *Leviathan*!" At those last words, he and his crew broke into another round of evil pirate laughter.

***

Daniel glanced back at the galleon. Sadness crept over him as he watched the once magnificent *Majesty* slowly sink into the ocean. The ships headed south, further away from his home, and he wondered if he would ever see his home again.

Chapter Twenty

A New Friend

Abner, a brown-haired pirate, with a long, partially braided beard, shoved Daniel across the deck of the ship, heading for the brig. "Consider yourself lucky, very few prisoners get to be cooks on the *Leviathan*," he barked into Daniel's ear.

The young man took a quick look around. He discovered that the environment here was very different from that of the *Majesty*. Waving in the gentle breeze from one of the masts was a black flag with a white skull and crossbones. Unlike the *Majesty*, the *Leviathan* was filthy.

The crew was dressed differently, too. While their captain wore an elegant, black, military-style frock coat with deep burgundy turned-back lapels and cuffs. Some of the men wore soft, stylish, and drapey cotton shirts. Others wore shirts with chest laces of heavy cording and slimmer fitting lower sleeves. The clothing was more colorful, too. Their hats often had a feather tucked in them. Daniel later learned that the sailors believed the feather would protect them from becoming shipwrecked.

The crew was a rough band of thieves, killers, and thugs. Although the captain's word was law, the men were harsh, quarrelsome, and rowdy. It was survival of the fittest in every sense. Those unfortunate enough to become prisoners of the pirates had limited options. Die, become a slave, or try to prove oneself worthy enough to join up with Captain Jacques Dupree's crew.

Daniel wanted no part of it. Although he was no match for these men, something in him finally snapped. He had lost the *Majesty* and Captain Stewart, but he was not about to lose his dignity. He spun around and took a swing at his captor. Before his fist could connect, the pirate wrapped his powerful arms around him and lifted him off the deck, bringing hoots of laughter from the crew.

"Okay, okay, I won't fight you anymore," Daniel yelled. "Put me down."

His words brought more laughter.

"That's not fighting," Abner said, setting him down. "It's more like a rooster scratching the dirt and puffing himself up for the chickens."

"I can entertain you with magic tricks," Daniel shouted over the laughter.

"You're entertaining enough," one of the pirates yelled. "We ain't interested in no magic tricks."

Looking around in desperation, Daniel saw that he wasn't the only member of the *Majesty* made into a laughing stock. Pirates shoved and tripped his former crewmates, laughing at their misfortune as they carried cargo to the hold in the ship. After that, they would be sent below to row for Captain Dupree's dark vessel.

"You're nothing but a bunch of bullies," Daniel yelled.

"Aw, now ain't that too bad," Abner said. "Get moving."

The pirate took Daniel to a cell and locked him up.

"Let's see how you feel after you cool your heels down here for a while."

Left alone, Daniel paced the floor and began talking to himself. Like the rest of the ship, the cell was filthy and smelled of stale sweat and other nastier things left behind by other prisoners.

"This is great. Things were just getting good on the *Majesty*. Now I have to start all over again from the bottom." He kicked the bars of his cage then sank to the wooden planks that served as a bed. Drawing up his knees, he dropped his head with a sigh of desperation. "Things will never be that good here on the *Leviathan*."

In the cell next to his, a young man the same age. But, smaller than Daniel, emerged from the darkness. "Did they destroy your ship?"

Daniel looked up in surprise and stared at him. Although light streamed in through a nearby porthole, he couldn't ultimately make out his features. "Yes. The *Majesty* was a fine ship. Now she's nothing more than a hunk of wreckage at the bottom of the ocean. What about you?"

"They took my family's sloop. It's built for speed and one of the fastest ships around."

"If it was so fast, how were you captured?" Daniel argued.

"The pirates waited until dark, and then snuck aboard from smaller boats. We never had a chance to run," the boy argued back.

Daniel stood up and moved to the bars that separated them. "Was that the second ship that came at us?"

"What of it? Are you going to blame that on me?"

His remarks calmed Daniel down. "What happened to the rest of your family?"

"They're dead by now." Tears ran down his cheeks, and he angrily wiped them from his face with his sleeve. "The pirates put my parents in a dinghy. We were too far from shore for them to make it to safety. They never had a chance."

"I'm sorry about your parents. That's awful. Why'd they take you, prisoner?" Daniel asked.

"My parents pretended I was just another member of the crew. Hoping I could escape, they thought I'd have a better chance if the pirates took me. I would rather have been cast off with them."

Daniel's voice softened. "You would have died, too."

"I don't care! I least we'd have been together."

"Don't give up so easily. They might still be alive," Daniel suggested.

"Why would you say that?"

"If you're not dead, there's always a chance. I'm assuming your father followed the regular sailing route. If he did, another vessel could come along and save them."

"Do you really think so?" The young man's voice filled with hope.

"Yes, and you should, too. Never give up. Look, once we're back on land, I'm going to escape. Come with me," Daniel said.

"I don't need your help. I can take care of myself."

"Okay, fine. I just figured we'd have a better chance if we stay together." Daniel looked away from him.

"Is such a thing possible?"

"Yes, we'll have to be careful, but with determination, I believe we can make it. The pirates won't stay at sea forever. They'll have to return to their base and unload their loot."

"Okay. I'm in, but we may never get that chance."

"Why would you say that?" Daniel asked.

"There are so many things that could happen: We could be tied to a mast, flogged, and die of our injuries. We might be sold into slavery."

"They do that?" Daniel asked in horror.

"All the time, they can't keep everyone they take prisoner. They'll kill people just for kicks. They could dunk us in the ocean and drown us. We might even be forced to walk the plank."

"Couldn't we swim away from the ship?"

The boy shook his head no. "We'd be too far from land, most likely. Besides, this far south, sharks are everywhere. The pirates could cut us, and our blood would draw them so fast we wouldn't stand a chance. Don't you know anything?"

"I've had some close encounters before," Daniel admitted, his thoughts went back to the near-death experience that he faced on the *Majesty*.

"Oh. Of course, they could just shoot us. I've heard they sometimes maroon people on islands where no one lives."

"We'd have a chance if they did."

"Yes, as long as there is food on the island to sustain us."

"We could catch fish, too."

"How? You could make a pole with a branch, but what would you use for line, a hook, or bait?"

"I don't know, but I'd think of something."

The young man's stomach growled. "I'm so hungry."

"How long has it been since you've eaten?" Daniel asked.

"It's been days. How many, I can't remember. My last meal was dinner with my family." He choked back the tears again.

Daniel stood up and went to the bars that separated them. Reaching through, he patted the inmate's arm. "I know how you feel." He related the story of how his Uncle had deceived him.

"That's terrible!" The prisoner said in a voice higher pitched than before.

Daniel took a closer look at him. The young man's features were softer and more feminine than that of a teenage boy. Of course, with all the dirt on his face, it was hard to tell for sure.

Noticing Daniel's change of expression, he asked, "What's wrong?"

"I don't know, but I just got the strangest feeling." He paused then asked, "Are you a girl?"

Rebecca's eyes widened. "Please, you can't tell anyone. If the pirates find out, they'll…"

"Don't worry," Daniel promised. "I won't say a word, and I'll do whatever I can to protect you. I can teach you some mannerisms that won't give you away so easily."

"You would do that for me?" she asked.

"Why not? We're in this together, aren't we?"

"I suppose so. My name's Rebecca. You can call me Becka."

"Not here, I can't."

She blushed. "Of course not, any suggestions?"

"How about Robert?"

"That's good. I like it."

"It should be easy for you to remember."

Daniel spent the next two hours working with her, trying to erase some of her feminine ways and make them more boyish. When they finished, he said, "That should help. Make sure you keep your voice pitched as low as possible."

Approaching footsteps sent Daniel and Becka to opposite sides of their cells. Abner stopped in front of Daniel's cell.

"Captain's hungry," he said, unlocking the door. "Time to earn your keep."

"Fine, but I'll need help." Daniel pointed to Becka. "Can I use him?"

"We already have one cook. Get a move on."

* * *

When they arrived in the galley, the cook's back was to them.

"That you, Abner?" he asked.

"Brought you some new help," Abner replied. "Cap'n says he was a good cook on the ship we just captured." He shoved Daniel toward the cook, who, hearing the sound moved out of the way. "Better make something good if you don't want to be keelhauled."

As soon as Abner left, the cook spoke up.

"The name's Jacob, although most people call me Cookie. What's yours?"

"Daniel."

"Glad to meet you. Just don't use my real name in front of the crew. They don't know it, and I want to keep it that way."

"Not a problem."

"Everything is stored exactly where I like it, so don't change anything around."

He turned and held out his hand. Daniel shook it and took note of the appearance of the pirate cook. His hair was tinged with gray, as was his small beard. Though both were kept fairly decent as compared to the rest of the pirates. He was dressed in a striped shirt and ripped pants. While Daniel couldn't identify his age, he could tell he was older than Grubb.

"You don't act like the other pirates I've encountered so far," Daniel said.

"That's because I'm not a pirate. They captured me, just like you, and made fun of me. I'm a bit clumsy, and they would have killed me, but my friend stood up for me and told them I could cook. The last one they had was terrible."

"What happened to your friend?"

"He's dead. He tried to escape the last time we docked." Cookie shook his head sadly. "They've sent me a helper now and then, but it never worked out. The helpers didn't know anything about making a proper meal, let alone a shipboard one."

Meeting Cookie made Daniel's spirits rise, even though he was distressed to hear about the last helper's failed attempt to escape. This cook was very different from Grubb. Unlike the rest of the *Leviathan*, the galley was sparkling clean.

"I'm sure we'll work quite well together," Daniel said.

"So, you're a cook, too. Any suggestions on what to make? It can't take too long. Dupree gets meaner when he's hungry," Cookie said.

"The pirates confiscated our remaining vegetables and livestock from my ship," Daniel said. "I'd just made chicken stew. My captain liked it. I don't know how many chickens you have. We lost some of ours in the transition. Why don't I make beef stew instead?"

"Excellent idea, I haven't had a chance to see what foodstuffs they stole from your ship. The storeroom is next to the mess. You'll have to use the salted beef. No time to butcher anything now."

"I'll be right back," Daniel said.

Gathering up the ingredients he needed, he carted everything back to the galley. He and Cookie start peeling the vegetables, but they kept getting in each other's way. The cook's clumsiness was also a problem. He bumped into open drawers, the corners of tables, and other furniture. As this continued, Daniel realized that Cookie was nearly blind, but he said nothing.

As they peeled and chopped vegetables, some of Cookie's hit the floor. Daniel leaned over and picked them up.

"What are you doing?" Cookie asked.

"Uh, some of the vegetables landed on the floor."

"Don't be so sloppy. Now you'll have to wash them all over again." Cookie sounded angry.

Daniel was about to protest when a realization came over him. Jacob was hiding his poor eye-sight. He was cross and blamed the dropped vegetables on Daniel because he feared someone would discover his secret. The pirates would consider him worthless and probably throw the cook overboard.

"Sorry," Daniel said at last. "This isn't working; we keep getting in each other's way. Why don't we set you up at one of the tables in the mess with the rest of the vegetables? I'll work here. I can handle the heavy stuff and get the pots cooking. After all, you're the boss."

Cookie was startled that Daniel would accept the blame so easily. Had he guessed his secret?

"Good idea."

Now that they weren't under each other's feet, things progressed smoothly, and before long, pots of stew were bubbling on the cookstoves. Daniel was amazed at how many things Jacob could do, even though he was nearly blind.

When the meal was ready, Abner walked into the mess. "Where's the captain's dinner. He wants it now, or heads will roll."

"It's ready," Daniel said, scooping up the trays that he had prepared.

He took the meal up to the Captain's quarters. Unlike Captain Stewart, Captain Dupree wasn't refined or gentry. Daniel didn't have to first take up dishes and set the table. He piled the plates and food on his tray, and upon arrival, he would arrange everything on the table.

As Daniel carefully made his way to the Captain's quarters, he feared he would never arrive with everything intact. Various members of the crew were fighting all around him. He had to protect the food from spilling or falling off his tray while trying to defend himself. He ducked fists and sidestepped around the combatants. It was survival of the fittest and every man for himself. Arriving safely, he reached for the handle on the cabin door, but it burst open, and Dupree appeared.

"Arr, ye scourges of the earth, quiet down!"

Amazingly, the men grew quiet, and the fighting stopped.

"Now git yer mangy hides down to the mess and eat. I'd better not hear another sound for the rest of the night."

144

Daniel scooted inside the cabin, set down the plates, forks, and mugs in their places, and put the food in the center of the table. There would be no napkins, and instead of coffee, he brought a jug of rum.

The captain and his lieutenants were quiet as they ate until Dupree said, "More rum!"

Daniel hurried to the mess, amazed that there, too, no one spoke above a low murmur. When he entered the room, some of the pirates made crude remarks. Others said nothing. The delicious smell of food made their mouths water, and they helped themselves, delighted to have fresh biscuits for a change, brought over from the *Majesty*. Once they began to eat, many offered compliments. The ones too mean to compliment, nodded grudgingly.

"You've got a great cook," Daniel told them. "He just needed the right help."

His words surprised Cookie, and as the days passed, the blind man would learn to trust Daniel.

Returning to the Captain's cabin, he refilled everyone's mug.

Dupree took a long swallowed and belched. "Not bad," he admitted. "You'll do."

A look of relief crossed Daniel's face.

"Good stuff," Enos, one of the lieutenants said.

"Keep it up," another chimed in.

"Since ye did such a fine job," Captain Dupree said. "I'll grant ye a boon. Whatever ye want, short of leaving the ship."

His words brought laughter from the others.

"Come on, lad. What'll ye have?"

145

"Can I think about it?"

"Take yer time and get back to me when yer ready."

Daniel nodded, removed the empty dishes, and left.

Chapter Twenty-One

Cookie's Confession

Rather than sleep in the crew quarters, Daniel returned to his cell, leaving the door open. The company here was much better, and he didn't have to worry about the crew's fighting. Besides, it enabled him to sneak food down to Becka. She was asleep when he arrived.

He kept his voice low so no one would overhear. "Wake up, Becka."

She didn't stir.

"Wake up," he said a little louder.

She groaned.

"Hey, wake up. I have something for you."

He didn't know if it was his insistence or the smell of food, but Becka suddenly jumped to her feet and turned to face him. Seeing the bowl of stew and two biscuits, she rushed to the front of her cell and eagerly accepted his offering through a slot in the door made just for that purpose. Taking the food to the side of the cell, she sat down and tore off a massive bite of biscuit, jamming it into her mouth. She only chewed enough to swallow it before digging into the stew.

One biscuit and half her bowl were gone before she said anything. "Mmm, this is so good. It's heavenly," she said between bites. "Thank you. You're a lifesaver. Did you make it?"

"Me and Cookie, but it was my recipe. The crew of the *Majesty* liked it a lot. So does the pirate crew, apparently."

She said nothing more until she finished, mopping up the last of the gravy with her remaining biscuit and swallowed it. Settling back against the wall, she sighed with pleasure. "I was so hungry. I've never been that hungry before. Of course, I'm used to more elaborate meals, but as far as I'm concerned, this tasted better than all of them."

Daniel smiled. "Pass me your bowl and spoon. I'll sneak it back to the galley."

Becka rose and handed them to him. "Can you get me anything to drink?"

Daniel thought about it.

"Please, anything will do, water, even rum."

"We'll pass on the rum. If you get drunk, you might forget you're supposed to be a boy. I'll see what I can do."

It seemed to take forever before Daniel returned. When he did, he handed her a mug of hot coffee. "Sorry, it took so long. I had to wash your dish and make the coffee."

"Do you have to hurry back with the mug?"

"No. If anyone sees me with it, I'll say it's mine."

They both sat by the bars dividing their cells.

"Don't you have to get some sleep?" Becka asked.

"I'm sleeping here. The pirates stink worse than the *Majesty*'s crew. At least they occasionally bathed in the ocean."

"Neither one of us smell that good either, but we don't have the stench of rum seeping through our pores," Becka agreed.

"I think I have a way to get you out of here."

Interest lit her features. "Off the ship?"

Daniel frowned. "In time, but no, out of this cell. One step at a time."

"How?"

"Dupree liked his meal so much, he granted me a boon. I told him I wanted to think about it. In the morning, I'll ask for your release."

Hope crept into her features. "Do you think he'll do it? He doesn't like me very much."

"I'm not sure, but it's worth a try."

Daniel thought about the secrets he still hid in his shirt. He would have to find a safer place for them. He couldn't let them see the treasure map. *If the pirates got their hands on the treasure, they might build more ships. They could even side with the British.* The first chance he got the next day, he would look for a hiding place.

* * *

"Wake up," Abner said, giving Daniel a not so gentle kick in the side.

The pain brought him awake. "What's wrong?"

"Wrong? I'll tell you what's wrong. What are you doing down here? You don't have to be in that cell any longer."

"I know," Daniel replied as he got to his feet. "The company down here is better."

"Look, I don't care where you lay your head just so I know where to find you. You need to get down to the kitchen right now."

"Okay. I'm going."

Daniel hurried away, forgetting the mug Becka had returned to him the night before.

Fortunately, Abner didn't notice it.

Daniel hurried into the kitchen. "What's wrong?"

"Time to cook," Jacob replied. "Fortunately for you, I've already made the oatmeal. Start the coffee."

Daniel did so. As he stirred the oatmeal, he noticed a sack of rat poison next to the stoves. Suspicious, he wondered how he could test the oatmeal until he spotted a rat in the corner of the room. He spooned a small amount on a plate and approached the rodent.

"It's okay. Don't run. I've got food for you."

"What are you talking about? I've already got some food," Jacob said.

Daniel ignored him. The rat was about to run, but when it picked up the scent of food on the plate Daniel set down, it wiggled its whiskers and stopped. Daniel backed away and watched. Still cautious, the rat inched forward and sniffed.

"Come on, boy. Go ahead. Eat it," Daniel whispered.

The rat sniffed again and took a bite or two. It was about to eat more, but as its nose approached, it sniffed and squealed, running away as fast as its little legs could go. It would take too long for the rat to die to prove his point, but Daniel had seen enough. Cookie had grabbed rat poisoning instead of salt. He opened the porthole and was about to grab the pot of poisoned food when Cookie dipped a spoon into it and brought it up to his lips.

"No!" Daniel yelled. Rushing over, he knocked the spoon from the cook's hand.

"What do you think you're doing?" Cookie yelled.

"You can't eat that. It's poisoned."

"You're out of your mind. My food isn't that bad. You've got a lot of nerve…"

"Listen. If you had eaten that oatmeal, it would have killed you. You put rat poison in it."

"You're crazy. The only thing I put in that pot, other than oatmeal, was salt."

"It wasn't salt." Daniel waved his hand in front of Cookie's eyes. "You're blind. Aren't you?"

The cook was about to deny it, so Daniel told him about the rat.

Cookie calmed down. "I'm not completely blind. I can still make out shapes and some things, but it's harder in the dark. Look, I really appreciate you saving my life. I'll do whatever I can to help you escape and send you back home. I just need time to figure it out."

Daniel dumped the contents of the pots out the porthole and grabbed a clean one. The other pot would need a thorough scrubbing, but first, he had to make more oatmeal. The oatmeal had barely begun to boil when the crew filed into the mess and sat down. When they realized there was no food on the tables yet, they picked up their spoons and pounded the table.

"Where's the food?" one man yelled.

"What's the holdup? Bring it on!"

Then the men began to chant. "We want food! We want food!"

"If we don't do something soon, we'll be in deep trouble," Cookie told Daniel.

Pulling his deck of cards out of his pocket, Daniel ran into the mess. "Ah, breakfast will be ready before you know it," he shouted. Still, it took a while to get their attention. "Soon. I promise."

"We want it now!" Someone yelled.

"It's coming. It's coming, but until it does, let me show you a magic trick."

As he started shuffling the cards, some of the men protested.

"Don't want to see no magic trick. We want food."

Daniel tuned them out and started the trick. Before long, he had everyone's attention. After the first trick, the men laughed and eagerly participated in the entertainment. Between tricks, he told funny stories until Cookie entered the room.

"If some of you will help carry out the food, we can eat."

Cheers went up, and soon everyone was eating. One of the lieutenants entered the room.

"Eat hearty, mateys. Cap'n wants you rowing today. There's no wind."

The men groaned. After the mess emptied and they were alone, Cookie told Daniel his story as they cleaned up and washed the dishes.

"I grew up in Jamaica, where my family had a small sugarcane plantation. Pirate coves are all over the islands. My twin brother and I were fifteen when they attacked us. They killed our parents and most of the slaves. Jeremy got away, but I was captured."

"How long ago was that?" Daniel asked.

"Thirty years. I've wanted to escape ever since, but with my bad eyesight and no one I could trust, I never could. Maybe together, we can pull it off."

"I'm all for that as long as we can take someone else with us."

"Who?"

"There's another boy my age locked in a cell," Daniel replied.

Cookie thought for a moment. "Yes, I think I know who you're talking about. They took him aboard several days ago. He's a real scrapper, fought tooth and nail to get away. He even took a bite out of Captain Dupree."

Daniel's eyes widened. "He did?"

"Yes, didn't get him anywhere, though. Cap'n backhanded him. He flew across the deck and hit his head on a rail. Thought sure he was a goner."

"No, he's alive."

"How you gonna get him out?" Cookie asked.

Daniel told him about Captain Dupree, offering him a boon.

"Well, don't know as the Cap'n will agree, but you can try."

"I'll go ask him now."

* * *

Chapter Twenty-Two

Secrets and Storms

"Ye want me to release who?" Captain Dupree asked.

"Robert, the boy you took aboard some days before you captured the *Majesty*," Daniel replied.

"Is he still alive? I thought he'd be dead by now," the pirate captain laughed. "Didn't feed him, did we, boys?"

"Not one morsel," came the reply.

"He's not dead yet. Will you release him?"

"No."

"Please, I promise I'll keep him in line. He won't trouble you at all," Daniel tried to reason. Just then, a small, arrogant smile came across his face. "You remember your boon to me, correct? You did say I could have anything I wanted."

Dupree thought it over. "All right, but yer responsible for him. If he causes any trouble, you'll be punished right along with him."

"Thanks." Daniel hurried below deck. Taking the cell key from the hook where it hung, he released Becka.

"He agreed? Really?" Becka asked, amazed.

"Yes, but under one condition. You can't cause any trouble, or they will punish us both. Deal?"

"Deal. What now?"

"Come to the galley with me. I'll see if Cookie is willing to put you to work."

"I'm no kitchen maid," Becka protested.

"Shh."

Becka looked around worriedly. No one had heard her.

"I don't know who you were before they captured you," Daniel warned her. "But here, we are just cabin boys. All right?"

Becka nodded with a firm frown on her face.

***

When they reached the galley, Daniel introduced her to Cookie.

"Nice to meet you, Robert. Glad you're still with us."

"Can he help out here?" Daniel asked.

Becka rolled her eyes, trying to keep her selfish whining to herself.

"Maybe you'd prefer to muck out the room where the animals are kept," Cookie said, narrowing his eyes. Even with his visual limitations, he could tell that the young man was feeling a bit entitled for being a cabin boy.

She blanched, but before she could say a response, Daniel put his hand over her mouth. "We have to let him in on your secret."

Ripping his hand away, she said, "Are you crazy?"

"No, he has a secret, too. That should keep you both honest," Daniel replied.

He told her about the cook's blindness and revealed her gender to Cookie.

"Don't worry," Cookie assured her. "I'll keep your secret, *Robert*, as long as you keep your mouth shut about mine. Deal?" He extended his hand.

"Deal," she replied a bit reluctantly, but she shook hands with him.

* * *

During the next few days, Cookie and Daniel taught Becka how to cook and clean, much to her chagrin. During one of her lessons, while Cookie was instructing her on how to check the freshness of the bread, Daniel seized his opportunity to tuck away the map. He found a cupboard in the back corner that was rarely used. He placed the oilskin with the map into a pot and carefully put it back. *Cookie has plenty of pots and pans, he shouldn't notice this one missing.* While the three galley cooks were bound together by shared secrets, Daniel was not ready to share these with them just yet.

* * *

The weather remained hot and steamy for days. There was so little wind that the sails remained useless. The men were tired of rowing and grew bored. They weren't used to spending so much time at the oars, but even with the number of slaves they had, it wasn't enough. Tempers flared, and fighting broke out frequently. By the end of the week, superstitious sailors became antsy.

"Better get below," Abner told Daniel and Robert one afternoon.

"Why?" Daniel asked.

"Some of the men think the wind stopped blowing due to black magic," Abner replied.

Daniel blinked in amazement. "That's crazy talk."

"Crazy or not, that's what they're saying."

"And they think it's my fault?" Daniel asked.

"Who else? You're the magic boy."

Becka pulled Daniel's shirtsleeve. "We've got to move now," she urgently whispered, pointing to a group of angry men heading straight for them.

They turned to leave, but one of the men yelled.

"Stop right there!"

Becka stepped aside and looked for a weapon. "Run!"

Daniel didn't get far before the group of men caught up with him.

"Lift yer curse and call back the wind," Enos, one of the pirate lieutenants, shouted.

"I had nothing to do with it. I swear!" Daniel shouted.

"Yer lying. Take him, boys!"

Two of the pirates grabbed Daniel's arms and started dragging him toward the side of the ship.

"Let go of him," Becka yelled. She hadn't found anything she could use as a weapon, so she raised her fists.

The men ignored her.

"Remove the curse, or we'll cut ya and throw ya overboard to the sharks," Enos warned.

As he spoke, a member of his group dropped a couple of dead and bloody rats into the water. Enos shoved Daniel against the rail and forced him to look down, so he could see what was happening. The young man's eyes grew large when two sharks moved in to grab the floating carcasses. A feeding frenzy ensued.

Daniel grew frantic. "I swear! I had nothing to do with it. I don't know how to control the wind!"

Abner came over. "That's enough! The boy had nothing to do with the weather."

They wouldn't listen. Two pirates lifted Daniel in the air, while a third drew his knife.

"Stop it!" Becka shouted, struggling to keep her voice low pitched. She beat her fists against the back of the nearest man.

He shoved her away. "Off with ya, whelp. Ya hit like a girl." The rest of the company snickered at the insult.

His words froze her in her tracks.

Daniel continued to struggle and beg. He was never so afraid in his life. The men holding him lifted him higher and prepared to toss him overboard when there was a shout.

"Stop!" Captain Jaques Dupree yelled as he unsheathed his sword. "Dump him overboard, and I'll cut yer livers out."

The men grumbled but set Daniel down on his feet.

"Yer want to kill the one who puts good food in yer bellies?" Captain Dupree asked angrily. He looked at Daniel. "Give Cookie credit all ye want, but I know why the food's gotten better."

Becka got to her feet, and feeling something brush her arm, she glanced upward. "Look!" she shouted.

Puzzled, the men looked at where she pointed. High above, the Jolly Roger flapped in the breeze. A shout of joy went up from the crew of the *Leviathan*.

"Set the sails, boys," Captain Dupree shouted. "We're back in business."

Cheers filled the air, and soon men were crawling up the scaffolding like ants. As soon as they fastened the sails, the wind caught the canvas, and the ship began to move at a good clip.

Dupree turned to one of his lieutenants. "Tell the extra rowers to take a break and assume their normal duties." Before he left the deck, he grabbed Enos by the scruff of his neck and shook him. "No one dies unless *I* say so."

"Aye, Cap'n," he replied dejectedly.

* * *

Daniel and Becka stood on deck beneath the stars. The evening meal was over, and they were free for the rest of the night. They talked about their families and other adventures they had before being trapped on the *Leviathan*.

"I've always wanted to be a sea captain. Just like my father. What about you?"

Becka made sure no one was around to hear them talking. "My family is wealthy. I want to marry rich and have my own plantation with lots of slaves."

"It's not right to turn people into slaves."

"You only say that because you've never had any," Becka replied.

"No. That's not it."

"Then what?"

"Look around you. Look at your crew and mine. Do they deserve to be slaves?"

"That's different. They were captured by pirates," Becka replied.

"What about the people kidnapped from Africa and forced into slavery?" Daniel asked. "Weren't they taken by pirates of another sort? They had families and life. Do they deserve to be treated that way?"

159

"They were poor and lived like savages," Becka argued. "At least here they have a home, clothing, decent food, and clean water to drink."

"At what price? Do you think that because they're poor, they deserve to give up their freedom and live at the mercy of cruel overseers? What about their living conditions?"

"We provide them with clean, dry homes and all their needs."

"Your family may do that, but what about the rest? Not everyone does. I've heard stories of the atrocities committed by some owners. Some slaves live in far worse conditions than they did in Africa. Some owners beat and abuse their slaves, force their women to have sex with them, and separate them from their families."

"My parents have never raised a hand against our slaves. Neither have I," Becka responded defensively. "And my father wouldn't dream of being disloyal to my mother."

"Good for you. I wish everyone were like your parents, but they aren't. Do you think that because I lost my father, which made my mother and me poor, that we deserve to be slaves?" Daniel stared at her intently.

"I never thought of it that way."

"You should."

They stood there quietly until the first one, then another fat raindrop hit their faces.

"We'd better go below," Daniel said.

Before they walked more than a few feet, a downpour soaked them thoroughly, and a fierce wind blew up, forcing them to grab hold of something substantial so they wouldn't be blown overboard. The storm grew quickly. The ship bucked, tossed about by huge waves that crashed on deck, washing some of the men over the side. Panic overwhelmed the pirates. They'd been in plenty of storms before, but never one this bad.

The deepening darkness made it impossible to see. Captain Dupree and his lieutenants shouted orders fast and furious. Still, no one saw the approaching rocks until it was too late.

"Rocks to the port side!" The man in the crow's nest shouted.

The man at the tiller struggled to spin the wheel to the right. His efforts were useless. A terrible grinding noise filled the air as the rocks tore into the hulls of the *Leviathan*.

"Man the lifeboats! Abandon ship!" A pirate screamed with fear.

Captain Dupree punched the quivering pirate square in the face, so hard that he crumbled to the deck without a sound.

"Last time I checked, *I* am Captain Jacques Depree." He looked to his men with a wild and savage look. "I'm not abandoning me *Leviathan* to Davy Jones's locker just yet. We ride out this storm until *I* say otherwise. Back to yer posts ye dogs!"

The pirate crew scrambled back to their posts, knocking over anyone and anything in their way.

Daniel panicked. "I've got to get something," he told Becka. "Wait for me."

"What? No, come on. We have to leave the ship, we might not get another chance like this," Becka insisted.

Daniel didn't listen. He fought the rest of the way and headed below. He had to get the treasure map. Without that treasure, he would never realize his dream of becoming the captain of his own ship. *If I don't try to go after that treasure, with or without any help*, Daniel thought. *I would feel like I let Captain Stewart down.*

Below deck, things were just as chaotic. Daniel had to struggle against the men fighting to get topside. It seemed to take forever, but he finally made it to the galley and retrieved his treasure from the hiding place. He was about to leave when he heard a moan and saw Cookie trapped by an overturned table. Daniel stuffed the paper filled oilskin into his shirt and ran to help him. Desperation filled him with newfound strength. He pulled the table off and freed the cook.

"Come on. I'll help you. It's madness out there."

Relief washed over Cookie's face. "Thank you, Daniel. I thought I was a goner. Where's Robert?"

"Waiting for us above. Let's go."

It was just as hard to get back to the deck, as it was to leave it. Men pushed and shoved each other in panic. The lieutenants, forced to retrieve a large chest of gold from the captain's cabin, struggled with their heavy load.

When Daniel and Cookie finally made it topside, the boat groaned again. It shifted further into the water, flooding the ship and making it nearly impossible to move without slipping and falling into the treacherous sea.

One of the pirates screamed.

"We're all going to die!"

And since they were in the outer bands of a hurricane, it seemed his words would come true. Daniel tried to get Cookie through the insanity when a strong gust of wind blew over, carrying a massive wave with it.

"Daniel!" A voice cried above the storm.

Daniel looked up as the wave caught him and dragged him to the mast. Hitting his head hard, he fell into blackness and remembered nothing more.

Chapter Twenty-Three

After the Storm

Daniel awoke to a light fluttering down beneath a green canopy. He felt warm sand beneath him, and a cool breeze blowing around him. He tried to sit up, but then a wave of pain came to his head. Touching, he felt a bandage wrapped around his head. He slowly leaned up on his elbows, trying to get his bearings on where he was.

The first thing he saw was the *Leviathan*, it was stuck on some rocks a bit away from the shoreline. At first glance, Daniel did not see too much damage, but he knew better than to give in to false hope. He scanned the beach, seeing the pirates and oarsman working on reclaiming debris from the ship, building makeshift tents, and a few keeping a massive fire going.

"You're awake!" Daniel heard a familiar voice as he slowly turned around to see Becka and Cookie walking towards him from the trees. Both were carrying strange and exotic fruit in their hands, and Cookie had a sack slung over his back.

"What...happened," Daniel struggled to ask.

"A miracle," Cookie answered.

"If you can really call it that," Becka sarcastically spoke under her breath.

"We are alive, aren't we?" Cookie challenged his companion. "And we found some food at least. Count your blessings, *Robert*." Daniel chuckled as Cookie delivered her fake name with the same amount of sarcasm as she had previously done.

Daniel, suddenly remembering, quickly felt around in his jacket, he felt the oilskin which held the treasure map. He sighed a silent prayer of gratitude. It really was a miracle.

"The storm brought us to this island," Cookie began, interrupting Daniel's train of thought. "You were knocked out when one of the waves hit us. Thankfully, Robert here and I took ya down below. We waited until the *Leviathan* got marooned on those rocks you see there. Once the storm passed, Cap'n sent out the few lifeboats we had left to check out the island. Deeming it safe enough, we disembarked here. That was about two days ago."

Two days! I really have been lucky on my time out at sea, Daniel thought.

"We lost more oarsman than anything, which is bad, but we still have most of the crew." Cookie continued to Daniel.

I wonder if Tom met his end there, Daniel reflected, remembering the former steward of Captain Stewart was also aboard the *Leviathan* with him.

"You seem to have come back just in time," Becka said as she pointed to the sky. "Looks like another storm is brewing."

The three companions looked up to see more dark clouds approaching, for what Daniel figured would not be the last time.

***

The storm did not let up, but Captain Dupree and his lieutenants didn't want to wait it out. They knew something bad was coming, and if they couldn't get the ship back out to sea, it would be smashed to pieces. They went below deck and inspected the damage.

"The hole in the hull isn't as bad as I feared," Dupree said. "I think we can repair it enough to get her home and fix her up proper."

His lieutenants agreed. Battling the fierce winds and stinging rain, the crew cut down two tall trees, which they used as, braces to lift the ship off the rocks. The men repaired the hole with the spare wood from the hold, kept for just this purpose. It was better to use seasoned wood than green.

It took two days before they were ready to sail. During that time, Daniel and Becka kept close to Cookie as possible. Venturing off to get food or firewood and helping with the limited cooking they could do on land. Cookie needed the assistance to get around; he was clumsy on a ship, but even clumsier on dry land. Captain Dupree and his men were too focused on getting the *Leviathan* repaired, and eating when they could, to suspect anything.

On the last night on the island, the three companions cleaned up the salvaged cookery in the ocean, far away from the ears of the pirates.

"I'm glad they can repair the ship," Daniel said. "It would be terrible to be stranded here. I need to get word to my mother that I'm okay."

"She's far from sound," Cookie said. "There's a lot of damage elsewhere, including a crack in the mainmast. The patch on the hull is only temporary. She'll need some lengthy repairs before she's seaworthy again."

"It's a good thing the *Swift Bounty* was able to find us," Becka added. "Had we been stranded here, well, I don't want to think about that."

"If the crew had been forced to leave on your sloop, the trip back to base would have been overcrowded and miserable," Cookie said. "Another blessing is that it survived the storm better than the *Leviathan*."

The next day was bright and sunny, a perfect day to get back on the voyage. As soon as everyone was back on board, the captain ordered his men to cast off.

Many men had died during the terrible storm that brought them to the island, but there were still enough to get the ship moving until the wind could blow over the sails again.

That evening after cleaning the galley and mess, Daniel, Becka, and Cookie sat at the table furthest from the door to the corridor and talked.

"Any idea how far we are from the pirate base anyway?" Daniel asked.

"I'd say a fortnight at the most," Cookie replied.

"Then that gives us fourteen days to make plans for our escape," Becka said.

"Before we get into that subject," Cookie said, "I overheard two of the lieutenants, Enos and Abner, talking about a treasure map."

"A treasure map?" Daniel asked. He struggled to keep his anxiety inside.

"Any idea where it's being kept?" Becka asked.

"Maybe in Dupree's quarters," Cookie replied. "Maybe not."

Daniel wondered if the map they spoke of was similar to the one he'd gotten from Captain Stewart, or if it was for a different treasure. He decided not to mention his own map yet. Although he believed he could share the knowledge of the Golden Chest with Becka, he wasn't quite ready to tell Cookie about it.

"What kind of treasure?" Daniel asked.

"Could it be that you haven't heard of the Golden Chest?" Cookie asked.

"Yes," Daniel replied. "The *Majesty*'s crew talked about it. Are you saying this map would take us to it?"

"What Golden Chest?" Becka wanted to know. Clearly, she hadn't heard of it.

Cookie told her the story of Black Bart.

"If everyone's been looking for it all these years, what makes you think it still exists?" Becka asked. "Someone may have found it, but never told anyone."

"No. Had someone discovered its whereabouts, believe me, they'd be bragging and strutting about like a proud rooster," Cookie said.

"What makes you think this map is the right one?" Daniel asked.

"Personally, I haven't seen it, so I don't know one way or the other. Cap'n, however, is convinced it's the genuine article," Cookie said.

"If we take the map, Dupree will eventually find out. We'll be caught red-handed and made for walking the plank," Becka said.

"Not if we make a copy of it," Daniel said thoughtfully. One way or the other, he needed to find out if the map was the same as the one he had. If it was, both maps might be worthless, or it could be that Captain Stewart wasn't the only one to have purchased a copy. "How good are your drawing skills, Becka?"

"My drawing is above average."

"Good. Any idea where we can get the materials we need to make a map?" he asked Cookie.

"I do."

"Then Becka and I are going treasure hunting for that map."

168

"If Dupree discovers you with it, or even finds out about you looking for it, he'll kill you both," Cookie warned.

"Then we'll have to be very careful," Becka said.

Chapter Twenty-Four

Hunting for the Treasure Map

At lunchtime, Becka did not show up to do her work.

"Where could he be?" Daniel wondered aloud, careful to use her male persona in case someone was listening.

"He's probably just trying to get out of his chores," Cookie replied. "Before now, I don't think that boy ever did a lick of work."

"I think you're right," Daniel agreed. "He was a spoiled rich kid."

"Are we going to let him get away with it or punish him?" Cookie asked.

"Hmm, what do you have in mind?"

Cookie's eyes lit with amusement. "I'll send him to feed and clean up after the animals."

"Good idea."

* * *

After lunch, Daniel went in search of Becka. He couldn't find her anywhere until he spotted her coming out of a room in a seldom-used corridor.

"Robert!"

Startled, Becka turned and sighed with relief when she realized that it was Daniel.

"Where were you at lunchtime?"

"Busy," she replied coyly.

"Really? Cookie's angry. You're supposed to do your job, not leave it for us to do."

"It's not a big deal. I'll be there to help with dinner."

"You need to see the cook right away and straighten this out if you don't want to get into further trouble," Daniel said.

"Okay, okay, I'll go see him now," Becka replied impatiently.

They walked together as they headed for the galley.

"What were you doing in that room?"

"Nothing much just wanted to see how this ship differs from my family's sloop."

"You were looking for 'it' without me, weren't you?" Daniel accused her.

"I was not."

"Yes, you were."

She sighed. "Alright, maybe I was."

"We're supposed to do it together," Daniel reminded her.

"You're right. I'm sorry."

She was a lot sorrier when she arrived in the galley and learned what her punishment was to be.

"I won't!" she said stubbornly.

"You will unless you want me to complain to the captain that you're not doing your job. Believe me, cleaning up after the animals is a lot better than getting twenty lashes," Cookie said, his arms akimbo.

"Not to mention that as soon as he stripped off your shirt, your secret would be out," Daniel whispered in her ear.

She turned and glared at him. "This was your idea, wasn't it?"

Daniel shook his head, no. "I had nothing to do with it."

"I'll bet."

"He's speaking the truth, *Robert*." Cookie slightly inclined his head toward the door of the mess.

She glanced over and saw Enos and one of the other lieutenants looking at them as he spoke with a crewman.

"Fine. Let's get it over with."

* * *

After she finished the work, Becka and Daniel decided to do some more searching until it was time to start dinner. They began where she had left off, investigating two more rooms. They were about to enter a third when Captain Dupree ran into them.

He gave them both the fisheye. "You're not up to anything, are you boys?" Dupree asked as he grabbed Daniel's arm and twisted it.

"No, no, I swear!" Tears of pain streaked down Daniel's cheeks, but his mind recognized an unexpected opportunity. As he struggled in the Captain's grip, he used his free hand to lift a key from Dupree's pocket.

Dupree finally released him. "Make sure you don't," he said and walked away.

"Are you okay?" Becka asked as she gently touched his arm.

Daniel's face turned red with embarrassment. Under ordinary circumstances, he would never show fear in front of a girl.

"I understand," she said softly. "That really hurt."

"At least I got the key to his quarters," Daniel said with a grin.

Becka beamed. "Smart move."

At that moment, their friendship grew considerably. Whenever they were together, Daniel felt nearly the same way he did when he was with his friend, Michael. They still argued on occasion and often saw things differently, but their friendship overshadowed everything.

***

A few hours later, they looked for Captain Dupree's location. He was up on deck, taking a turn at the wheel.

"Good," Daniel said when they found him. "He'll be there for a while. Let's go check out his quarters."

"What about the man guarding the door?"

"He usually falls asleep. Maybe we'll get lucky."

Sure enough, the guard sat against the wall across from Dupree's door, snoring loudly. Daniel put his finger to his lips. She nodded. As quietly as possible, they tiptoed to the door and unlocked it.

Once inside, Daniel whispered, "You take that half of the room, and I'll take the other."

"Okay."

They looked everywhere, starting with the chest containing the captain's gold. Becka checked the bedding, under the mattress, and beneath the bed itself. Daniel examined the shelves containing souvenirs taken from other ships. Then Becka observed the chest that held Dupree's clothing and personal articles. At the same time, Daniel looked around and under the remaining furniture. Halfway through the search, they froze when they heard footsteps approach.

Daniel pointed to the porthole. They would have to escape through it to avoid discovery. Opening the hatch, he signaled Becka closer, but before she could move, the footsteps moved away.

"Whew!" Daniel wiped his brow and closed the hatch.

"That was too close. We'd better hurry up and get out of here," Becka whispered.

They continued their search, looking behind pictures, and everywhere they could think to look. No map.

"Where would a pirate hide a map?" Becka asked Daniel.

He shrugged.

They even checked the bottom of an empty rum jug. Nothing.

Moving to the Captain's chest filled with gold, Daniel raised the lid to take a better look. The sight dazzled them both. So much so, they almost didn't see the map attached to the lid.

"Daniel," Becka whispered urgently. She pointed to the lid.

Grinning, Daniel removed the map and tucked it under his shirt. "Let's get out of here."

Slipping out the door, the pair had taken only two steps when the guard snorted and sighed. If he opened his eyes, he would see them and become suspicious.

They hurried away. Becka covered her mouth to stifle a nervous giggle as they ran back to the galley.

* * *

Cookie had the materials ready that Becka would need to copy the map. She took everything, found a discreet corner in the supply room, and got to work, while Daniel and Cookie started dinner. When she finished, Daniel took the original.

"I gotta get this back before he misses it."

Becka took over peeling potatoes and mentally crossed her fingers. *Please don't let him be caught putting it back.*

The guard was still asleep when Daniel slipped inside and carefully put the map back where he found it. Opening the door, he checked the guard and the hallway. It was empty except for the sleeping pirate. He was almost clear of the corridor when he heard approaching footsteps. Daniel turned around and started walking toward the captain's quarters.

"What are you doing here?" Captain Dupree called.

He moved up quickly, nearly bumping into the young man. The sound of thunder could then be heard above. Startling Daniel even more.

Daniel turned around. "Oh, Captain, I was just looking for you. Cookie and I are making your favorite dessert tonight. I just thought you'd like to know." While he spoke, he slipped the key back into Dupree's pocket.

"Cookie told me. Now get back to the galley."

"Aye, aye, sir."

Daniel's excuse didn't sit right with Dupree. *That boy is up to something.* Hurrying to his quarters, he fished out the key to unlock the door and kicked the guard.

"Git up, ye lazy git!"

The man jumped up. "Sorry, sorry, Cap'n, I wasn't asleep for long."

"Was anyone sneaking around here? Anyone enter my quarters?"

"No, sir, I'd have heard someone trying to get inside yer quarters."

"Ye better be right. If not, I'll keelhaul ye."

Not satisfied, Dupree went inside and looked around. His suspicions were on high alert. He knew his quarters blindfolded, and he studied them carefully. It wasn't much, but he found two items slightly out of place. Alarmed, he hurried to his chest of gold and opened the lid. Was anything missing? No, nothing had changed. The gold was all there. Then he glanced up at the lid. The map was there, but it was slightly askew.

That son of a sea dog found my treasure map. He must be planning to steal it and escape the ship. Well, we'll see about that!

Dupree's face turned red with anger as he marched to the galley, the rain had started to fall lightly. Once he entered, he looked for the boy and then grabbed Daniel by the scruff of the neck.

"Lousy, no good thief, I'll teach ya to try and steal me treasure map."

"What?" Daniel protested. "No! I don't know what you're talking about!"

"Shut yer lying mouth," Dupree ordered as he dragged him out of the mess. "I'll show ye what we do to thieving scum."

As the Captain dragged him up to the deck, Becka and Cookie followed, protesting Daniel's innocence. More thunder sounded above the protests. Another storm had come back unexpectedly.

"He stole something of ours!" Dupree told his crew.

The men hissed and booed.

"I say we cut off his hands!" The captain shouted. He signaled his lieutenants to grab Daniel and hold out his hands. The wind was now blowing hard, making walking difficult as the rain soaked everyone.

"No!" Becka screamed.

Dupree drew his sword and raised it high over Daniel's outstretched hands. The young man struggled mightily, but he could not pull free. One lieutenant, Enos, wrapped his arms around his chest. One each held out one of his arms.

Fear tore through Daniel's heart, making him shiver violently. If he lost his hands, it was all over, his dream of becoming a captain gone. It would ruin his life, leaving him little more than a beggar.

The crew cheered and began to chant.

"Off with his hands! Off with his hands!"

"No," Daniel cried. "Don't. Please! I beg you."

Raising the sword even higher, the Captain brought it swiftly down.

Chapter Twenty-Five

Unexpected Company

Daniel closed his eyes and gritted his teeth, waiting for the agony that would come when the sword struck his hands from his arms.

An inch from his wrists, the sword stopped. "I've changed me mind," Dupree said.

Daniel's knees gave out. He'd have hit the deck without the support of the lieutenants. Becka wobbled, feeling faint, but Cookie placed a supporting arm around her waist.

"Git the plank ready! We got us some fish bait. Tie him up!"

"No!" Becka begged. "Please, he doesn't know anything about a map."

The plank was set up, and one of the lieutenants tied Daniel's hands behind his back and shoved him onto the narrow board. Becka grabbed Dupree's arm.

"Please, don't do this!"

He shoved her aside, making her lose her balance. When she jumped up, Becka began to cry. "Don't! Please!"

"Take him," Dupree said, shoving Daniel at his lieutenant. Then he spun around and studied her. Grabbing her arm, he scrutinized her face.

"No wonder things have gone so badly as of late," he said, pulling the cap from her head. As her long golden hair tumbled out, angry shouts and curses filled the air.

"It's a woman! Ye was right, Enos. We were cursed! Ye can walk the plank with him," Dupree snarled.

"Please, Cap'n," Cookie begged. "They're just kids. Don't make them walk the plank."

"You, too?" He asked the cook. "You three are as close as a flea on a dog's skin. Don't think I wasn't watching y'all back on the island. Were you a part of this, too?"

Before Cookie could answer, Dupree, shoved him toward Daniel and Becka. "Fine, ye can all die together."

Suddenly, the wind, which had been growing increasingly powerful, became worse. It violently rocked the ship and brought even more rain.

The captain turned one of his men. "Keep an eye on them. The rest of ye, man yer posts. We're headin' for the eye of a hurricane!"

The crew scattered like mice, including the one who was supposed to watch the prisoners. Those who could lash themselves to anything that wouldn't blow away.

Becka pulled Daniel off the plank and, with Cookie's help, untied him. Struggling against the wind and rain, they grabbed one of the ropes the pirates had stretched across the deck to hold onto.

"We'll never make it," Cookie yelled.

"Yes, we will," Becka hollered back.

Men bellowed, but the horrible sound of the storm blew away their words, and their voices quickly grew hoarse.

Halfway to their destination, Becka lost her grip on the rope and screamed. Holding on with one hand, Daniel surged backward and grabbed her as her body partially lifted off the deck. From that point on, the three linked up, holding the rope with one hand, and the hand of the person in front of them with the other. Becka's thoroughly drenched long hair flew out around her head. Thick clumps of strands blew into her face and over her eyes, making her nearly blind.

"Hang on," Daniel shouted. "We're almost there!"

* * *

Captain Dupree was back at the tiller with his helmsman. He tied himself to the mast behind him, and the two men struggled to maintain control of the wheel. It was nearly impossible. The helmsman slipped and fell, pulling the tiller in the wrong direction. A strong gust of wind within the hurricane lifted the helpless man off the deck. A death grip on the wheel was the only thing that kept him from blowing away.

Unable to steer in the direction he wanted it, Captain Dupree lashed out.

"Let go! Yer pullin' us in the wrong direction. We have to ride with the wind."

If they hadn't been in the midst of a hurricane, the remark might have been funny, since the storm had already shoved them in the wrong direction. Dupree's next move was far from unusual. Lifting one foot, he kicked at one of the helmsman's hands until the helpless pirate lost his grip.

"Noooo!" The man screamed in helpless terror.

Dupree attacked his other hand. "Let go!" The captain shouted in frustrated fury. His kicks were punctuated by each word. "Let!" Kick. "Go!"

The helmsman's fingers slipped. Unable to hold on any longer, the wind sucked him the poor man's screams away as the hurricane caught his body and sent him flying through the darkness.

* * *

The final five feet to the stairway seemed like five hundred. The same gust that cost the helmsman his life grabbed Daniel, Becka, and Cookie and lifted them into the air. Letting go of each other, six hands hung onto the rope for dear life. As the wind and their bodies violently pulled on the hemp, they watched in horror as a knife, belonging to a pirate that was washed overboard, flew through the air. Its blade nicked the rope between Becka and Cookie. Between the wind and the pull of three pairs of hands, it began to fray.

"Hurry!" Becka screamed at Daniel.

It took a Herculean effort, but Daniel pulled forward and grabbed hold of the railing along the stairway. He let go of the rope as soon as he was inside the stairwell. Becka came next. She grabbed his hand, and he pulled her inside. Cookie passed the frayed portion of the rope, but the individual threads of the hemp unwound rapidly.

"I can't make it," Cookie yelled.

"Yes, you can!" Daniel shouted. "Stretch out your hand!"

Cookie did so, but he was still too far away. "It's no use!"

As the words left his mouth, the rope snapped in two. Still holding one end of the rope tied to one of the masts, his body flew past the screaming Becka. Then, at the last second, Daniel grabbed his hand. Their hands were too slippery, causing a lack of grip, he felt Cookie's body jerk in the opposite direction until Becka reached out and added her strength. Together, they pulled the man to safety.

Exhausted, they dropped to the floor in the first corridor. A hurricane could rip a ship to pieces. Although there was little chance of surviving if sucked away, being below deck when a vessel ripped apart was a surefire death sentence.

181

The storm lasted for hours as the ship passed through the eye of the hurricane and out the other side. No one dared move until the wind died down, which took several hours more while it raged through the night. Then suddenly, without warning, it was over, and calm descended upon the ship.

The exhausted crew, what remained of them, collapsed into unconsciousness. Daniel, Becka, and Cookie were no exception. They slept on the floor of the corridor. The ship listed in the now calm waters. No one awoke until mid-morning the following day. It was a miracle; it remained afloat. However, the ship has sustained a lot of damage. While the crew slept safe and sound, water was starting to sink the mighty *Leviathan*.

Chapter Twenty-Six

Water, Water, Everywhere

When Captain Jacques Dupree awoke, he untied himself and surveyed the damage. A third of the crew had lost their lives during the storm. Some pirates were awake, doing what little they could to brace the doomed ship. In the waters surrounding them, cargo, supplies, and part of the patch that had covered the hole in the hull bobbed in the now gentle waves. The *Swift Bounty* was gone, blown far from her sister ship if it even survived the storm. Her fate would remain unknown until the pirates reached their hideaway if they ever made it. Frowning, Dupree remembered what he was doing before everything had turned to chaos.

"Git up!" He shouted, kicking a crewman.

They got to their feet, still somewhat groggy.

"Find those three and bring 'em to me."

"Aye, Captain," the men replied.

***

Daniel woke first and headed to the captain's quarters. In Dupree's cabin, he found a flask of water. It wasn't nearly large enough, especially for three people, but it would have to do. He was tempted to steal some of the gold, but he realized its weight could become a problem once he was in the water.

He went to the galley next and retrieved a few things. He removed both copies of the map, still safe in the oilskin, and tucked it into the waistband of his trousers. Then he dumped the rum out the porthole and filled the flask with water. This went into the inside pocket of his coat, along with three eating knives. They wouldn't be much of a weapon, but it was better than nothing.

When he returned, Becka and Cookie were awake. They were no longer alone. Some of the pirates had managed to go below during the storm and were scattered helter-skelter throughout the corridor. Getting to their feet, Becka and Cookie joined him. They headed for the deck. Their fate was sealed. There was no point in putting it off any longer. If they had to leave the ship, they wanted to do it on their terms. They met Enos and the rest of the crewmen Dupree sent on the stairway.

"Cap'n wants ya," Enos said.

When they reached Dupree, he pulled out his sword and pointed it at Daniel.

"Git a move on!"

Frightened and wondering how they would survive this, all three put on a brave front. This time, they wouldn't beg for their lives. They wouldn't give the Captain and his crew the satisfaction. If they hurried, they might escape without their hands tied behind them. Daniel, Becka, and Cookie headed for the plank, but it was no longer there.

The ship groaned loudly and shifted suddenly. Several members of the crew tried to brace themselves on the ship, but a few had fallen over.

The *Leviathan* was sinking!

Daniel looked down and saw sharks in the distance. He prayed they had feasted on the dead crewmen flung overboard during the storm. If so, they might have a chance.

"Tie them up!" Dupree shouted, but as his words left his mouth, he watched in angry fascination.

Splash! Splash! Splash!

All three had jumped off the ship!

"Arrr!" In his anger, Dupree pulled a pistol from his waistband, aimed it at Daniel's head, and fired.

Becka screamed and tried to shield him. It was an unnecessary move. The gunpowder in the weapon was too wet. Dupree pulled the trigger repeatedly, but it didn't matter. The gun wouldn't fire.

The pirates were torn; no one wanted to cross the captain. However, the thought of diving into shark-infested waters also was not a pleasant one. Breaking their ideas, Captain Jacques Dupree barked another order.

"Ferget them! They are off the ship, the curse should be lifted." As he spoke, the rest of his crew looked around to see water rising from various points in the *Leviathan*.

Turning to his sole remaining lieutenant, Dupree shouted his next order, "Get busy! We need to shore up this ship if we're ever going to make it home."

"Aye, Captain."

* * *

Daniel and his companions swam for the broken portion of patch that had once covered the hull. It would become their life raft. Using their hands, they moved the raft toward a broken dinghy. The boat was worthless, except for the paddle that remained attached to one side. Pulling it free, Daniel used it to row away from the ship and into the current. Even though they escaped the pirates, the three of them were still in danger. They were in shark-infested waters, vulnerable to storms, and had no food and very little drinking water. Their only chance was to steer in a direction they hoped would lead them to shore.

They drifted for days. After the first two days of taking turns rowing, Daniel used the oar only occasionally to keep them steady in the current he hoped would take them to safety. He'd taken only two swallows of the water in the flask to wet his parched throat, giving the rest to Becka and Cookie. Still, the water soon ran out. Scorched by the sun, the refugees were starving, their throats dry, and their lips cracked. None of them had the strength to continue rowing.

Talking kept them awake during the day, so they could sleep when it grew dark. On the fifth day, a shark approached their raft.

"It senses our weakened condition," Cookie said. "Keep your hands and feet away from the edge."

That wasn't easy. The raft was too small for even one of them to lie down. Then the shark began to circle them, raising their adrenaline as it swam a few feet away.

"It's leaving," Daniel said, relieved.

Cookie's eyes went wide with alarm. "No, it's not. Hang on. It's going to ram us!"

Realizing the cook was right, all three grabbed onto the sides of the raft away from the shark. A moment later, it turned and swam full speed toward them. Daniel pulled back one of his legs. When the shark hit, its head came up onto the raft, jaws wide open.

Becka screamed.

"Don't let your leg go into its mouth!" Cookie shouted. "It'll bite it right off!"

Daniel kicked the shark between the eyes as its mouth snapped shut. Disoriented, it swam away.

"That'll show it," Daniel said with a grin, but as he turned around, Becka was no longer on the raft.

He looked around frantically. "Becka!"

"She was knocked into the water when that beast hit us!" Cookie shouted.

Without thinking twice, Daniel kicked off his shoes, took a deep breath, and dived overboard. Going deeper and deeper, he frantically looked for her. Although the water was clear, as soon as he passed the depth where the sun's rays penetrated, it was too dark to see much. Running out of air, Daniel surfaced and then dove once more. His mind shouted for her. *Becka! Where are you?*

Running out of air again, he was about to swim upward, when he spotted her. Fearing to lose sight of her, he swam faster until he could grab her hand. His lungs burned with the need for oxygen as he swam for the surface as fast as he could. With his vision beginning to go black, Daniel had to fight the temptation to stop struggling and take a breath, even though he would get nothing more than a lung full of saltwater. Closing his eyes, his body began to relax. He had to shake himself to dislodge the lethargy that told his brain to stop struggling and just give up.

That might have been the end for both Daniel and Becka, but suddenly, his wrist was enclosed in a tight grip, and he was pulled upward. He gasped for breath as he broke through the surface with a mighty splash. Cookie pulled him onto the raft. Then he pulled Becka aboard. Shaking with exhaustion, Daniel grabbed her shoulders and shook her.

"Becka, Becka, say something." He placed one hand beneath her nose. "She's not breathing!"

Cookie leaned forward and gave her a hard thump on the back. Becka gasped and repeatedly coughed, bringing up water each time. When she finally stopped, Daniel was so thrilled to have her back; he pulled her into a fierce hug.

"Don't ever scare me like that again!"

"Thank you, Daniel," she said, pulling back slowly and revealing a deep blush. "You saved me." She turned her head and looked at Cookie. "Both of you."

Amazed, Daniel stared into her eyes, realizing that their relationship had just gone from friends to something much more profound.

Cookie's shout broke the spell. "Land ho!"

Becka and Daniel broke eye contact and looked to see where he was pointing. Sure enough, there ahead of them, the waves rolled up onto a sandy beach. Trees and foliage lay beyond. With a burst of adrenaline, Daniel picked up the paddle and rowed for shore. When they reached the part where they could leave the raft and stand, they pulled it onshore and headed for the nearest stand of palm trees. Sinking down, Daniel closed his eyes and immediately fell asleep.

Becka and Cookie joined him, and as they, too, drifted off, the realization of how Daniel had saved their lives filled them with gratitude.

"I just hope we can find food and fresh water here," Becka murmured.

"You and me both," Cookie added.

Chapter Twenty-Seven

The Adventure to Town

They awoke the next morning, hungry, thirsty, and filled with hope. Daniel had awakened first and took the opportunity to compare his two maps. They were identical, but he wasn't sure if that was good or bad.

"Any idea about where we are?" Daniel asked Cookie.

"I think we're somewhere south of Savanna unless the hurricane blew us further off course. It's difficult to say. We may even have traveled as far as the Bahamas."

"Well, wherever we are, I hope it's somewhere close to civilization," Becka said.

Daniel stretched his cramped muscles. After the crowded conditions of their makeshift raft, it felt good to move about again. "Let's explore our surroundings," he said. "We need food and water, and who knows, maybe we'll stumble upon a town or village."

"We should follow the coast," Daniel said. "If there are any settlements, we'll find them close to shore."

"I agree," Cookie said. "Do we go north or south?"

Daniel thought about it, but Becka spoke first.

"North. If we're on the mainland, there are fewer settlements along the southern part of the east coast."

"If we're on an island somewhere, it probably won't make any difference which direction we go. North it is," Daniel agreed.

Becka took Cookie's arm. "I'll be your guide," she said, smiling.

"That's right kind of you, miss."

As they walked through the trees and foliage, Cookie stumbled over tree roots, and an occasional rock or two, only Becka's assistance kept him from falling. Seeing this, Daniel looked around until he spotted a sturdy tree branch lying on the ground. He retrieved it and, using his knife, removed the smaller branches until he ended up with a relatively smooth walking stick.

"Here, Cookie, use this. It should help," he said, placing the walking stick in the cook's hands.

"Thank you, Daniel." The former ship cook said.

***

They moved further inland, where they had a better chance of finding food and water. Walking for the next hour, the three fugitives discovered a stream and drank their fill, soothing their parched throats. They wondered if they would find any inhabitants on the island.

"If we find any people, their language will tell us if we're in French or Spanish occupied territory," Becka said.

"How come you know so much?" Daniel asked.

"My father wanted a son. He got me, instead. Mother lost the next three pregnancies, and after the last one, the doctor told my parents that if she became pregnant again, it would kill her. Therefore, my father decided to make the most of having a girl. He hired the best tutors, taught me how to ride a horse, manage the plantation, everything he would have taught his son. Mother schooled me in the feminine arts whenever I wasn't busy with everything else. I guess that's why I'm a bit of a tomboy."

"So, is that why you were dressed like a sailor when we met?" Daniel asked.

She blushed. "Yes."

"It's a good thing you were," Cookie said.

"I know," Becka replied, looking at Daniel. "How does that make you feel?"

"A bit jealous," he admitted. "Nevertheless, I admire you. Not many girls can boast of having such a fine education."

They trod on, through overhanging trees and dense foliage. This was the only time since when they were first shipwrecked that Cookie had been on land for longer than a few hours. Becka, while used to this climate, was struggling due to her privileged upbringing. Daniel felt that he was in another world. Only having lived in Boston, before living on the *Majesty* and *Leviathan*, he was astounded by the native flora and occasional fauna.

Further along, a blackberry bush provided enough berries to take the bite off their hunger, but it wouldn't last long. They left the now empty bush behind and forged ahead until the sound of voices stopped them in their tracks. Daniel put a finger to his lips and motioned the others over to a nearby mangrove tree. The trunk and broad expanse of roots above ground was the perfect place to stay out of sight. "Wait here," he whispered. "I'll check it out."

Daniel moved toward the sound, careful not to step on any twigs that could snap and give away his presence. As he got closer, he was able to make out a few words. Most were English, although a few people spoke Spanish. As he moved closer, he saw the road and studied the people walking or riding along with it. Satisfied, he returned to the others.

"There's a road over there. The people are mostly English and seem okay. I don't think they're pirates. At least, I didn't recognize anyone."

"Thank heavens," Becka said. "Where there are people, there should be a settlement not far off."

When they stepped onto the road, no one paid any attention to them.

Walking was easier for Cookie on the packed dirt road. As they followed the others, they talked about what to do next.

"I'm getting a message out to my mother as soon as I can," Daniel said. "What about you, Cookie? Do you have any family you could contact?"

"Please, call me Jacob. Cookie is the name I acquired shipboard because I wouldn't tell the pirates my real name. Now that I'm rid of them, I want to use my real name again."

"Understandable, what's your last name Jacob?" Becka asked.

"Fremont, and no, I'm sure there are relatives somewhere overseas, but I have no way of knowing who they are or where they live. After the pirates killed my parents, there was only my brother and me, and I have no way of knowing if he's still alive."

"Then you'll just have to come with us. Besides, once we find the treasure, you can purchase a house and hire servants to help you," Becka added. "And Daniel can buy his own ship if he wants and sail back to Boston."

Daniel still hadn't told them about the second map.

"We must be extra cautious, regardless," Cookie said. "There are pirate hideouts everywhere, some on the islands, and others along the coastline of the mainland. That map and our talk of it could bring a lot of attention if we aren't careful."

The three companions walked back on the dirt road. They were the only ones walking. They had agreed that since A short while later, the unmistakable sound of horses' hooves came toward them from the opposite direction. No one said a word as they scurried off the road and ducked behind some bushes. They didn't have long to wait. A troop of English soldiers rode past, returning from patrol.

"Maybe we could go with them?" Becka asked, hopefully.

"Better not," Jacob said. "We're at war, remember? They might not be too friendly."

"Wouldn't we be safer? If we're with the soldiers, we would have protection, and no one would bother us."

"Jacob's right," Daniel said. "Until we learn more about the people here, we had best be cautious."

When the troop was finally left, the three friends returned to the road. An hour later, they came to a sign outside what appeared to be a thriving city.

"The town ahead is Port Royal. It's located on the western end of Palisadoes in Jamaica. The English founded it, and the British Royal Navy maintains a permanent presence here," Becka supplied. "It's a wealthy and civilized place and is the center of Caribbean trade. The only problem is it's also a perfect spot for pirate raids."

"Great. At least we know where we are," Daniel said. "We'll have to take the chance. They shouldn't be looking for anyone in the colonial militia down here."

"A word of caution," Jacob added. "There are several pirate coves located on these islands. We must tread carefully, and hope the authorities don't think we're pirates."

As they entered the port town, Daniel and Becka were impressed with the differences they saw there, compared to the cities of their birth. A wall surrounded the city, and its streets were narrower and paved with brick. Bold primary colors were used everywhere: on homes and shops, banners, clothing, and even the flowers in boxes under the windows, making the city a delight to look at.

The people wore lightweight clothing, including white pants and skirts, topped with more colorful shirts and blouses. The smell of fish was strong. Smalltime merchants fried fish on open grills along the main thoroughfare. The delicious odors made their stomachs rumble.

Being dirty and looking unkempt, the local citizenry ignored them. Whoever looked at them wrinkled their noses and frowned. As far as they were concerned, these three must be beggars, and they wanted nothing to do with them.

Without money for food and new clothing, Daniel, Becka, and Jacob had no way to relieve their hunger and little chance of finding a job. They went down to the harbor, where Daniel performed a magic trick. He earned enough coins to purchase a small amount of fish, which they shared. Returning to the dock, they watched a beautiful sunset.

"Red sky at night, sailor's delight," Jacob said.

"What's that mean?" Daniel asked.

"It means the weather tomorrow will be perfect for sailing," Becka responded.

Daniel and Jacob looked at her in surprise, making her blush.

"As a child, my father used to tell me about the superstitions the sailors had."

Daniel looked out to the sea. "We'll have to sleep in an alley tonight and look for jobs tomorrow."

"I'd rather sleep here with the sweet smell of saltwater and fish in my nostrils," Jacob said.

"So would I," Becka added, although she would never consider the scent of fish sweet.

"Me, too, but the guards would never allow it. We'd better find a spot before it gets too dark," Daniel said.

They settled on a section of an alley located behind a pub. Jacob examined a couple wooden boxes of trash next to the back door. Becka and Daniel watched in amazement as he dug through the refuse and pulled out pieces of discarded, uneaten food.

"You can't eat that!" Becka exclaimed.

"Why not," Jacob asked. "It's clean. If it's good enough for the dogs, it's good enough for me."

Daniel took Becka's hand. "Come on. I'm still hungry."

They found enough food to fill their mostly empty bellies. Becka balked at first, but after watching Jacob and Daniel eat hungrily, she quickly joined them. Their stomachs full, they curled up among boxes and barrels, covered themselves with discarded newspapers, and dropped off to sleep. Just as they attempted to get comfortable, two men crashed through the back door of the pub and continued fighting.

Others soon joined them, cheering on the combatants until one man was knocked to the ground and remained there.

"The winner!" One onlooker shouted, raising the other man's arm in the air. Laughing and going over the highlights of the fight, everyone went back inside the pub, leaving the injured man where he was.

As soon as they left, the loser staggered to his feet and rambled off.

Daniel had a difficult time falling back to sleep. He was awake long after the others. *I need to take them into my confidence.* He thought. *I could search for the treasure on my own, but I don't want to leave Becka.* He shook his head sadly. He wasn't quite ready to admit his feelings for her, even to himself. Becka still had a plantation, friends, and possibly her family. She would return home, and who could blame her? Looking over and seeing her shivering in her sleep, he covered her with his newspapers and gently stroked her hair. *Should I tell them about the other map?* His mind was still in a quandary; he finally fell back to sleep.

* * *

Chapter Twenty-Eight

Libraries and Pubs

The next morning, the pub's owner, who did not know that anyone was sleeping in the alley, brought them awake when he threw trash on them. All three jumped to their feet and brushed the refuge off. Having turned his back to reenter the pub, the owner still didn't notice them.

Daniel stepped forward. "Excuse me, sir."

"Huh?" The owner turned around, finally noticing them. "You three sleep in the alley all night?"

"Yes, sir," Daniel replied. "Please, can you give us a job?"

The owner, Cornelius Edward, wrinkled his nose and shook his head. "I'd like to help you out," he said, "but I don't have enough patrons to hire even one of you. The Squawking Parrot doesn't need any help. I do everything myself."

"What if we increased the number of patrons for the Parrot?" Daniel asked.

"How do you think you're going to do that? You are nothing more than a bunch of beggars."

"We're not beggars, and I have a surefire way to increase your clientele. Tell you what. Hire us for one day. If we don't make a difference, you can let us go."

"Even with the increased business, I can't hire all three of you."

"Then we'll work as one for one wage. Becka will be your waitress. Jacob will wash dishes and help me cook. We have lots of shipboard experience."

Realization dawned on Cornelius. "You were shipwrecked?"

"Yes, sir," Becka replied. "That's why we're so dirty and disheveled."

The pub owner felt sorry for them, which was unusual for him. "All right, I'll let you work tonight, and then we'll see what's what after that. In the meantime, come inside." He took them up to the third-floor attic. A curtain hung, splitting the room in two. "This side's yours, Becka. Daniel and Jacob can use the other. Clean yourself up. I can't have you working for me in smelling like you came slept in a pigsty."

He pointed to a trunk at the end of the room. "There are some clothes in that trunk. See if you can find something that fits."

"Thanks," Daniel and Jacob said, grateful to get out of their dirty clothes.

"As for you," Cornelius said, turning to Becka. "My late wife was about your size. I can't have you dressed like a boy. Follow me."

He led her down to the second floor and a three-room suite.

"These are my quarters," he said in explanation. "Wait here."

He went into the other room, giving Becka a few moments to look around. She stood in the parlor, the room where a family would spend time together, reading, sewing, playing games, or only talking. The furniture was old but serviceable. It was apparent a woman had once lived here. Feminine touches were a reminder of her former presence.

There's the kitchen, so the other must be the bedroom.

She'd barely finished her thought when Cornelius reentered the room.

"These should do for now," he said, handing her two well cared for dresses, unspectacular but serviceable.

"They're beautiful. Thank you."

198

She hurried to her side of the attic, which was furthest from the door. Daniel and Jacob hauled buckets of hot and cold water up to their makeshift rooms. As Becka soaked in a round wooden tub, she looked at the dresses lying on the bed. Before her disastrous sea voyage, she wouldn't have given them a second thought. Now, after all she'd been through, she thought they were the most beautiful dresses she had ever seen.

When all three were clean and dressed, Cornelius met them downstairs.

"You can have the rooms for as long as you work for me, no longer. It'll be considered a part of your wages." He offered them bread and three oranges. "It's not much, but it'll fill your bellies."

All three thanked him.

"For now, why don't you explore the town? Make sure you're back by four o'clock. You'll need to start dinner."

From the time they met, Cornelius spoke gruffly.

"Seems a bit of a grouch," Daniel said when they were out of earshot. "Still, he must have a big heart, or he wouldn't have helped us."

"Not us, lad," Jacob said, "Becka. She reminds him of his deceased wife."

Becka had explained earlier where the clothing had come from, telling them about the death of the pub owner's wife.

"I think you're right. He's kept her things the way she left them," Becka agreed. "Anyway, since we have time to kill, why don't we find out where the island with the treasure is located?"

"How are we supposed to do that?" Daniel asked.

"There must be a library or something with maps of the islands around here. We should check there first."

"If you don't mind, I think I'll remain here," Jacob said. "I can't read, so I'll only be in the way."

"That's okay," Becka said. "Why don't you familiarize yourself with the kitchen?"

"Good idea."

***

Becka followed Daniel outside through the front door of the pub. The sun was shining, there were bird calls in the distance, and they had no idea where to begin their search.

"Let's try this way," Daniel said, pointing to the left. "The buildings are bigger and look more important."

"What makes a building look important?" Becka giggled.

"Hard to explain, they just do."

Coming from Boston, the city that he saw didn't overwhelm Daniel. Yet there were distinct differences. Because of the heat and humidity, awnings made of canvas shaded most of the windows, helping to keep the rooms more refreshing in the afternoon sun. Having a diverse population of nationalities, some of the buildings had a more Spanish flair, allowing better airflow.

Like any port town, sailors came and went with their ships. Street merchants were everywhere, selling food, lightweight fabrics, handmade jewelry and crafts, seashells, and numerous other things. Street musicians played merry tunes in hopes of earning a few small coins from passersby. The city also had its fair share of pickpockets and beggars.

Becka stopped to admire a shell bracelet. She wanted to purchase it, but without pieces of eight, one of the main currencies in the colonies, it was impossible. She sighed and smiled.

"It's beautiful."

"Thank you, miss."

When they finally found the library, a clerk took them to a room filled with boxes and piles of books on the shelves and floor. They looked through the piles of written work, brushing aside dust, spiders, and bugs that covered nearly every surface. Time passed too quickly. In another hour, they would have to return to the pub.

"There's nothing here," Daniel said at last. "Let's go back to the main room and see if we can find anything there."

 The scanned several books in the appropriate section. Finding nothing, Daniel slammed his last book shut. The sound brought dirty looks from patrons and librarians alike. He was about to give up and head back to the pub when he turned and found Becka staring at a mural of the islands on the wall behind him.

He scooted back his chair, drawing more dirty looks, and hurried over to her. "That's it!" He whispered as quietly as possible as he checked the mural with his map.

"I know," Becka replied. "Now we know where to look."

"It isn't that far away. All we need is a way to get there." He paused for a moment, then decided to plunge ahead. "I have something to show you."

Curious, she followed him back to the table where he pulled out both maps.

"You have two maps?" She asked, amazed. "Does that mean there are two treasures?"

"No, they're both the same. Captain Stewart of the *Majesty* had it before the pirates captured us. I was able to get it before I was brought on board. When we heard about the one Dupree had, I wanted you to copy it, to check to see if they were the same. They are."

Becka studied his expression. "So, are the maps real or not?"

"I don't know. Captain Stewart thought so. Though, I'm wondering if there were other duplicates made. If so, there's no telling how many others may have this map."

"If it is real, the pirates will be after it as soon as they find another ship," Becka said.

"My thoughts exactly. If it isn't, we'll be placing ourselves in danger for nothing," Daniel warned her.

Becka looked into his eyes. "We have to try. It's the only way you'll ever get your own ship. Besides, Cookie, I mean, Jacob, needs his share. Otherwise, he'll be homeless and destitute because of his eye problems."

"What about you? Don't you want a share?"

"Sure, who wouldn't, but I don't need it the way the two of you do. My family is rich. Once I return to my plantation, I'll be fine. You should hide one copy of the map just in case someone else tries to take it from you. I don't think we'd get so lucky to get it back again."

Daniel nodded. "Good idea. Then it's agreed. We'll go after the treasure as soon as we find a boat to take us."

Excited to have found the location, at last, they started to leave. A large clock in the town's bell tower chimed four o'clock. They were late. Becka and Daniel ran, but when they reached the library's entrance, they spotted Captain Dupree, Enos, and Abner, heading in their direction.

Daniel grabbed Becka's hand and pulled her away from the door. "This way."

They hid behind the front desk.

"What on earth do you think you're doing?" The librarian whispered angrily.

Becka raised a finger to her lips and pointed at the pirates entering the door. Understanding, the librarian remained silent as Dupree and his men approached her desk. She didn't know why they were afraid of the pirates, but she wasn't about to allow them to become victims of such brutes.

"Where do ye keep yer maps?" Dupree asked in a loud voice.

"Shhhhhhhhhh!"

The patrons' response was nearly as loud as Dupree's voice.

"Keep your voice down, sir. This is a library," the librarian said. "If you'll follow me, I'll take to the room where the maps are kept."

Once they were out of sight. Becka and Daniel scooted out from behind the desk and ran outside.

"Looks like the *Leviathan* made it to shore, after all," Daniel said as he ran.

"Or at least some of the pirates did. Do you think they're looking for the island, too?" Becka asked.

"Without a doubt. I should have taken the original, too."

"It wouldn't have mattered. The pirates would have taken it from you before making you walk the plank. Nothing we can do about it now. I just hope they don't discover the mural."

They quickly exited the library and headed for the back door of the pub, and ran straight into the kitchen. Jacob was already hard at work, peeling potatoes when they joined him. For the next hour, all three talked and laughed as they worked. Occasionally they would throw little things, like potato or vegetable peel,s at one another or teasing each other like best friends. For the moment, life had become fun again.

"What's that delicious odor?" Cornelius asked when he later entered the kitchen.

"A hearty beef stew," Daniel replied as he pulled freshly baked biscuits from the oven. "When it gets closer to six, why don't you open the front door? The smell should bring them in off the streets."

"Good idea," Cornelius said.

"This should do nicely for the stew," Jacob said, pulling out stacks of wooden bowls.

That evening, the Squawking Parrot was full of customers. Daniel's cooking was quite a hit. The presentation was successful, and the crowd appreciated Becka's hard work. Unlike the grouchy owner who often yelled at his customers, she was pleasant to everyone, and their tips showed their appreciation for the attractive waitress.

All three worked hard to make the evening a success. People were so happy with the excellent food, not a single customer picked a fight. Afterward, Daniel, Becka, and Jacob cleaned the pub, making it shine like new.

"This place hasn't looked this good or been this busy since my wife passed," Cornelius admitted. "Thank you for your hard work."

He went to bed, and the friends pulled up chairs in front of the fireplace and watched the dying embers. They were too excited over their success to seek out their own beds yet.

"Now that we know *where* to look for the treasure," Daniel said. "What do you plan to do with your share?"

"I'm going to build that house, Becka suggested," Jacob said.

"I think I'd like to travel around Europe for a while," Becka said dreamily. "Maybe I'll meet someone rich, a duke, or an earl, and get married who knows." She looked at Daniel to judge his reaction and found him frowning. "Of course, you'll buy a ship and your mother a house. Right?"

Daniel withdrew from his disturbing thoughts and nodded.

Becka reached out and took his hand. "If you buy a ship, you could take me wherever I wanted to go."

Her words brought hope to Daniel's eyes. "I could. Couldn't I?"

That night Daniel slept better than he had since he'd unwillingly shipped out in Boston.

* * *

Chapter Twenty-Nine

The Price of Popularity

Word quickly spread throughout the city. So many people came looking for lunch that Cornelius added the mealtime to the Squawking Parrot. After his wife had died, he'd closed the kitchen, except for the evening meal. Suddenly, the business was back to what it had been so long ago. At the end of the second day, Cornelius offered each of his new workers a private room on the second floor and a better wage.

"I used to rent those rooms out," he told them. "I haven't had much business there, either, probably because I'm not good at cleaning and all. You might as well use them."

Daniel and his friends were thrilled. Things were looking up. "We appreciate the rooms. What made you decide to pay us separately?"

"Truth be told, the owner of the 'Hog's Head' pub down the street came by. He was willing to offer you more money. So I matched it and threw in the rooms as a bonus. Naturally, you'll have to clean them yourselves."

"That's not a problem," Becka said. "We'll be happy to do it." Later she thought about her words. She'd never cleaned her room before, never did much housework of any kind. She'd had maids to do that. She was surprised how much satisfaction she got from accomplishing such a simple task.

***

Becka stepped back and scanned the room. At a table at the far end of the pub, Captain Dupree, Enos, and Abner sat down and waited to order. It was a nightmare.

Things weren't so bad for Jacob and Daniel. Working in the kitchen kept them mostly out of the public eye, except when Daniel had to help Becka carry a heavy tray of food to a table.

Heading to the kitchen, Becka pulled her hair back into a ponytail and placed a mop cap over the rest that nearly covered her eyes. Whenever they entered the dining room, they were careful to keep their backs to the pirates. She and Daniel looked comical as they ducked and slipped around the tables to avoid discovery. Then Becka remembered the owner had reading glasses, and she slipped upstairs and grabbed them from the table in Cornelius' parlor. Returning to the kitchen, she handed them to Daniel, who parted his hair in the middle, pulled it back, and fastened it. Putting on the glasses, he felt his eyes cross. The lens was strong, but as he looked at his reflection on the bottom of a shiny pot, he was satisfied with the disguise. He would only have to wear them when he left the kitchen, and he would still avoid frontal contact with their enemies.

Happy diners filled the pub, making Cornelius proud of his new employees. He approached the table that the pirates occupied. "What'll you have?"

"Rum and plenty of it," Dupree ordered.

"Can I interest you in one of our fine meals?"

"Nah," Dupree replied.

"You really should try something," Cornelius insisted. "I have a new cook, and he's really good at his job."

Dupree still refused, but the pub owner's words caught Abner's attention.

"What's this new cook look like?"

"I'm not much for describing people, but I could take you back and introduce you."

"I ain't interested in some cook," Dupree said. "I need a ship. Just keep the rum coming."

"I think I'll take ye up on the offer," Abner interrupted the captain. "We lost a good cook recently, and I may know him."

Daniel had watched the interplay from the kitchen door. When Abner, left his chair and followed Cornelius, he grabbed Jacob and together, they slipped up the stairs to the second floor. He didn't want to go into the alley as the owner might look for them there.

Stepping into the kitchen, Cornelius's expression went from happy to puzzled. "That's strange, where'd he go?" He looked out the door leading to the alley. No one was there.

"Where's me, rum?" Dupree's shouted from the dining room.

"Must've gone to relieve himself," Abner said, losing interest.

The pirates had the original map, so it wasn't necessary to find Daniel and the others, even though it would be satisfying to get his revenge. Abner returned to his table as the owner hurried for the rum and mugs.

Cornelius trotted back and forth, pouring mead, rum, and other drinks, and delivering them to customers. At one point, after noticing the changes to Daniel and Becka's appearances, and the strange way they were acting, he popped into the kitchen and took a good look at them.

"What's going on?" He asked. "Why have you changed your hair? And you, what are you doing with my glasses?"

Turning to Becka, he asked, "Why haven't you served table three? If you screw up my newfound prosperity, I'll fire every one of you."

Seeing his anger, Daniel explained about the pirates and thieves. "So you see. We can't let them know we're here. Our lives are in danger."

Cornelius nodded. "I understand now. Don't worry about their tables, Becka. I'll serve them. Just make sure they don't get a good look at any of you. I don't want trouble. They'd tear my place apart."

As the pirates drank, they talked about stealing a ship and going after the treasure.

Becka served a table nearby, keeping her back to them. As she did, she listened to every word until she felt a pinch on her behind. Her initial reaction was outrage, but remember who was behind her, she pulled her cap lower and turned slightly, so he couldn't make out her features.

"Hey there, girlie, why don't ye fetch us more rum and come sit on me lap for awhile," Dupree said.

Not trusting her voice, she nodded and hurried away to find Cornelius.

"You okay?" He asked. "Did they recognize you?"

"I don't think so. The Captain wants more rum and me to sit on his lap."

"I'll handle it," the pub owner said. "He won't like *me* on his lap."

Becka giggled, and then rushed into the kitchen. She told Daniel and Jacob about what she'd heard.

"They won't leave the city until they find another ship," Daniel said. "Which must mean the *Leviathan* did sink or is too damaged."

"And the *Swift Bounty* never reconnected with them. I wonder if it too sank," Becka added.

"And it means we're in danger again," Jacob said. "We need to earn enough money to get out of here and buy passage to the island. Failing that, we might have to steal a ship of our own."

***

The days passed pleasantly. Aside from staying out of sight from the pirates, things were working out well. Whenever they weren't working at the pub, Daniel and Becka kept an eye on the pirates. This was easier in the evenings whenever Captain Dupree, Enos, and Abner sat in the pub drinking rum until closing, making it simple for Becka to listen in. If Dupree and his men reached the island before they did, it would ruin their plans. Daniel and Becka would be stuck without a way home.

Daniel made inquiries into how much it would cost the three of them to book passage on a boat traveling to the next island. That night after closing the pub, he calculated the amount against what they earned working for Cornelius.

"It's not enough," Becka said, discouraged. "It'll take forever to earn that much money, and before we do, Dupree will have his ship and go after the treasure."

"What if I start entertaining the customers while they eat?" Daniel asked.

"How would that help? You can't run the shell game here like you did in Boston," Becka said. "Cornelius would never allow it. It would hurt his business and could get you killed, or at the very least, tossed in jail."

"You're right, but I'm sure he wouldn't mind if I entertained his customers with card tricks and funny stories," Daniel replied.

"I still don't see how that would provide us with extra money," Becka insisted.

"Pass the hat," Jacob said simply.

"What?" Becka asked.

"*Pass the hat*," Jacob repeated. "Street musicians, jugglers, and other entertainers keep a hat on the ground or pass it to collect tips from their audience. This would be no different except that instead of roaming the streets, Daniel will be performing for a specific audience."

"That just might work," Daniel said thoughtfully. "As long as Cornelius doesn't object."

"I'll handle Cornelius," Becka said. "Once I explain that the entertainment will keep customers here longer, which means they'll be eating and drinking longer, he'll be all for it."

Daniel's entertainment worked so well that his tips added up faster than he could have hoped. They packed the pub to capacity every day. During the times that Dupree and his men were there, Daniel remained out of sight. Fortunately, the pirates didn't like the crowded conditions.

One night, they sat down at the only remaining empty table. Cornelius hurried over to them. "What'll it be, boys?"

"Rum for the three of us," Dupree said.

"And what would you like to order for dinner. Our special tonight is…"

"I don't give a rotten porpoise tail what yer serving for dinner," Dupree growled. "Just bring the rum."

"I'm sorry, gentlemen, if you aren't ordering a meal, you'll have to give up the table to someone who is."

Dupree narrowed his eyes. "Who's going to move us? *You*?" he laughed.

Part of the Squawking Parrot's regular clientele included several burly men. It didn't take them long to figure out that whenever the pirates were there, the entertainment wasn't. They preferred the entertainment. Overhearing the conversation, six men stood up and joined Cornelius.

"Sounds like you've got a bit of trouble here, Cornelius. Shall we toss them out?" one of the men asked.

The pub went very silent.

Dupree looked up, a defiant remark on his lips, but when he calculated the size of the six men, he changed his mind. "We're leaving," he told Abner and Enos. "There's a better pub down the street where they'll give us the *proper* respect."

Once they were gone, Daniel left the kitchen. "Anyone for a card trick?"

The crowd broke into cheers.

* * *

Chapter Thirty

Cornelius' True Colors

After working a month for Cornelius, it was time to be paid. The pub closed at the usual time, and after cleaning up, Daniel, Becka, and Jacob went looking for Cornelius. They found him in the back room, counting the day's receipts. He whistled and smiled as he finished. Looking up, he saw the three friends looking at him in anticipation.

"Business is booming, thanks to the three of you. What can I do for you?"

"We've come to collect our pay," Daniel said. "It's been a month."

The owner's smile slipped just a little. "About that, I've meant to tell you. I've changed my mind. Your meals, room, and board cost me a pretty penny. So I've decided that will be your pay, nothing more."

"What?" All three yelled at once.

"You can't do that!" Becka protested.

"Oh yes, I can. And there's nothing you can do about it."

"Then we quit," Daniel said.

"Who cares?" Cornelius responded. "I ran this place by myself for years. I can do it again. You can sleep here tonight, but in the morning, grab your gear and clear out."

"You're bluffing," Jacob said.

"Try me."

* * *

The next morning, Daniel, Becka, and Jacob stood on the street outside the Squawking Parrot. Over the past month, other than the clothes given to them by the pub owner, they hadn't accumulated much aside from a few things for personal grooming. They each carried those things in small sacks.

"Why are we waiting around here?" Jacob asked.

"He's got to come to his senses at some point," Daniel replied.

Cornelius did not come out.

"Now what?" Becka asked. "Without our pay, we'll never come up with enough money to go after the treasure."

The words no sooner left her mouth when she spotted Captain Dupree and two of his men in the shadows.

"We have to hide," she said, grabbing Daniel and Jacob by the arm and pulling them between two buildings.

They hid behind some crates and waited. As the pirates walked past, Daniel slipped along the side of the pub to listen to their conversation.

"That's it, then," Dupree told the others. "Gather the rest of the men. We'll make our move tonight."

Enos gleefully rubbed his hands together. "Before we know it, the treasure will be ours!"

Once they were out of sight, Becka and Jacob joined Daniel.

"They're making their move," Becka said. "What are we going to do?"

"First things first," Daniel said. "We have to slow down those pirates and have a talk with the Harbormaster."

As they went in search of the Harbormaster, the cook made a suggestion. "I think it's best if I talk to him," he said.

Jacob's appearance had changed during the past month. Dressed in town clothes, clean-shaven, with his hair neatly combed, he looked like any other person in the town who wasn't on the street. Daniel had also cleaned up nicely, and Becka was as pretty as a picture.

"You're right," Daniel agreed. "He might think Becka and I are too young to take seriously."

They found the Harbormaster checking in a newly arrived ship. It was a brigantine, swift, and beautiful.

"I wonder if that's the one they want to steal," Daniel said.

"I wouldn't be surprised," Becka said. "She'll be fast."

They waited until the Harbormaster finished before speaking to him. When he was about to walk away, Jacob cleared his throat.

"Excuse me, kind sir. Would you be the Harbormaster?"

"I am. What can I do for you?"

"My friends and I overheard a disturbing conversation that I think you'll want to hear."

The Harbormaster smiled condescendingly. Whatever Jacob had to say, he was sure it wasn't as important as the man seemed to think. "Really?"

"Yes, sir, we overheard three men talking about gathering the rest of their crew and stealing one of these fine vessels tonight. "

The Harbormaster examined three very serious and concerned faces. "You're sure this wasn't some kind of joke?"

"No joke, sir," Jacob said. "They looked like pirates and talked about killing the crew and taking the ship to an island just south of here."

"Pirates!" the Harbormaster swore. "They've attacked us plenty over the years, but to outright steal one the ships in *my* harbor; it's an outrage." He called to a man working with a manifest list. "Williamson!"

"Yes, sir?" The man answered as he came closer.

"Triple the guard on the docks. I've gotten word that pirates will attack tonight and try to steal a ship."

Williamson frowned. "I'll take care of it right now. We'll have a little surprise party-ready when they come. With luck, there'll be pirates hanging from the gibbet tomorrow."

* * *

"Where are we going to sleep tonight?" Becka asked as they headed away from the dock.

"There's always the alley," Daniel said.

Becka wrinkled her nose. "I do not intend to get filthy again. Can't we use a little of the money for a room?"

"We're already using it for food. If we have to pay for a room, it won't last long," Jacob said.

"I have a better idea," Daniel said. "Once the pub closes down, and Cornelius goes to bed, we break in and take what is ours."

"How are we going to do that?" Jacob asked. "The doors will be locked."

Daniel pulled out the lock pick.

"Where'd you get that?" Becka asked.

"Richard, a friend on the *Majesty*, gave it to me during one of the meals we had together." His head dropped in sorrow. "I never got the chance to properly thank him, or even to tell him the truth about the treasure."

Becka hugged him. "It's all right. I'm sure he would be glad that you still have it."

He hugged her back. "It's the only thing I have to remember him by."

Cookie spoke, "and I am sure he would rather you have the treasure than the pirates."

The Parrot's door opened, and the last two customers left. Without Daniel, Becka, and Jacob, the business had dropped off considerably. They heard the lock in the door stick shut. Moments later, the light from a lantern in Cornelius' rooms turned on. It went out shortly afterward.

"Good," Daniel said as he watched the windows. "Cornelius must have undressed and gone straight to bed as usual. We'll give him time to fall asleep, and then make our move."

They waited ten minutes before going to the alley behind the building. Daniel inserted the pick into the lock and worked it until the lock clicked. Before he could open the door, a drunk walked into the alley, singing some ditty about sirens tempting sailors to their death at sea. Jacob moved away and sat down, pretending to sleep. Daniel was about to do the same when Becka pulled him into her arms and kissed him, making it last until the drunk passed and disappeared down the alley.

Surprise and happiness filled Daniel. When she pulled away, he did not want to let her go.

"I hope you don't mind," Becka said softly. "I figured it was the best way to remain unnoticed."

"Remain unnoticed?" Daniel asked, his voice squeaking.

"I'm sure that man sees plenty of tarts kissing men. It's so common, he wouldn't notice, and he didn't."

"You're no tart," Daniel protested.

"Of course not, silly." Becka blushed. "You didn't answer my question."

"Question?" Daniel had to think for a moment."Oh, yes…I mean, no. I didn't mind a bit. It was nice, wasn't it?"

"Very," Becka replied with a smile.

"If you two love birds are finished, we'd best get back to business," Jacob said.

"What? Oh, yeah," Daniel said, embarrassed.

He released her and turned, quietly pushing open the door of the pub. Hoping the drunk's singing hadn't woken Cornelius, they snuck through the kitchen and into the back room.

"He keeps the money in here," Daniel whispered.

Going to the desk, he pulled out the second drawer on the left and removed the sack of money. Daniel counted out one month's wages for each of them. Then put back the rest, he closed the drawer.

"Let's go," Daniel said after handing Jacob and Becka their share and pocketing his.

"Why don't we just take it all?" Jacob asked. "He cheated us. It would serve him right."

Daniel shook his head. "No, we're not thieves, at least not technically. You're still thinking like a pirate, *Cookie*. We take only what is rightfully ours."

Jacob hung his head, the weight of Daniel using his pirate name sank in. "You're right. Now that I'm no longer a pirate, I must strive to remain honest."

Daniel smiled. "Let's get out of here."

They were nearly home free. Opening the back door, Daniel started out.

"Move another step, and I'll shoot your girlfriend."

Daniel froze in his tracks. All three turned to find Cornelius there, pointing a flintlock at Becka.

Chapter Thirty-One

The Magistrate

"I thought you might pull something like this," the pub owner said.

"You cheated us!" Becka accused him.

"So you say. Tell it to the magistrate."

Cornelius took them to the constable. Arrested and thrown into a filthy cell with a drunk and a petty thief, things looked hopeless.

"That's it," Jacob said. "We'll be in prison for years."

"The pirates will steal a ship and recover the treasure," Becka moaned. "We'll never see home again."

"They may even cut off our hands," Daniel added.

The others looked at him in horror.

"It's a common punishment for theft," Daniel said. "If they do that, we're finished."

The night seemed to drag on forever. Becka cried, and Daniel tried to comfort her, but their fate weighed heavily on her mind.

"I'd rather be dead," she said.

"Don't say that," Daniel said. "As long as we're alive, there's always hope."

She shook her head, no. "Without hands? Left to rot in this prison for possibly the rest of our lives? No, Daniel. It's hopeless. We wouldn't even be able to feed ourselves."

The following morning, the constable and his men escorted the drunk, the thief, Daniel, Becka, and Jacob to court. Spectators, who had nothing better to do, filled the spectator seats. Cornelius and the petty thief's accuser sat in the front row, behind those accused. When the magistrate, wearing black robes and a powdered wig, entered the courtroom, he took his seat and shouted for silence.

"Quiet! You know the rules. If you can't keep your mouths shut, I'll have you escorted from the room and thrown in jail."

The room grew so quiet that when someone coughed, it sounded as loud as an explosion.

"Okay, who's first?"

The constable stood up. "You, you, and you," he said, pointing to Daniel, Becka, and Jacob. "Stand before Magistrate Fremont."

"What's the charge?" Magistrate Fremont asked as they stood before him.

"Robbery," the constable said. "They broke into Master Edward's pub last night and stole his money."

The Magistrate studied the three of them as the Constable gave their names. The Magistrate asked to hear Jacob's name again. He then studied the man like he was going to throw him into prison for life. Suddenly, Magistrate's mouth opened in surprise. There, standing in front of his bench, was his brother, Jacob. While the magistrate could see that is was, in fact, his own brother on the bench, Jacob knew it as well when he heard his brother's voice. Jacob was about to open his mouth, but Jeremy shook his head, and his expression turned serious once more.

"Is Master Edward here?" Jeremy asked.

"Yes, Magistrate," Cornelius said, standing up.

"Do you concur with this charge?"

"I do. They broke into my pub last night and stole my money."

"Is that true?" The magistrate asked Jacob.

"We broke into his pub, sure," Jacob said. "But we only took what was ours. He promised us wages then refused to pay us."

"And how much was that?"

"A month's wages of twenty pieces of eight for each of us." A piece of eight was the equivalent of one Colonial dollar.

Magistrate Fremont turned to Cornelius.

"Did they take more than what was owed to them?"

"No, sir," Cornelius replied. "But I gave them food and a place to sleep. I figure that was worth more than twenty pieces of eight. As far as I'm concerned, they're paid in full."

"That's a lie!" Daniel shouted. "He promised the wages in addition to meals and a place to stay. He wasn't using the rooms anyway. They were so filthy, no one wanted to stay in them."

"We had to clean them before we could use them," Becka added.

The magistrate turned to Cornelius. "Seems to me, the only thief here is you. A gentleman's word is his bond. I would suggest you drop all charges against these three right now." He leaned forward on his bench. "If not, the constable has a cell ready for those who cheat others."

Cornelius blanched. "I'll drop the charges."

"Good, this case is dismissed."

Daniel, Becka, and Jacob hugged each other as the magistrate called a clerk over.

"Take those three to my chambers. I'll join them shortly."

* * *

Magistrate Fremont made quick work of the last two cases, chastising the drunk and fining him for public disturbance. He gave the petty thief six months of hard labor. Returning to his chambers, he greeted Jacob with a bear hug. Because they were nearly identical, Daniel and Becka had figured out who Jeremy was.

"I never thought to see you again," Jeremy told his twin. "When I learned that the pirates had gotten hold of you, I figured you'd be killed at sea."

"I thought that a few times myself," Jacob replied. "I wondered what had happened to you."

"It's a long story, for both of us, I'm sure. Come to my home." He looked at Becka and Daniel. "That includes the two of you. I imagine you both have equally intriguing stories if you were aboard a pirate ship."

"We do, sir," Becka said. A tear ran down her cheek. "My parents were set afloat at sea in a small boat. They're probably dead."

"I was kidnapped by my uncle and forced into labor on the *Majesty*," Daniel added.

"The *Majesty*, you say? What happened to her?" Jeremy said.

"She's at the bottom of the sea, I'm afraid," Daniel replied. "Pirates sunk her, the same ones who are trying to steal a ship here. We warned the Harbormaster. Were they caught?"

"I'm sorry to say that only Dupree, the scourge of the high seas, as he likes to call himself, was apprehended. The British have him in a cell on their ship. You won't have

223

to worry about the likes of him ever again," Jeremy said. "He'll be hung by the end of the week."

All three sighed with relief, but it wouldn't last.

* * *

When Dupree was captured last night, he'd asked the Harbormaster how he knew about the attack.

"A blind man and his two companions warned us."

The response infuriated the pirate. "I'll break out of this cell," he mumbled to himself. "Me men will rescue me, and when they do, I'll find those three and make them wish they had died on the *Leviathan*."

* * *

Dinner that night was delicious.

"I haven't eaten this well since I left my parent's plantation," Becka said.

"I'm glad you enjoyed the meal," Jeremy told her. "So, what happens now? What are your plans?"

Daniel told him about the treasure. "All we need is a boat to get us there."

"I have a small sailboat that would be perfect for the trip. I'd be happy to lend it to you," Jeremy said. When Daniel looked at him in surprise, he added, "As you can see, I'm a very wealthy man. I don't even want a share."

"That's very generous of you, sir. In that case, we'll still split the treasure three ways," Daniel said.

"Two," Jacob said.

"What do you mean?" Becka asked.

"I'm not going with you. Being practically blind, I'll only get in the way."

"You've worked as hard for this as we have. You deserve a share, whether you go with us or not," Becka said.

"Absolutely," Daniel agreed.

Jacob smiled. "That's very generous of you, but I've finally found my brother. I want to stay here with him."

"He'll want for nothing," Jeremy said. "We have a lot of years to catch up on."

Becka and Daniel were sad to leave Jacob behind. The three of them had bonded so closely, it felt like losing a member of their family.

"At least we won't have to worry about Dupree," Daniel said as they headed for their rooms.

"What about the rest of his men?" Becka asked. "They may decide to go after the treasure without their captain."

"Even if they do, they still have to get their hands on a ship, which won't be easy with the British navy on the alert for them," Daniel said. "I think it's safe to say that Cap'n Dupree and his crew won't be bothering us any longer."

Daniel could not have been more wrong.

Chapter Thirty-Two

The Escape

The next day, Jeremy took them shopping for supplies and a map of the island they would be landing on, which he insisted on paying for out of his own pocket. Daniel asked about getting a message to his mother, but the next ship going north wasn't due for at least a month. The message would have to wait.

Early the following morning, Jeremy and Jacob accompanied Becka and Daniel to the dock and helped them load everything into the sailboat. It was the perfect size for the two of them.

"When this is all over, I hope you'll come back and see us," Jacob called as the boat moved away from the dock.

"We will," Daniel called back.

"We promise," Becka added.

They were sad to leave their old friend behind, but they realized that Jacob was happy and belonged with his brother.

***

The next evening, Enos, Abner, and four other pirates sat around a table in the Squawking Parrot, discussing ways to rescue their captain and steal a ship. Jeremy sat at a nearby table, pretending to ignore them while listening to every word.

Desperate to keep from losing any more customers, Cornelius had rehired Jacob to cook. This brought back some of the customers, but without Daniel's entertainment, and Becka's smiling face, the atmosphere just wasn't the same.

When he'd heard enough, Jeremy slipped back to the kitchen and told Jacob what the pirates said.

"I'm worried about Daniel and Becka," Jeremy said. "They have a head start, but a larger ship could easily overtake them."

"That's not good," Jacob replied. "If the pirates see them, they'll either mow your sailboat down or shoot it out of the water with cannon fire."

"The only thing left to do is to pray that doesn't happen."

* * *

Dupree paced his cell, while elsewhere, his men made plans to set him free. They would wait until dark. Then slip aboard the H.M.S. *King George* while most of her crew were onshore. It was a daring plan, but one that was sure to work. The pirates would take out the skeleton crew and steal the *King George* out from under the Brits' noses. With their captain freed, they'd go after the treasure, and anyone getting the way would pay the ultimate price.

Death.

* * *

Thanks to his lessons with Captain Stewart, Daniel had no trouble piloting the sturdy little sailboat.

"We're finally on our way," Becka said as she watched the sunrise over the ocean. "What a beautiful sight. I never get tired of it."

"Me neither," Daniel replied. He glanced down at the map and adjusted his course setting. "Becka, I was wondering about something."

She turned her head and looked into his eyes. "About what?"

227

"I suppose you still have some family back home. Right?"

"My grandparents on my Mom's side live with us, but most of my family is still in England. Why?"

"Once you return home and tell everyone what happened, are you still planning to tour Europe? Will you go to England and visit relatives there?"

"My grandparents won't be eager to let me leave so easily."

"With the war on, it's better if you didn't. You should wait until the war is over before you do any traveling," Daniel said. "It's too dangerous on the water. If pirates don't get you, the British may."

"I hadn't thought about that. I mean, pirates are always a danger, but the British might be just as bad. I guess I'll have to wait."

Daniel hesitated. He knew what he wanted to ask her, but was afraid she'd say no. "Would you like to come with me to meet my mother?" He asked at last. "She'd like you, and I know you'd like her, too."

"I don't know," Becka replied. "I really do want to return home."

"Please don't say no right away. Think about it."

The look on his face caught her heart. "I'd have to do it before I went home," Becka said, thoughtfully. "I suppose I could send my grandparents a message once we reached Boston, but I couldn't stay long."

"I know. As soon as I get my mother set up, maybe I could travel to Roanoke with you. You shouldn't go alone."

"Would you really do that?" she asked. The thought made her breathless.

"Yes, mother would understand, and it's not like I'd never see her again. Maybe she and I could move to Roanoke, too. We'd leave my uncle behind, and I know mother would love the warmer weather."

"I'm sure she'd be a lot happier without him around," Becka added. She smiled broadly. "Why not?"

Daniel hugged her. Suddenly, their future looked even brighter.

* * *

The sun's remaining rays slipped into the ocean. Under the cover of darkness, the pirates piled into stolen boats and, as quietly as possible, paddled to the starboard side of the H.M.S. *King George*. Once in place, they tossed grappling hooks up over the side of the ship, hooking onto the rails. Then like eels, they slipped up the side and onto the deck. The guard on duty was asleep. He never heard a thing until it was too late. Enos broke his neck and pulled the body into the shadows. Once the ship was theirs, and they were out to sea, they would dump the bodies of the remaining crew overboard.

Each pirate held a knife in his mouth. They could not afford to fight with swords or pistols. That would make too much noise. For this job, they needed stealth more than might. Alerting the guards on the dock would bring them running, and the British sailors would not be far behind. Moving on silent feet, the pirates spread throughout the ship, eliminating everyone still on board. While that was going on, three other pirates, led by Abner, went to break out Captain Dupree. They picked the locks to the jail and their captain's cell and scurried back to the docks.

"The ship is ours, Captain," Abner spoke. "We'll be ready to cast off shortly."

"Ye've taken the ship?" Dupree asked. He was incredulous. "Are all me men on board?"

"Aye, sir. They be eager to cast off and leave this cursed place behind."

"Then let's oblige them."

***

As they walked up the gangplank, Enos hurried to deliver his captain a salute.

"Nothin' to it," Enos said with a grin. "It had only a skeleton crew."

Everything was quiet. So far, no one on land had any idea of what was happening.

"No shouted orders," Dupree warned. "We slip outta here like thieves in the night."

"Aye, sir, I'll pass the word."

Every minute that passed in preparation set Dupree's nerves on edge. When everything was finally ready, he gave the signal. One sailor used his sword to slice through the thick rope that tied the ship to the dock. Others raised the anchor. A brisk wind blew in the pirates' favor. Gently lowering the sails, the pirate captain steered the ship out of the dock and into the night.

When they were far enough out, the pirates dumped the bodies of the skeleton crew overboard.

"Well done, mates!" He yelled, receiving shouts of joy and laughter.

"The crew would never let you down, Cap'n," Abner said.

"And so they shouldn't," Dupree replied. "Once we nab that treasure, there'll be bonuses for all of ye!"

This brought more shouts of glee. Captain Jacques Dupree was a man of his word. His crew happily set to work, whistling, singing, and talking about what they would do with their share of the treasure.

They sailed deep into the night. Numerous lanterns hung about the deck so the men could work. Several hours out, the man in the crow's nest called down to the captain.

"What is it?" Dupree asked.

"Boat ahead. Can't tell its size yet, Cap'n."

Dupree looked through his telescope. He didn't see a thing until he spotted a single lantern. "It must be small, with only one light. Not to worry. This ship is loaded with some of the most powerful cannons they make. If he's trouble, we'll smash him to pieces."

He was about to turn away, but something niggled at him. He raised the telescope once more and focused on the lantern. It didn't give off much light, and Dupree couldn't make out anything more until a face moved closer to the light.

"Daniel! It's that thieving cook from the *Majesty*," Dupree growled.

"They must be after the treasure, too," Enos said.

"Blow him out of the water!" Dupree shouted. "Payback for him, sinking me lovely *Leviathan*."

Arming one of the cannons, the gunner crew fired at the tiny target.

"It missed," he said, passing the words along with the crew until they reached the captain's ears.

"Fire again!"

That one also missed. "They too far off," Enos said.

"Then we'll wait until we catch up. This ship should easily overtake them."

* * *

When the first cannonball hit the water several yards away, the small boat rocked violently.

"What's happening?" Becka asked, alarmed.

Daniel turned around and looked through the telescope that Jeremy had generously provided. What he saw made him turn pale.

"What?" Becka asked, tugging on his arm. Now she was alarmed as well.

"Cannon fire," Daniel told her, lowering the telescope. "I can't make out the ship, but it has to be Dupree. Somehow he must have escaped and stole a ship."

"Oh, no!"

"We can't outrun them. Douse the lantern; we'll have to lose them in the darkness before they get closer."

Becka blew out the light. She held her hands fisted in her lap, while Daniel steered the boat on a different course. Neither said a word as the ship drew closer. By now, the young man had maneuvered his boat off to the right so that when the ship passed, the pirates couldn't see their boat. They heard Dupree shouting.

"Where'd they go?"

"Don't know, Cap'n," Enos replied. "With their light out, they could be anywhere, and we'd never see them. Do you want to keep looking?"

"Bah, forget them and put us back on course. If they're foolish enough to go after the treasure, we'll be there waiting for them."

As soon as it was safe, Daniel relit the lantern and turned to Becka. "It's the *King George*."

"What is?" Then it hit her. "The British naval ship back in the dock?"

"Yes."

"How on earth did they manage to steal it? There aren't enough pirates to overpower the entire crew unless Dupree took on more back at Port Royal."

"They didn't have to," Daniel replied. When a ship's in the dock for a while, the Captain allows his crew to take shore leave. There would only have been a skeleton crew on board."

"Are you sure?"

"Yes, that's what they did in Boston Harbor."

"So, those men are dead now."

"I doubt any were allowed to escape and give the warning. If there was a battle before the pirates escaped, more would have been killed," Daniel said. He reached over and took one of her hands, squeezing it.

"You were wrong. Dupree escaped, and we're back in danger again."

"I'm sorry."

"Will it ever end?"

* * *

The *King George*'s actual captain, Captain Meriwether Banks, enjoyed a leisurely breakfast at the home of friends, he visited whenever his duties allowed. Thanking his hostess for the lovely meal, he pulled on his uniform coat, placed his hat on his head at a jaunty angle, and left, heading for the ship. He couldn't see the dock until he passed

233

several tall buildings. When he did, a puzzled expression crossed his face. He kept walking. Something was out of place, but he couldn't think what until it hit him like a cannonball.

"The ship," he mumbled to himself. "The ship." This time his words were louder. "The ship!" He yelled. "The ship! Someone's stolen my ship! To arms!"

Alarmed soldiers, dockworkers, and citizens poured out of the buildings. Many of the soldiers ran out in their nightwear, struggling to pull on pants and shirts as they ran. The dock was total chaos, and it grew worse as everyone realized what had happened.

When he reached the docks, Captain Banks shouted. "Quiet down."

Some did, others continued to question and exclaim.

"I said *shut up*!"

That got their attention, and it grew quiet except for the sound of the waves lapping against the dock and the call of seagulls flying overhead.

The captain stared angrily at the spot where the H.M.S. *King George* was supposed to be. How would he ever explain this to the admiral?

"Curse you, Dupree! You've stolen my ship!"

Chapter Thirty-Three

The Deserted Island

The following morning dawned sunny and beautiful without a cloud in the sky. Daniel loved piloting the small sailboat. Becka sat across from him. They both enjoyed the serenity that surrounded them. Seagulls flew overhead, occasionally swooping down to the water to snatch up a fish swimming close to the surface.

Becka pulled out some bread and two pieces of fruit, handing half to Daniel. When they began eating, a gull swooped down and landed on the rim of the boat. This delighted Becka.

"What a beautiful bird you are," she told it.

"He probably wants some food," Daniel said.

"What makes you think it's a boy? It could be a girl, you know." She turned back to the bird. "Are you a girl?"

The bird squawked.

She broke off a small piece of bread and held it in her outstretched hand.

"Careful, it might bite you."

"No, it won't. Seagulls are used to people offering them food. Wait and see." As she spoke, the gull hopped closer. It angled its head sideways and studied the offering, then looked up at Becka.

"Go ahead. Take it. It's okay. I won't hurt you."

Looking back at the bread, the bird leaned forward and snatched it out of her hand, then flew off.

"Great," Daniel said. "Now, they'll all come looking for food."

He no sooner finished speaking when half a dozen gulls swooped down and landed on the boat. They hopped toward Becka. She laughed and broke off six small pieces, making sure that each bird received one.

"You'll be sorry."

As soon as these six flew off, more and more gulls swooped down. So many landed on one side of the boat, the vessel began to tip in that direction.

"Shoo," Daniel shouted, waving his hands to scare them off.

They flew away, leaving Becka laughing.

"I told you they were trouble," Daniel said.

"I know, but they're so cute."

"Yeah, so cute, they nearly tipped the boat over and dropped us into the sea." His voice was gruff, but her laughter soon brought a grin to his face.

All the commotion brought other curious creatures to the boat. Dolphins swam around them, clicking and making different vocal sounds. Some showed off, standing straight up in the water and with their tail fins, moving backward as easily as a person skating on ice. Daniel and Becka both clapped and cheered. A few came so close to the boat that the two friends cautiously reached out and rubbed their snouts, much to the delight of the dolphins.

"This is how sailing should be," Daniel said as he settled back in his seat.

The dolphins moved away from the boat, but continued to escort them, diving, swimming, and calling out to each other.

"Look! One has a fish in its mouth," Becka exclaimed. She turned to Daniel. "I see what you mean: No pirates, no bad weather, just calm seas, a gentle breeze, and nothing to worry about. I wish it could always be like that."

"Me, too," Daniel replied.

Late that afternoon, Daniel's eyes lit with excitement. "Land ho!"

Becka turned around. The island lay ahead of them, surrounded with rocks of various sizes sticking out of the water. Over the past few hours, the wind had steadily increased, making stronger waves. It wasn't dangerous until they found themselves speeding toward the rocky barrier around the island.

"I'll look for obstacles," Becka yelled over the sound of waves crashing onto the rocks ahead. "You steer." Her keen eye studied the water. "Move right! Quick to the left!"

The last rock had come up so quickly that when Daniel shoved the tiller in the opposite direction, he nearly tipped the boat over.

"Careful!"

Daniel nodded.

This went on for five minutes, yet it seemed endless. With Becka calling out warnings and directions, it was like moving the boat through a dangerous maze. When they finally reached the shore, Daniel and Becka jumped out and pulled the boat onto the sandy beach. Daniel secured the sail and removed the gear.

"We made it!" Daniel laughed.

The joined hands and danced around the sand until they dropped to the ground, tired and happy. They were silent, reveling in the fact that they had landed and were about to take the final step toward finding the treasure.

"We'd better gather some wood for a fire," Daniel said. "Sunset isn't far off.

Once the sun was down, it was so dark the campfire did little to dispel it. The moon was only a sliver, which did nothing to lighten up things. To take their minds off things, the two friends talked about their families until the deafening sound of a wild animal brought their words to a halt.

They turned to stare at the trees behind them. Three pairs of shiny yellow eyes looked right back, then the sound returned in triplicate. Fear ran its icy fingers up Daniel's spine. He'd never heard such a howl before.

"You're scared, aren't you," Becka asked, reaching out and taking his hand.

"What? No, just surprised," he fibbed. His expression denied his words as he stared back at the yellow eyes.

"You're safe with me, Daniel," Becka assured him.

Daniel continued to watch the trees. Becka laughed.

"What's so funny?"

"Nothing," she giggled. "It's only howler monkeys. The first time you hear them is quite scary, but once you know what they are, you're fine. It takes some getting used to."

"So, they don't attack humans?"

"Only if provoked."

Daniel still watched the eyes as more pairs joined the original three.

"Look away, unless you want to aggravate them."

He turned back to the fire, and seeing her relaxed expression, finally settled down and pulled out the treasure map.

"We're on the right island," Daniel said, looking it over. "Now we have to figure out what all these clues mean."

Becka moved closer and held one side of the map while they studied it, careful not to allow any burning embers near it.

"It looks like we go through these trees, cross a valley and climb a hill," Daniel said.

"What are these things?" Becka asked as she pointed to different markings on the map.

"I'm not sure, but they may be traps. We'll have to be careful. Then once we reach the other side of this hill, we should find a ring of trees, the bark on one of the trees looks like a face."

"We'd better get some rest if we're going to start off early tomorrow morning," Becka said.

Daniel folded up the map and placed it back in the oilskin. He took two blankets from their supplies. As Becka got comfortable next to the fire, he carefully covered her up. She smiled and closed her eyes. Daniel lay down on the opposite side of the fire, and pulling his blanket over himself, he was soon asleep.

* * *

In the morning, the island natives spotted the smoke rising from the dying campfire. Moving soundlessly, they hurried through the trees toward the shore, but when they arrived, the camp was deserted.

Becka and Daniel had left at sunrise. They were unaware of the natives. They were also unaware of the other potential dangers until they spotted a sloth ahead of them, slowly making its way up a tree. Neither of them knew anything about it, but with three, three-inch claws on each foot, they made a wide path around it.

"What was *that* thing?" Daniel asked.

"I'm not sure. Father told me about the poisonous spiders and frogs, but he didn't mention any mammals."

Daniel was intrigued. "Poisonous frogs?"

"Yes, just touching them can kill you."

"Wow, I'm glad you told me that. This place is more dangerous than I thought."

As they continued walking, Daniel pulled out the map and studied it again. He was so engrossed; he didn't see where he was going. He stepped into a loop of rope, and when he lifted his foot to move on, it pulled tight and jerked his body into the air.

Chapter Thirty-Four

Looking for the Treasure

Daniel yelled.

Becka stopped in her tracks. "Daniel, are you all right?"

"I'm hanging upside down by my foot. So no, I'm not all right." Then, to punctuate his situation, his knife slipped out of his pocket and hit the ground.

"Becka, my knife, you have to find it."

The foliage was nearly two feet high, so the knife was not in plain sight. She dropped to her knees and searched the area directly below him. Nothing.

"It's not here!"

"It has to be, try further out."

When the knife dropped, neither realized that it had bounced off a fist-sized rock. Becka looked further and further, going around in a circle since she hadn't seen what direction it flew. The longer it took, the more panicked Daniel became.

"Hurry, Becka. Whoever set this trap will be back to check it."

"I'm going as fast as I can," she replied, slightly irritated.

"The pirates probably set the trap."

"I'm hurrying, Daniel. Be patient." She continued looking until she held up the knife at last. "Ah, ha! Found it."

Rushing back to Daniel, she looked up. "I have to find where the rope is fastened near the ground."

"Never mind that," Daniel replied. "Give it to me. I'll cut it from up here."

She looked at him doubtfully but handed him the knife anyway. It took a couple tries, but Daniel finally swung up enough to grab his legs. He pulled the rest of his body higher until he could reach the loop around his legs. The knife was sharp. It cut through, and he dropped to the ground.

"Ouch!"

He wanted to lay there awhile and recover, but he didn't dare waste any more time. Becka helped him to his feet, and they hurried away, careful not to step into any more snares. When they had put a considerable distance between them and the trap, Becka started giggling.

"What's so funny?" Daniel asked.

"You should have seen yourself dangling upside-down. You looked so funny."

Daniel was about to snap out a remark when a mental picture of what he must have looked like popped into his head. "I guess you're right." He laughed with her.

They continued on, changing directions when necessary until they came to the first prominent marker on the map.

"The tree with the face should be around here somewhere," Daniel said.

They looked everywhere, but no clue was in sight.

"We must have missed it somehow. I guess we better backtrack," Daniel said.

Becka didn't move. "Wait a minute. It has to be here. Maybe we're not looking low enough."

She stopped at the nearest tree and brushed aside the overgrown foliage that covered the bottom of the trunk. "Here it is!" She said excitedly.

Daniel joined her. "Yup, that's a face, all right. Kinda creepy if you ask me."

242

"Regardless, we're on the right track. Let's keep going," Becka said.

"Okay," Daniel said, looking at the map. "From here, we go…" he paused and pointed his finger to the left. "That way. We need to find a small circle of stones with this strange mark on them." He showed the drawing to Becka.

"Got it," she said. "Let's go."

They walked until they found a single stone with the correct marking next to a tall palm tree. It, too, was almost completely buried in the foliage.

"This is it," he said, uncovering the remaining stones.

They both grinned until they realized that the only way to go now was down a sheer rock face.

"How are we supposed to get down there?" Becka asked.

Daniel looked around until he found a sturdy vine. Using his knife, he cut it loose and brought it to the edge of the cliff where he tied it tightly around the palm tree. Then he dropped the other end over the cliff.

"Wait," Becka said. "What about me?"

"Here," he said, handing her the map. "Hang onto this and wait here. This looks like a dangerous climb."

Grabbing the vine with both hands, he gave it a pull to test its strength. It held. Backing up to the edge, he looked down, took a deep breath, and started down. The rock face was slippery with different sections sticking out farther than the rest, making the climb difficult. Partway down, his foot slipped, and he lost his grip on the vine.

"Daniel!" Becka screamed. Her heartfelt ready to burst.

Daniel slipped five feet before he was able to grab the vine again. Both sighed with relief. Working around the jutted sections, he continued downward. His weight pulled the vine above him taut, and although he avoided the juts, the vine did not. Sharp edges rubbed against it, and the vine began to fray.

"Daniel!" Becka called a warning, but it was too late.

The vine snapped, dropping Daniel the rest of the way to the ground.

* * *

On the other side of the island, three dinghies carrying a score of pirates from the *King George* headed for the shore of the island. As they headed for shore, Captain Dupree stood in front of his boat, reflecting on when he first got the map.

* * *

The map had originally belonged to another pirate, who claimed to have won it in a bet. One night when deep in his cups, the pirate pulled out the map he'd drawn and showed it to Dupree.

"I've hung onto it for a long time, saving it for a rainy day."

"Wise thing to do," Dupree replied. His eyes shone with greed as they stared down at the map while he calculated his next move. "Let me buy ye another bottle of rum."

The pirate put the map away and drank more rum. "Mighty accommodating of you, Dupree."

Half a bottle later, he drooped over, resting his head on the table and snoring loudly.

"Finally," Dupree said. He grabbed the map and returned to his ship.

At the time, the *Leviathan* was off the coast of Georgia. He'd make a few more raids as he headed south, and then go after the treasure. From what the other pirate said, it contained a fortune in gold and jewels. Dupree couldn't wait to get his hands on it.

* * *

Pulling the boats onshore, Dupree and his men climbed onto the sand. Prior to stealing the map, the captain had been to this island several times, and he had a fair idea where to find the treasure.

"We'll go after it this way," Dupree said. "If Daniel and that girl have made it to the island, they go in the front way. We'll take the back paths and be waiting for them."

The men nodded and smiled as they left the beach and headed into the jungle. Dupree led them two by two. Enos, one of his few remaining lieutenants, stood beside him. Several feet in, a quiet whoosh cut through the air and the lieutenant slapped his hand to his neck. He turned and looked at Dupree, eyes wide with shock, before sinking to the ground. He was dead.

"We're under attack!" Dupree yelled. Another dart swooped past, just missing his cheek.

Whoops, and hollers cut through the air as a tribe of natives attacked. The pirates pulled out swords and knives and took cover from the darts. Most of the natives carried spears. The pirates attacked them first, while Dupree aimed for the two still shooting darts. A flick of his wrist and the first one went down with a knife in his chest. A second knife took out the other before he could even react.

Spears are dangerous weapons, but against a sword, it was hardly a fair fight. The natives calculated the loss of their men and ran away, disappearing into the jungle.

* * *

Daniel picked himself up off the sand.

"Are you okay?" Becka called down.

"Yes, just shook up a bit. There's a cave down here. I'm going to check it out."

It was low tide when Daniel went inside. The cave wasn't deep, and the sun's beams lit more than half of it. He looked around for something that would tell him where to dig. There was nothing. Going back outside, he yelled up to Becka.

"There has to be another clue on the map. I can't find anything in there."

Becka examined the map carefully. Then she looked up at the sun. It was directly overhead. She smiled. "I figured it out, Daniel."

"Good. Where do I look?"

"Go back inside and walk to the spot where the sunlight stops, and the darkness begins. There should be two small rocks there."

Daniel ran inside, returning a moment later. "You're right! Toss down the shovel."

"Look out," she called as she dropped it.

Daniel stepped aside. The shovel hit the ground and bounced. Grabbing it, he ran back inside and started to dig.

"Finally," Daniel said aloud. "This is it."

Chapter Thirty-Five

The Find

Daniel dug down a foot before the shovel struck something hard and bounced. He didn't react right away. It might just be a rock. He dug around the object, but kept hitting it and had to dig farther and farther out. When he completed an oblong space, he dropped to his knees and used his hands to brush the rest of the ground away, revealing a very large treasure chest.

"I found it!"

His yell was so loud that Becka heard him above. She danced around excitedly.

He grabbed it on either side and pulled, but he couldn't budge it. Standing, he used the shovel as a lever, struggling and grunting as he strained his muscles until it finally popped out of the ground. He rested for a moment. Then using the shovel once more, he broke the lock and opened the lid. His eyes nearly popped out of his head as he gazed in amazement.

Running out of the cave, he shouted up to Becka. "It's huge! The chest *really* is gold! There is so much gold and jewels inside, it must be worth a fortune."

Becka squealed and clapped her hands. "How are we going to get it out of there?"

"I don't know yet, but we'll figure out something." Daniel beamed at her. *Finally, we got it!*

* * *

With the natives gone, the pirates continued their trek through the island jungle. The further they walked, the more difficult it became. The men used their swords to hack at the vegetation along the way, leaving a clear trail that anyone could follow. They kept at it all morning until they reached an area that was impassable.

"Arr," Dupree swore. "Check around for another way."

The pirates did, but none of them got very far. They returned with gloomy expressions.

"I'm sorry, Cap'n," Abner said. "There's no way through."

"Then we'll have to go back the way we came and take the ship around to the other side of the island."

With the path already cut, the walk back was quicker. The pirates climbed into their boats and rowed back to the *King George*. Once everyone was on board, and the boats hauled up and stored, Dupree gave his next orders.

"Haul anchor and follow the island around. We'll be taking the front entrance after all."

* * *

Becka tossed down a new vine, and Daniel climbed back up. They hugged each other fiercely.

"I think I know a way to get the treasure out," Becka said.

"How?"

"Let's go back to the boat and follow the island around until we reach the beach in front of the cave."

"Great idea."

"Do you think we can get it all aboard without sinking the boat?"

"We'll have to distribute it evenly so as not to tip it over. If we can't take it all, we'll have to be satisfied with as much as we safely carry and head back to Port Royal," Daniel said.

After taking note of the sun's position, they joined hands and retraced their steps back to the spot where they'd left the sailboat. Becka climbed inside, and Daniel pushed it into waist-deep water before hopping onboard.

"Which way?" He asked.

"That way," Becka replied, pointing in the opposite direction of where the boat pointed.

Using the oars, Daniel turned the sailboat around and rowed. He didn't dare use the sails this close to the rocks. After the near-disaster they'd had coming in, he did not want a repeat performance. Becka handled the tiller as they maneuvered through the treacherous coastline. While he rowed, he also kept an eye on the sun, which had crossed the sky and was moving down the western side of the horizon.

* * *

The *King George* sailed towards the treasure, sails out as they sped around the island. So as not to incur any damage, Dupree kept the ship away from the rocks, which stretched out quite a distance from shore. As they headed for the cave, he thought about the vessel they'd stolen.

"It's a fine ship," he told Abner.

"Aye, Cap'n."

"Kinda puts the old *Leviathan* to shame."

"Yer right, of course. Now we have his majesty's finest, built just for us."

Abner glanced over at Dupree. Had he said the wrong thing? The captain had loved that old ship. He relaxed when he saw the smile.

The men laughed.

"I'm thinking of naming her *Dupree's Revenge*. Whadda ya think?" Captain Dupree asked his lieutenant.

"A fitting name it is."

"And a perfect way to rub the Brits' noses in it," Dupree said. "As soon as we get home and set anchor, have someone paint on her new name."

"Aye, sir, it'll be a pleasure."

* * *

"There it is!" Becka said.

Daniel brought the boat as close as he dared and dropped anchor. When he hopped out, Becka saw that the water came up to his knees. She joined him, holding two sacks high above the water. They hurried into the cave, and when she got her first glimpse of the treasure, she gasped.

"There's a king's fortune there."

"I told you," Daniel replied, grinning. "Let's start hauling this stuff out."

Becka grinned, and they both began to shovel gold and jewels into their sacks, careful not to make them too heavy to carry. It took several trips before they got it all out of the cave. The chest was the last thing they took. They would need it when they returned to Boston. The boat was grounded in the shallow water.

"We'd better hurry," Daniel said. "The tide will be coming in soon. When it does, it'll lift the boat higher, and we can sail out of here."

They were about to place the chest on their ship when Enos walked out of the shadows, sword in hand.

"That's mighty decent of you to dig up the treasure for us."

"No!" Becka screamed in frustration. They had been so close.

Daniel spun around, wishing he had a weapon in his hand. "The treasure is ours. We found it first," he shouted.

"Not so, Cap'n Dupree found it first. He took the map off another pirate who couldn't hold his rum. You made a copy so you could steal the treasure from us. We don't take kindly to that," Enos said.

"Jump into the boat, Becka. We're leaving."

"I don't think so," Dupree said as three dinghies pulled up, blocking them in. He climbed out. "Transfer the treasure to our boats and take it to *Dupree's Revenge*." He stopped to look as his once again prisoners.

"Do ya like the new name?"

Daniel and Becka sat with angry expressions, too shocked and angry to reply.

"After that lads," Dupree turned his attention back to his crew. "Put it back in the chest and stash it in my quarters. I'll hand out yer shares later."

The sailors got to work while Enos and another pirate pulled Daniel and Becka back onshore.

"Now, what am I going to do with the two of you?" Dupree asked thoughtfully.

It was all a ruse. Two men grabbed a large cage from one of the dinghies and pulled it across the sand and into the cave.

"Ah, yer fate has arrived." Dupree pulled his sword.

251

He and Enos marched Daniel and Becka back into the cave and shoved them inside the cage. The pirates then wound the thick rope around it, making a great show of it, until the door was securely fastened.

"You can't leave us here," Becka protested. "Look at the waterline on the cave wall. When the time comes in, we'll drown."

Dupree fixed her with an evil grin. "How fitting. Ye should have drowned in the hurricane. Or when you snuck off the *Leviathan*. Funny how fate eventually catches up with everyone."

"I wouldn't want to be you when fate catches up to you," Becka said.

"Tsk, tsk, little girl, show some respect," Enos reprimanded her.

"Let us out!" Daniel shouted.

Jacques Dupree cocked his head. "Nope. I don't think so. Farewell. It's so nice to know ye will never bother me again." He turned as he and Enos boarded the last dinghy.

Daniel and Becka continued to yell until Daniel realized it was too late. The boats were long gone. As soon as the treasure was loaded on *Dupree's Revenge,* the pirates would sail away.

"It's no use," Daniel said at last. "This is it. We're done for."

Becka looked into his eyes, tears streaming down her face. "I don't want to die."

"Neither do I, but I don't think we're getting out of this one."

She nodded.

He pulled her closer, and they wrapped their arms around each other for comfort.

"At least we're together," she said, snuggling against his chest.

"Yes," Daniel replied softly. "At least we have that."

When the tide came in, the water slowly rose higher and higher, moving up their bodies until it reached their necks.

"This is it, Becka. It won't be long now."

Becka shivered in the cold water. "Daniel."

"Yes."

"I wish things would have worked out differently. I was looking forward to meeting your mother and seeing what the next adventure would be," Becka said.

"Me, too."

Chapter Thirty-Six

The Rescue

Ever since the pirates stole the H.M.S. *King George*, Jacob and Jeremy had been worried about their two young friends.

"We have to help them," Jeremy said during lunch.

"How?" Jacob asked. "There won't be another military ship in port for weeks, maybe even months, depending on how long it takes a message to reach England. Then it may take a while for the Brits to send a replacement for the *King George*. The war with the colonists could delay it even longer."

"I'm afraid we can't wait for military help. I have a friend with a boat. It's larger than mine and needs a crew of twelve to sail her. She's no match for the *King George*, but she does have two cannons, which should help somewhat," Jeremy said.

"Will he let us borrow his ship?" Jacob asked.

"I believe so. Let's take a ride and see."

It was so long since Jacob had ridden a horse that Jeremy decided to take a carriage. They rode to a large sugar plantation, owned by the magistrate's neighbor.

"Jeremy." Albert Wilkerson greeted his neighbor with a handshake. "Could this be Jacob?"

"My brother escaped the pirates and has finally returned to me," Jeremy beamed.

"That's wonderful! Reunited at last. So what can I do for you?" Albert asked.

Jeremy explained the situation to his friend. "So you see, if we don't go after them, I fear their fate is dire."

"My ship is yours," Albert said. He called to a manservant. "Gather the crew and prepare the *Rachael Ann* for departure within the hour."

"Yes, sir." The manservant rushed away.

An hour later, Jeremy and Jacob boarded the ship and stowed their gear.

"Captain Aveno is in charge of the ship," Albert said.

The men shook hands.

"He's a good man. If your friends can be rescued, he will find a way to do it."

As soon as the tide was favorable, the *Rachael Ann* set sail. She was a sleek ship, and with the wind in her sails, they made good time, arriving at the island shortly after the *King George* left, on their way to the pirate cove.

"We're too late," Jeremy told Captain Aveno as he watched the British frigate disappear in the distance. "The only way that ship would leave is if they have what they came for."

"That may be true," Captain Aveno said as he looked through his telescope. "Nevertheless, we don't know the fate of your friends. Isn't that your boat over there?"

Jeremy looked where the captain's finger pointed. "Yes. I believe it is. They may yet be alive. Can we get closer?"

"Yes."

The captain gave the order, and the ship moved in as close as the rocks would allow. From there, Jeremy, Jacob, and two crewmembers rowed a dinghy the rest of the way, sliding up next to Jeremy's boat.

"Daniel! Becka!" Jacob called. "Where are you?"

In the cave, Daniel and Becka were completely underwater, except for their mouths, pressed against the bars at the top of the cage. The waves from the dinghy covered even that, forcing them to hold their breath. When they heard the muffled sound of Jacob calling, hope sprang up within them, but time was running out. Would their rescuers be too late?

Unable to speak, Daniel kicked the wooden door of the cage, but under the water, very little sound escaped.

The water was so high now that at first, no one realized they were in front of a cave. Then Captain Aveno, who had sailed many voyages before taking the cushy job with his employer, took a deep breath and dove into the water. He disappeared. Seconds later, he resurfaced and took a breath.

"They're in the cave, locked inside a cage. We have to hurry. They're nearly out of air!"

Jeremy, Jacob, and the captain dove under the water and swam into the cave. Jeremy pulled out a knife and began sawing through the thick ropes that secured the door of the cage, but it was taking too long. Captain Aveno started working on the ropes on the other side. Jacob reached through the bars, he refused to let his failing sight hinder him from saving his closest friends. Daniel and Becka weakly grabbed his hand but had no strength left to squeeze. Their lungs were ready to burst, and they were at the point where their bodies would force them to gasp.

Jacob released their hands and swam around to the front of the cage. Grabbing the top edge, which had loosened as the ropes began to give way, he gave a mighty heave and pulled it free, snapping the weakened ropes. Jeremy and the Captain reached inside and grabbed Daniel and Becka, who was no longer breathing. They swam to the surface as fast as they could. The two crewmen pulled the freed prisoners into the boat and slapped them repeatedly on the back, trying to force them to dislodge the water they'd swallowed. Finally, Daniel and Becka coughed, spitting up water repeatedly until their lungs were clear. Together, they rowed back to the *Rachael Ann*. Jeremy's boat was tied to the larger ship and towed.

Wrapped in blankets, Captain Aveno went to his cabin to change, while the other four went below deck to dry off.

"We thought we were dead," Becka said, speaking for the first time since her rescue.

"What are you doing here?" Daniel asked.

"When we learned the pirates had stolen the *King George*, we feared you were in trouble," Jacob said.

"We had to help," Jeremy added.

"Thank you," Becka and Daniel said together.

"Now what?" Daniel asked.

"We go back to Port Royal," Jeremy said. "I'm sorry you didn't find your treasure."

"We found it, but Dupree stole it from us and left us to die," Daniel said. "We have to go after them."

"It's too dangerous," Jeremy said. "You'd be facing the lion is his den."

"They stole our treasure!" Becka said. "Daniel's right. We *have* to go after it."

* * *

After arriving in Port Royal, Daniel and the others returned to Jeremy's home to clean up and change. Jacob had to go to the Squawking Parrot to cook. The others arrived an hour later. Cornelius had already started the meal, using a recipe he'd learned from Daniel.

While they ate, Daniel tried to talk Jeremy into going after the treasure, but it was useless.

"Give it up," Jeremy said. "My little sailboat wouldn't do well that far out on the open sea. Take it from me. Sometimes revenge isn't worth the price you have to pay."

"I can't," Daniel replied. "It's not about revenge. I'm going after that treasure, even if I have to do it alone."

Becka looked at him, her expression sad. "Without a ship? How? Besides, we have no idea where their hideout is."

"I do."

Everyone looked up to see Jacob standing next to the table.

"I've been there many times over the years. I can take you right to it."

Jeremy looked at his brother. "I'm not so sure this is a good idea."

"Look. I know where they'll hide the treasure, and I know where the guards are stationed."

"Then we have a chance," Daniel said. He looked at Jeremy. "Are you with us? There's more than enough gold and jewels in that chest to make us all rich beyond our dreams."

"At what cost?" Jeremy sighed. "If I can't change your minds, then count me in. I can't allow you and my brother to go running off into danger alone." He turned to Jacob. "I can't lose you again."

* * *

It took two days to plan and gather what was needed for it to work. This time, they would sail on a privately owned sloop similar to the one Becka's family had owned. Seasoned sailors made up the crew, handy to have around in case of a fight. They set sail with the morning tide and reached the pirate cove that evening. Steering clear of the guard posts, they anchored the ship, leaving a skeleton crew aboard.

Onshore, Jacob spoke to the sailors that had come with them. "Wait here. Daniel, Becka, my brother, and I will scout ahead. If we need help, we'll yell. We won't be that far away."

After telling them the direction they needed to go, Daniel and Jeremy led the way to a cliff high above the cove. What none of them realized was that a pirate was silently following them.

Chapter Thirty-Seven

The Pirate Cove

On a hillside overlooking the cove, Daniel, Jeremy, and Becka laid on the grass looking down. Creeping up the hill behind them, a pirate with a sword in hand approached an evil grin on his face. His captain would be so pleased when he brought these two in. Dupree might even reward him with more treasure.

Becka looked through the telescope, trying to make out what was happening below. Daniel was about to ask her a question when a soft footstep alerted him. The hair on the back of his neck stood up. Then he relaxed. It had to be Jacob. Becka noticed his movement out of the corner of her eye and looked at him questioningly until she, too, heard the soft crunch of grass. Like Daniel, she dismissed it, figuring Jacob had finally caught up with them.

"They're too far away," she said. "I can see them moving around, but it's difficult to tell what they're doing."

"We have to get closer," Daniel replied.

"If ye want a better view, I can take ye a lot closer," the pirate sneered.

Daniel twisted and sprang to his feet, swinging his fist at the man. He missed it because he had to jump out of the way. Otherwise, the pirate's sword would have sliced him in two. His movement made him stumble. The man turned and raised his sword, but before he could swing it, Jacob hit him across the temple with his walking stick. The man dropped like a stone. Regaining his balance, Daniel joined Jacob and Jeremy, who had finally caught up.

"You saved my life. Thank you."

"Just returning the favor," Jacob replied.

"How did you know where he was?"

Jacob grinned. "I *saw* him with my ears."

Daniel shoved the pirate's unconscious body with his foot, and the man rolled back down the hill, coming to a halt when he hit a large boulder below.

"Let's move closer," Daniel said. "He won't regain consciousness for some time.

"Are you sure you know where they're hiding the treasure?" Becka asked.

"Pretty sure," Jacob replied, "but we won't know for certain until we can get a better look."

Using the trees for cover, the four friends crept down the hill on their bellies. When they were halfway down, Daniel crawled up to Becka and Jacob's position behind some thick bushes. She was guiding the cook down so that he didn't crawl off in the wrong direction.

"Look there," Daniel said, pointing at a spot behind all the activity.

At first, Becka didn't know what he meant. Then her eyes fastened on a cave entrance when two pirates walked through the opening. "It's a cave. Do you think it's their hideout?"

"No," Jacob replied. "They have a village further on the island. Normally this is where they wait for enemy ships approaching the island. They must have arrived too late to continue on to the village."

"With the area secured, there's no need for them to hurry." Daniel said. He pointed to a spot a hundred feet to the right of the cave. "We go there next, but we'll be in the open until we can make it to that grove of trees."

"It's too close to their camp. They'll see us, or at least, hear us," Becka worried.

"We'll wait until dusk to go closer. There will still be enough light enough to see where we're going. Then when everyone's asleep, we go after the treasure."

Becka nodded. "In that case, I'm taking a nap. I didn't sleep much last night, and I'm exhausted."

"Go ahead. We'll keep watch."

Becka curled into a ball. The moment she closed her eyes, she fell asleep. Feeling his own exhaustion, Daniel fought to stay awake, but soon he, too, was asleep.

Jeremy looked at his brother. "I guess we'll keep watch."

***

They awoke in time to see the sun's dying rays before disappearing behind another hill. Cramped from sleeping on the hard ground, Daniel and Becka stretched, got to their knees, and examined the camp. Many of the pirates lay on the ground, asleep. Captain Dupree sat with his back to a tree, talking with his lieutenants, Abner and Enos. Now that they were closer, the four of them could hear what was going on. The pirates laughed and drank, clearly celebrating their escape from Port Royal.

"We showed them red coats a thing or two," Enos bragged.

"I wish I could have seen their faces when they discovered their ship had been taken by a band of pirates," Dupree said.

"When do you think that happened?" Abner asked.

"Probably not till that morning," Dupree replied. "Someone saw the empty dock and yelled his head off, bringing the Brits runnin'."

Enos laughed. "Half of 'em probably ran out in their skivvies, hopping around trying to pull their britches up."

The mental picture his words created made Abner howl with laughter. "That sure would have been a sight to see."

The more the pirates drank, the rowdier they became. Fistfights broke out until the combatants dropped from exhaustion and from too much drink. Loud snores replaced the shouting and laughter, and the camp grew quiet.

"Time to move," Daniel said as dusk set in. "We'll have to be careful. We don't want to draw attention to ourselves."

The others nodded.

With Daniel in the lead, they crawled down the hill, Becka, Jacob, and Jeremy closely behind. They couldn't chance standing up until they reached their destination. It wasn't fully dark yet, one of the pirates still awake might see them. The journey was slow and nerve-wracking. They had stopped in a copse of trees when a nearby pirate woke up and started to stumble in their direction.

Daniel and the others dropped flat, hardly daring to breathe as the man came closer before veering left and disappearing into the bushes where he relieved himself. Becka made a face. They waited until the pirate went back to camp, laid down, and fell asleep.

Daniel looked at Becka, and when he saw her expression, he covered his mouth to stifle a laugh. "Let's go," he whispered.

They crawled the remaining distance to cover. Standing up was a relief. None of them had spent so much time on their knees since infancy. Jeremy looked around. The deeper dark of night would soon overtake them.

"There's still too many," Jeremy whispered. "Going into that camp is suicide."

"Where will the treasure be?" Daniel asked Jacob.

"Next to the Captain. He'll sleep with a sword in his hand."

"Doesn't he trust his men?" Jeremy asked.

"Not when it comes to treasure," Jacob replied.

"How are we supposed to get it away from him without waking everyone up?" Becka asked. "That chest is so heavy; it will take at least four men to carry it."

"An impossible task," Jeremy added.

"Can't we get the others to help?" Becka asked, referring to the sailors waiting on the other side of the cliff.

"There's not enough to fight all these pirates," Jeremy said.

"Then why bring them?" Daniel asked.

"I didn't think we'd have to fight an entire shipload of pirates at once."

Daniel's face fell. All their planning, their work, the dangers they faced were for naught. There was nothing left to do but take the boat back to Port Royal and look for work until he and Becka could save enough to return home. He pulled Becka to her feet and stared blankly at the dying embers of the pirates' campfires. Dupree lay next to one. Blinking, Daniel studied the pirate, and a flicker of hope sprang to life, filling him with a new purpose.

"Dupree doesn't have it. It must be somewhere else in camp. All we have to do is find it." He pointed to the drunken captain.

Jeremy and Becka looked. Daniel was right. There was no chest next to Captain Jacques Dupree.

"You're right," Becka said, brightening. "Now what?"

"We'll have to sneak around camp until we find it. When we do, we carry away as much as we can before someone wakes up."

Becka put on a brave front, but inside, the idea frightened her more than a little.

"Are you up for this?" Daniel asked.

She took a deep breath to steady her nerves. "I'm ready."

"Spread out. We'll cover more ground that way. If you see the treasure, stay put, and wave your arms."

Sneaking around the sleeping pirates was as delicate a mission as walking on eggshells. They carefully orchestrated each step to avoid trampling on anyone or anything that might make a sound and give away their presence. Whenever a sleeping pirate turned over, snorted, or coughed, Daniel and the others froze in their tracks until the pirate settled back to sleep. At this rate, it would take all night to find the treasure. They were getting nowhere.

Then the sound of a man's footsteps dropped all four into a crouch. They held their breaths and watched as a pirate staggered out of the cave with a heavy gold and ruby necklace around his neck. As he walked, he admired several chunky rings on his fingers.

Daniel and his companions now knew where the treasure was, but they didn't dare move. The pirate might be drunk, but he could still call out the alarm if he saw them. As he wove through the sleeping bodies, the pirate stumbled into someone sleeping on the ground. The man cursed him and rolled over, immediately falling back to sleep. The pirate staggered on until he finally found an open spot near one of the campfires. He tried to sit but fell instead. He lay there admiring the rings by the feeble light of the dying fire until finally, his hand dropped to the ground, and he began to snore.

Becka stood up, her legs were cramped from squatting for so long. Daniel also rose, but before he could take a step, the pirate next to him reached out and wrapped his fingers around his leg.

Trapped!

Chapter Thirty-Eight

The Fight for the Treasure

His heart in his throat, Daniel waited for the shout of alarm to go up. His body felt weak when the pirate who held him spoke.

"Get back to bed ya drunken sea slug. Some of us are trying to sleep."

Daniel was so relieved that he had been mistaken for another pirate, he nearly apologized, but reason stopped him. "Let go, ye mangy cur." He spoke in his best pirate accent as he shook his leg until the man released him. He had hoped his words had been enough to satisfy, but not too much to bring the manfully awake and ready to fight.

The man let go and rolled over. Daniel stifled a sigh and moved on. When the four of them reached the cave, they remained careful in case any more pirates were still inside. To their relief, it was empty, except for supplies and the large chest with the top open, leaning against a cave wall. Seeing it again was thrilling, but for Jacob and Jeremy, it was stunning.

"I never in my life have seen so much gold and jewels in one spot," Jeremy said.

"I have," Jacob said, "but even to these failing eyes, it's still a sight to behold."

Daniel's words brought them out of their stunned condition. "If we're going to get this out of here and live to tell about it, we need a plan."

"I think I have an idea," Becka said.

The four of them huddled together as she relayed her scheme.

"It's worth a try," Jeremy said when she finished. "Let's do it.

Becka left to get the sailors waiting on the shore. She led them back along a path that encircled the camp, stopping near the cave entrance. Jeremy explained what they had in mind, and everyone helped themselves to the supplies they would need. Following the route they used to come in, the men surrounded the camp and began building traps.

Sailors strung trip wires between the trees; others shimmied up tall palms, which seemed no different from climbing up a ship mast. They tossed coconuts down to waiting hands that set them aside to be distributed among them. The men pulled back low hanging branches of other trees as far as possible and tied them to stakes pounded into the ground. Rope traps like the one that had ensnared Daniel were also set. None of the pirates heard a thing. They were deeply asleep from exhaustion and too much rum.

The last thing Daniel and the others did was to build campfires around the circumference of the camp, giving the appearance that hundreds of men surrounded the pirates. It was time to attack. Daniel, Becka, Jacob, and a few of the crew remained with the traps. The rest would charge, fight, and chase the pirates toward those waiting in the jungle.

Shouting at the top of their voices, those attacking whooped and ran into the camp. Groggy from little sleep and too much rum, the pirates, at first, didn't realize what was happening. No one had ever attacked them on their island before. Captain Aveno led his crew and Jeremy into the fray, eliminating the pirates too slow to fight back. The camp was in chaos, with pirates running everywhere. Many of those who ran into the surrounding jungle, fell victim to the traps that had been set.

Seeing Becka as an easy target, one pirate ran toward her, his sword held ready. When he was ten feet away, she raised her hand and threw a coconut, hitting him right between the eyes. The pirate dropped like a stone. Daniel was having the time of his life. Two pirates ran at him, and when they reached the right spot, he used a sword, dropped by an unconscious pirate, and cut one of the rope traps. A heavy branch sped toward the villains too quickly to avoid. Both men flew through the air and slammed into the trunks of other trees. Daniel and his defenders were winning.

Back in camp, however, Dupree, Enos, and Abner gathered the remaining pirates to them. Heavily armed and focused, they fought off their attackers without giving any ground or quarter, and the battle took a turn for the worse. After dispatching the pirates in the area surrounding the camp, Daniel, still holding the pilfered sword, and the others charged forward and joined the fight. Captain Dupree spotted him and fought through the mob.

He stopped in front of Daniel. "Ye have no one to help you this time, magic boy."

"I don't need anyone's help," Daniel said, raising his sword.

Dupree sneered. "So brave for one so young. Let's see how you feel when me sword is at your throat."

Sword held high, Dupree moved forward and slashed. Daniel danced back, bringing his sword up to block the pirate's blade. Steel against steel rang out as both combatants put their weight on their front foot and pushed with all their strength. Dupree was stronger. Daniel's blade slid off. As he ducked, he felt the wind of the pirate's sword whip past, just missing his cheek. Three quick strikes followed. The young man blocked the first two, but the third sliced his sword arm. The sword dropped, and Dupree forced him back against a tree.

"At last," Dupree crowed. "I will have my revenge for all the trouble ye have caused me!"

* * *

Chapter Thirty-Nine

Captain Versus Cabin Boy

Before the *Rachael Ann* left port, the Harbormaster called together his men and Captain Banks of the *King George*. He brought everyone up to date on what was happening.

"These pirates have been the scourge of our island and the surrounding seas for too long. We have to make a stand now!"

Shouts of agreement met his words.

He turned to the captain. "What about you?"

"I'd do just about anything to get the *King George* back. As it stands, I'm a disgrace to the uniform, but without a ship, what can we do?"

One of the dockworkers smiled. "A brigantine arrived in port late last night. I've spoken with her captain. He is willing to allow us to use his ship. And the *Sea Witch* was about to set sail this morning, but her captain has also agreed to help."

"With two ships and a sloop, I'd say we have a fighting chance of bringing those pirates to their knees," the captain said. "All right, count my men and me in."

"How quick can we leave?" the Harbormaster asked.

"Within the hour."

"Then let's do it!"

True to his word, everyone was on board the three ships and ready to sail in no time. The Harbormaster had gotten the location of the pirate cove from Jacob before he left. The captains of the ships set course and sailed after the *Rachael Ann*.

Dupree pulled back his sword arm. Daniel was as good as dead. As the pirate captain prepared to finish off the young man, Becka reacted. With little thought to her own safety, she ran forward, kicked the pirate in the shin, and grabbed his sword arm, hanging on for dear life. Daniel used the distraction to duck and roll to where his sword lay on the ground. He snatched it up and jumped to his feet, ready to strike, but when he turned to face Dupree, his breath rushed out of his lungs.

The pirate held Becka prisoner with his left arm.

"Come one step closer, and I'll gut her like a fish. Now drop yer sword."

"No, Daniel! Don't do it. He'll kill us both," Becka begged.

What choice did he have? He couldn't stand there and watch the pirate kill her. Daniel dropped the sword.

"That better," Dupree said. "Now, which one of you wants to go first?"

"Me," Daniel offered.

"No!" Becka screamed.

"It's better this way," Daniel said. "You mean too much to me."

"Now isn't that sweet," Dupree sneered. "So be it."

Pushing Becka to the ground, he raised his sword and stepped forward. He was about to swing down when his arm froze in mid-air. Daniel was puzzled until he realized that the tip of a sword was sticking out of the pirate's chest. The British captain of the *Sea Witch* removed his sword and pushed Dupree to the ground with his foot.

"That'll teach you to steal one of His Majesty's ships."

Jumping to her feet, Becka ran to Daniel and fell into his arms. After their embrace, Daniel looked around. The place was swarming with men, some in uniform, some not.

"I don't understand," he said to the captain. "Where did all these people come from?"

"Port Royal," the captain said with a smile. "Seems you two made more friends than you realized.

British sailors gathered up the surviving pirates and placed them in the cells aboard the two large ships. The treasure was loaded onto the *Rachael Ann*. When the three ships arrived home, the remaining townspeople cheered. Daniel and Becka were glad it was all over, but they were also sad.

On the way back to Port Royal, Jeremy had some bad news.

"You will take a share," Daniel told both Jacob and Jeremy. "After all, you risked your lives to save us and bring it home.

Jeremy frowned. "I'm afraid that isn't possible."

"Why not?" Becka asked.

"This treasure already belongs to someone else."

"How can that be?" Daniel asked.

"I didn't realize it at first, but I've seen it before at the home of the father of a good friend. Pirates stole it years ago during a raid. I'm sorry, but we can't keep any of it."

Daniel and Becka looked at each other.

"Then, we're stuck here until we can raise enough money to book passage home."

"Now, I'll never find out if my parents survived." She began to cry.

Chapter Forty

Going Home

The captain of the *Sea Witch* ordered the remaining pirates hung. Afterward, the city held a big celebration. They realized that there were still pirates to deal with; at least Captain Dupree and his crew would no longer be a problem.

Neither Daniel nor Becka felt like celebrating. The underlying reason for going through the difficulties they had disappeared. Or it would as soon as the treasure's owner came to claim it.

Jeremy felt bad for them. Jacob was okay with losing his share. Now that he was living with his brother, he didn't need anything else. He continued cooking for the pub and even convinced Cornelius to hire back Daniel and Becka, along with another waitress. Cornelius asked Daniel to entertain, but the young man's heart wasn't in it. He was too depressed to make anyone laugh.

After taking care of the cases currently on his docket, Jeremy retired to his office to do some research. Something about the treasure had been bothering him for the last few days. First, he searched his old case files. Nothing there. Then he went through property deeds and other legal documents. He was about to give up when he finally found what he was looking for.

A slow smile spread across Jeremy's face as he hurried over to the pub. He caught Becka's attention and motioned for her to join him in the kitchen.

"Daniel, I have some news that will affect both you and Becka."

"What is it?" Daniel asked.

"Do tell us," Becka added. "Is it good news?"

Jeremy grinned. "Yes, indeed."

A glimmer of hope took root in both of them.

"Is someone offering to buy our tickets back home?" Daniel asked, hopefully.

"No."

Their faces fell.

"Something much better. I was troubled about that treasure and half-remembered, seeing a document about it somewhere. I've been looking for days, and today, I finally found it." He paused for dramatic effect.

"Tell us!"

"The document states that if the treasure is ever found, half would be given to the finder as a reward. It's signed and witnessed by the owner."

They were too stunned to take it in at first.

"How much is that?" Daniel asked.

"More than you can ever spend in a lifetime."

"Woo-Hoo!"

Daniel, Becka, and Jacob danced around, cheering and celebrating.

"Now that you don't need a house, what will you do with your share?" Becka asked Jacob.

"Me? No, no, you and Daniel will split the reward. I have what I want."

"You're sure?" Daniel asked.

"I know what I want. I'm content."

Daniel was sure he saw a small smile at the corner of Jacob's mouth. He remembered when he first met the cook he was tired and angry, now he seemed to be a completely different person. Or perhaps, he was acting like the person he always had been?

* * *

Farewells brought a mixture of emotions. Daniel and Becka promised to return for a visit someday after the war was over. Daniel bought a ship, a clipper named *Rebecca's Treasure*. They decided to stop in North Carolina for a quick visit with Becka's grandparents. To their amazement, her parents had made it home alive.

"We got lucky," her father explained after the excitement of their reunion died down. "After three days afloat, a Colonial ship spotted us and returned us home."

"We were so afraid you were dead," her mother sobbed and laughed at the same time.

Daniel and Becka stayed a week. By the end of it, her parents had heard the long tale of their adventure. They also realized that something more than friendship had developed between their daughter and Daniel. Both had turned seventeen while they were away. When it was time to leave, Becka's parents didn't want to let her go, but they realized she was a woman grown now, and a rich one at that. They agreed to allow her to travel to Daniel's home, providing she took her maid with her as a chaperone.

When they arrived in Boston, Daniel's mother was at the dock waiting to greet them.

"Oh, Daniel, I feared I would never see you again," Temperance sobbed, kissing him on the cheek and hugging him fiercely.

"How did you know I was coming today?"

"I didn't. I have been waiting here on the dock every day since you disappeared."

"I'm sorry, Mother. You've been through a lot, too, but I plan to make it up to you."

Temperance dried her tears and turned to Becka. "Who is this beautiful young woman with you?"

"Her name is Rebecca, Becka, for short," Daniel replied. "After the *Majesty* was captured by the pirates, I found her on their ship, dressed like a boy. She fooled everyone."

"Almost everyone," Becka smiled. "You discovered it soon enough."

"Then welcome to Boston. I'm sure you both have lots to tell me."

When they arrived at Temperance's small home, they found George amazingly sober. He stood up and hung his head.

"Sorry isn't enough," George told Daniel. "I had no right to do what I did."

"No, you didn't," Daniel replied. His face was without expression.

"I've been so ashamed, but I'm a different man now. Ask your mother."

Temperance nodded. "He's given up drinking and has taken a job."

Then Daniel remembered his father. "Did he tell you the truth about father?"

"Not at first," his mother replied. "It came out one night during a drunken nightmare. I was so angry, I could have killed him."

"But she didn't, and I've been trying to make it up to her since. I know I can never bring your father back, but I will do my best to take care of you the way I should have from the beginning. Can you ever forgive me, Daniel?"

Daniel didn't answer right away. He thought about all that had happened. George was right. Nothing would ever bring his father home again. He also thought about the hate, greed, and anger he had witnessed during his adventure. Such emotions poisoned a person inside. Finally, he walked over to his uncle and extended his hand.

"I forgive you as long as you never treat my mother badly again."

"I promise." A tear rolled down George's cheek. "Thank you, Daniel. Your forgiveness means more than anything to me."

That night they feasted with friends at one of the finest restaurants in Boston. Temperance was overwhelmed when Daniel told her about the gold and jewels.

"We can finally move back to our old home. You'll never want for another thing as long as you live," Daniel told her.

It took two days to pack and load everything up. Neighbors from all around helped, and when it was time to go, bid them tearful goodbyes. Two weeks later, they were home in Boston. The family home was reopened and put back into shape.

"Your father and I spent many happy years here. There are a few things I'd like to replace and update, maybe change some of the décors, but I'm right where I belong, and George," she said, looking at her brother-in-law, "You can have the guest room in the west wing."

* * *

Days later, things finally settled down. Daniel's mother took Becka and her maid shopping, so Daniel went to meet up with Michael. They sat on the knoll in their favorite spot, watching people go about their business. When two men carted a heavy chest off a recently arrived ship and looked around to see if anyone was watching, Daniel and Michael looked at each other and laughed.

"I'm not chasing after that one," Michael said. "I don't care if they are pirates. Haven't you had enough adventure for a lifetime?"

"For a lifetime? No," Daniel answered truthfully.

"I can't imagine, being abducted, getting kidnapped by pirates, tossed on islands and all the fights? I would think that would be enough for me."

As Micheal reminded Daniel of the adventures at sea, Daniel once again was reminded of Captain Stewart. *No doubt he died at sea*, Daniel thought. *I hope I made you proud, Captain Nathaniel Stewart. I won't forget what you taught me.*

"Now that you are the master of your own ship, you can take off whenever you want." Michael said interesting Daniel's thoughts.

"I could even join up and fight the British," Daniel said.

"You'd go to war?" Michael asked.

"Probably not," Daniel admitted. "With all that happened, I feel like I've already been through one. Besides, I'm no soldier. I still don't know how to properly use a sword."

"Ah, but you are an adventurer," a man's voice said.

Daniel and Michael looked up and jumped to their feet.

"Admiral Sir William Penn!"

The Admiral smiled. "I see my reputation goes before me. I wanted to personally thank you for helping Magistrate Freemont and his men with reclaiming the treasure. It's an admirable thing you've done, Daniel, especially in the face of what you experienced. You deserve a reward."

Daniel grinned. "Thank you, sir, but if you know the rest of my story, you'll understand when I tell you I don't need one."

"Not monetarily, no. However, I have something else in mind that might prick your interest," the Admiral said.

Daniel looked at him, quizzically. "I can't imagine what that would be, sir."

"I have a job for you. It's a mission of the highest forms of secrecy. Far too delicate for an army or ship full of sailors to handle. My employer and I need something...picked up, shall we say? You'll need your ship and a trustworthy crew."

Daniel smiled. "I am your man, sir. How soon do I leave?"

www.ingramcontent.com/pod-product-compliance
Lightning Source LLC
Chambersburg PA
CBHW031028260626
47153CB00016B/672